CAREFUL

WHAT YOU

WISH FOR

CAREFUL

WHAT YOU

WISH FOR

A NOVEL OF SUSPENSE

HALLIE EPHRON

wm

WILLIAM MORROW

An Imprint of HarperCollins*Publishers*

CAREFUL WHAT YOU WISH FOR. Copyright © 2019 by Hallie Ephron. All rights reserved. Printed in the United States of America. No part of this book may be used or reproduced in any manner whatsoever without written permission except in the case of brief quotations embodied in critical articles and reviews. For information, address HarperCollins Publishers, 195 Broadway, New York, NY 10007.

HarperCollins books may be purchased for educational, business, or sales promotional use. For information, please email the Special Markets Department at SPsales@harpercollins.com.

FIRST EDITION

Designed by Bonni Leon-Berman

Library of Congress Cataloging-in-Publication Data has been applied for.

ISBN 978-0-06-247365-3

19 20 21 22 23   LSC   10 9 8 7 6 5 4 3 2

For Jerry

CAREFUL
WHAT YOU
WISH FOR

SATURDAY

EMILY HARLOW WASN'T convinced that her sock drawer sparked joy. Her socks had once been a jumbled mess, stuffed in the top drawer of the mahogany bureau she'd inherited from her grandmother. She'd tried to follow the decluttering guru's mantra, keeping only those socks that "spoke to her heart" and arranging them so that they stood at attention, paired and folded just so (starting at the toe) and sorted by color. Months later, bright and early on this muggy August morning, as she stood in her sunlit bedroom in shorts, a tank top, and flip-flops, the message those socks whispered to her heart was more about privilege than joy. Who on earth needed so many pairs of socks?

Still, sock-sorting had been life-changing. On a whim, as she'd done it she took a sequence of snapshots, then assembled the stills into a stop-motion video, a herky-jerky animated progression showing the transformation from chaotic to tidy, with a few socks saluting the camera in the process, and ending with a selfie of her grinning as she deposited a bag of discards in a Goodwill collection bin. Dissolve to a final shot of her newly ordered sock drawer.

Watching that video *did* spark joy. She'd posted it on Instagram. Thousands of views and shares later, the *Boston Globe* ran a human-interest story on Emily and her sock-sorting video. A local morning TV talk show invited her on. And before she knew it, she had people reaching out and asking her to help them declutter their drawers and closets and film the process.

That had been just before the school year ended, at a time when she was susceptible to any excuse not to go back to teaching the next fall. Once upon a time, she'd loved teaching. Loved setting up her classroom in September. Sorting her supply closet and stocking it with reams of paper and art supplies. Meeting twenty-five fresh-faced third-graders and introducing them to the wonders of fractions, the solar system, and *Charlotte's Web*. But after eight years of the East Hartwell school system's relentless focus on tests, along with well-meaning parents who valued grammar and spelling over creativity and problem-solving, teaching itself no longer *spoke to her heart*. Not in the uncomplicated way that her sock-sorting did.

The outpouring in response to her video and the prospect of a stream of clients willing to pay for help decluttering their living spaces felt like a minor miracle. In short order, Emily had tendered her resignation, barbecued stacks of lesson plans and grade books, and given away a ton of teachers' guides and school supplies. She hoped she'd never have to smell another erasable marker or staple another corrugated border on a bulletin board.

She'd been pleasantly surprised when her husband, Frank, encouraged her to *go for it. Take the risk. Give it a year and see what happens.* Even though they were still paying off loans they'd taken out when Frank and his best friend, Ryan Melanson III, started their private-practice law firm. Compared to the emotional roller coaster that she and Frank had been on trying to conceive a child, the ups and downs of launching a new business seemed like a walk in the park.

The only thing that made Frank uneasy was her going alone into strangers' homes. You just never knew. So he'd set up location sharing on her phone so he'd know where to start looking if she didn't come home, and bought her a stun gun, baby blue, about the size of a TV remote. She'd fired it once. The sparks and lightning crackle had scared her half to death. She'd dropped the gadget into her gear bag and hoped she would never have to use it.

Emily had partnered with her best friend, Becca Jain, a one-time nurse turned social worker turned life coach, who was perfectly equipped to hold clients' hands and nurture them through the peeling away of personal property, as painful for some as peeling off layers of skin. Turned out people could part with that beloved herd of plastic horses that they'd collected when they were eight or that flowing chiffon they'd worn to their senior prom if they had its image saved in a digital archive. Emily made the freeze-frame videos capturing vanishing possessions. She and Becca called themselves Freeze-Frame Clutter Kickers, their logo a high-heeled boot kicking an unspooling reel of videotape.

Emily's sock-sorting had gotten them off to a good start. Now she was creating a closet-sorting video to grab the attention of more potential customers.

"Emmy, I'm off!" Frank shouted up to her. She'd left him downstairs in the kitchen, poring over yard-sale ads that he'd printed off Craigslist and Facebook. Every Saturday, with military-like precision, he plotted a route, then left the house no later than seven-thirty, because, according to Frank, no one meant it when they advertised *no early birds*.

Emily left the bedroom and crossed the upstairs hall that was narrowed by floor-to-ceiling bookcases loaded with Frank's books. Continued past the door to what was supposed to be the guest room but which was rapidly turning into Frank's storage closet.

When she got to the landing, Frank was at the foot of the stairs, grinning up at her. He went to weekend yard sales looking distinctly un-lawyerly in a pair of grungy Levi's and a T-shirt that Emily had had made for him. It featured a *New Yorker* cartoon of an elderly man, lying in a hospital bed and saying to the woman holding his hand, "I should have bought more crap."

"Need anything?" Frank said, brushing back a shock of hair from his forehead.

"No bedroom sets," she said.

Frank licked an index finger and chalked one in the air.

"But I could use a salad spinner."

He saluted and clicked his heels.

Emily returned to the bedroom. *No bedroom sets* was only half joking on her end. She suspected Frank had several headboards and bedframes, not to mention bureaus and vanity tables, stashed in their garage and basement. Lighter fare—radios and all manner of small appliances (he had a passion for vintage metal fans and porcelain-based soda-fountain milkshake makers)—he'd sneak up into the attic when he thought she wasn't looking. Even when Emily was shut away in her tiny upstairs office with its white pleated window shades, jar of freshly sharpened pencils (she never used them, but looking at them pleased her), and well-ordered files, she could feel Frank's finds restively revving up, like a phalanx of *Sorcerer's Apprentice* brooms mustering to invade the main house.

It wasn't all junk. Only last week he'd scored the original cover art for an issue of one of his favorite 1960s horror comics, *Creepy*. The signed watercolor had been tucked between the pages of a scrapbook priced at two dollars. So not Emily's taste, it featured a hairy beast, teeth bared and fist raised, threatening a voluptuous blonde who cowered in the foreground. When Emily looked up the artist, turned out individual pieces of his cover art sold for tens of thousands of dollars.

As if on cue, the house trembled. Emily recognized the sound of the back door slamming shut. She crossed to the window and looked down into the driveway. Frank's ancient Chevy Suburban (he didn't take his BMW Z4 to yard sales) lumbered below her as it backed out into the street.

Pick your battles had been her mother's sage advice on the day she and Frank married, and Emily had tried to do just that. Still, the irony of her upstairs, sorting and culling, and Frank out in the world, hunting and gathering, was not lost on her. She liked to think of theirs as a zero-sum game, though what she was about to rid from her closet was undoubtedly a spit in the ocean compared to what he'd soon drag into their house.

But there was no point dwelling on it. There were worse hobbies than compulsive yard-sale-ing, and he wasn't about to change. Besides, she had to get busy. She and Becca had an appointment to meet a new client this afternoon and it would take Emily hours to get this video done.

First off, she needed an establishing shot. She looked at her closet interior through her camera's viewfinder. Her clothes were hanging packed together on a single rod, winter at one end, summer at the other. Shoes and handbags were heaped on the floor. If she'd been triplets, she'd still have had more than enough.

She snapped a picture. Next, she had to set up the camera to record the stop-action series. She mounted it on a tripod in the corner of the room and set up a pair of LED light pads on either side of the bed to cancel out shadows. Closed the window shades.

Lit a scented candle on the windowsill. The candle was supposed to help you focus and find inner peace. It would also shrink as the filming progressed, a touchstone for the viewer.

Stage set, Emily pulled out clothing by the armload from the closet and mounded the pieces on one side of their king-sized bed. She set three empty plastic trash bags on the floor for discards, and tossed the orphaned clothes hangers in a corner, off-camera.

She looked at the pile through the viewfinder. What had seemed barely manageable hanging in a closet felt daunting piled on the bed. She adjusted the light and focus, then stepped back, making sure she wasn't in the shot. She pressed the camera's remote control, and she had her opening shot for the animation—the big mess. From now until she had the entire pile of clothing sorted, she'd have to keep the camera exactly where it was and take care not to bump the lights.

Emily snagged the topmost item, a pair of lined, cuffed wool trousers, an anachronism in today's world of leggings and jeans. She spread the pants out on the bed. Took a picture. Ran her palms across the surface. *Click.* Smoothed them. Another *click.* *Keep or toss?* Easy decision. Moth holes and a lining that was disintegrating did not spark joy.

She crossed the trouser legs. *Click.* Crumpled them up. *Click.* Threw them into a garbage bag, and took a final picture of the empty spot on the bed. Then she checked the camera, running through the sequence to be sure the images were coming out crisp and clear.

Next item: a silky (polyester) white blouse with (the term made Emily cringe) a *pussy bow.* She'd worn it on the first day of school every year since she'd started teaching. It was her version of a power tie, designed to convey to even the most rambunctious kid that this teacher was not to be trifled with.

No more first day of school, no more proving herself to eight-year-olds, so no need for a blouse with a pussycat bow. Best of all, no more time wasted teaching the fine art of filling in bubbles on answer sheets.

Emily took a picture of the blouse with its bow untied. Then, taking care not to disturb the rest of the pile, she took more pictures—bow tied, bow untied, sleeves folded across the front, as if the shirt were daring her to decide. And finally, gone.

She made short work of three boxy double-breasted blazers (one red, one black, one navy). First lining them up like soldiers. *Click.* Then, one at a time, arm bent in mock salute. After that, she whipped through a pile of dresses, dumping them all, including the bridesmaid's gown she'd worn to Becca's wedding.

She was stuffing the last dress into the garbage bag when she heard gravel crunch in the driveway. She stepped to the window and raised the shade. Frank had returned. His SUV was parked in the driveway below her. The driver's-side door opened and Frank got out.

From above, she could see the bald spot that he took pains to comb over. He must have bought something, because he popped the trunk and was bending down, reaching for the bulkhead door to their basement. The metal door creaked open.

Before Frank turned back to his car, he glanced up at her and waved. She waved back and dropped the shade. She really didn't want to see what he was bringing in.

She snapped another picture of her barely diminished clothing pile, and then picked up a turquoise zippered jumpsuit that she'd bought at a resale shop in Venice Beach. She'd been a different person back then, just out of college and getting her teaching degree. Frank was an idealistic, newly minted attorney, committed to human rights and equality, about to start what would be a two-year stint working in the Massachusetts public defender's office. Venice Beach had been fast changing from a neighborhood of aging hippies and secondhand stores to one with hipsters, yoga studios, and oxygen bars. She wondered if Frank remembered the amazing sex they'd had, camped out on a friend's covered porch overlooking the canal. Sex-without-thinking sex. Sex-without-checking-the-calendar-and-taking-your-temperature sex.

That had been years ago, back when she assumed that having a baby would just happen. Back when she'd never have considered pussy bows and blazers. Never dreamed how fast Frank would fill their house with more and more stuff.

If only he'd let her work her organizing magic on his clutter, Emily thought as she eyed the bulging drawers of his bureau. The door to his closet could no longer shut, either. Frank's "lawyer suits," hanging in garment bags squished at one end of the closet, would have so much more room to breathe if he'd only get rid of . . .

There was no point in finishing the thought. Because there was an ironclad rule of decluttering: You're only allowed to declutter your own shit. And it didn't seem like that big a deal when she and Frank were spooned, skin to skin, in bed on a lazy Sunday morning.

She shook out the jumpsuit and held it under her chin in front of the full-length mirror that hung on the bedroom door. It reminded her of her juicier, less mousy self, one she hoped she hadn't consigned to the rubbish bin on her journey from free spirit to elementary school teacher and on to professional organizer.

She threw the jumpsuit on the bed. Took a picture.

Had it been inevitable that Frank would become a rabid collector? Genetic, even? When they'd helped clean out Frank's grandfather's two-bedroom apartment years ago, there'd been piles of newspaper clippings going back to the forties. And what was a man whom she'd never seen dressed up except at their wedding doing with suits and sports jackets hanging double-deep in his closet? Turned out the pockets were an elaborate filing system. Frank had reached confidently into the breast pocket of a sports jacket and brought out a handful of solid silver quarters and dimes. From a pants pocket, a one-dollar bill with a printing error. A penny wrapped in a bit of toilet paper had a double-date stamp. The rest of his grandfather's treasures included a worthless stash of 1964 New York World's Fair pot holders and a mountain of hotel soaps and shampoos. Frank probably had all of it saved, only God and Frank knew where.

At their wedding, Frank's mother had confided to Emily that Frank's first word had been "Mine." Back then, Frank's redeeming features seemed to far outweigh what Emily then thought of as his quirky passion for collecting. He was handsome as hell, with that million-dollar smile. He was smart. He laughed at her jokes. And he didn't screw around like his law partner, Ryan, who'd recently divorced wife number two and was already cheating on his new girlfriend.

She turned her attention back to the jumpsuit. Ran her hands once again over the soft fabric, imagining that the jumpsuit was Frank himself. Gently she smoothed him. Straightened his shoulders. Unkinked his legs. *Keep or toss?*

She was considering when she heard a thud. Probably the steel bulkhead door to the basement slamming shut. She looked out the window in time to see Frank climbing into his car. No sooner had he pulled out of the driveway than there was a loud, discordant crash from the bowels of the house. Echoes sent a chill down Emily's spine. What on earth had he dragged home this time?

EMILY STOOD ON the upstairs landing and listened. There was a quieter, almost musical reverberation, but it was the sound of breaking glass that propelled her down the stairs. She doubled back from the foot of the stairs to the kitchen, her turf, with its white walls, glass-fronted cabinets, and navy blue Formica counters. The spices that stood on a long narrow shelf were sorted in alphabetical order. Even the cleaning supplies, invisible in the cabinet under the sink, were in order, sorted in a double-decker wire-mesh storage rack. The room smelled of coffee and dishwasher detergent.

Emily continued through to the little laundry room and hesitated at the door to the basement. Unless a fuse blew, she had no reason to go down there and many reasons not to. She pulled open the door, gazed down into murky darkness, and listened. Silence and moist, cool air rose to meet her. She flipped on the light switch, waiting for the energy-efficient light bulbs to flicker on and brighten.

Clearly Frank wasn't using these stairs for speedy access to the basement: the risers were crowded with boxes and bags. Sticking out of one box was a *MAD* magazine "What—Me Worry?"

board game. Frank had a soft spot for Alfred E. Neuman. Emily reached into a bag and eased out an old horror comic, *Tales from the Crypt*. She slipped it carefully back. Her hand came away smelling of mildew.

She cleared a narrow pathway, descended the stairs, and picked her way across the basement toward the opposite wall and the bulkhead door. She passed a rockerless rocking chair, occupied by the skeleton they put out every Halloween. A Ping-Pong table covered with stacks of picture frames, a pair of life-sized ceramic cats that one of Emily's students had given her as a Christmas present, a grinning, garishly colored glass clown that she had won in a raffle, and a pile of three-ring binders. The picture frames Frank had surely picked up at yard sales, but the binders, clown, and cats—Emily had put all of them out for charity donation pickup. Apparently Frank had had other ideas. This was why she hated coming down here.

So far, nothing to account for the crash she'd heard. She'd nearly reached the far wall when she spotted what looked like a gold-painted, person-sized harp. On closer inspection she recognized it as a piano frame. Too small to have come from a grand piano, it was still formidable. Even she could appreciate the gracefully arched frame that was dotted with large and small crater-like holes. Along one edge, the letters MUSKEGON MICH were embossed. Poor thing was a long way from home. It was leaning against a utility table, the floor around it littered with broken glass and china. She tried to shift it, but it was too heavy for her to manage on her own. Frank could deal with it when he got home. Or not. It wasn't her problem.

Emily climbed the stairs and returned to the kitchen. Sitting on the counter in the drying rack was a blue plastic salad spinner. Frank must have picked it up for her. He'd even washed it.

She put the lid on and gave it a whirl. She felt a pang of guilt. If Frank could bag her a salad spinner, the least she could do was sweep up the mess in the basement. It would take only a minute.

Emily went back with a broom, a dustpan, and a paper bag. Crouching beside the piano frame, she reached across and began to sweep up the pieces. It was a mixture of glass and china, maybe a vase and some wineglasses. She dumped a load into the bag, then crouch-walked farther in. Sneezed. Swept up more pieces. Added them to the bag.

She was straining forward, pressing her shoulder against the utility table, trying to reach the last shards, when the bulkhead opened. Light streamed in, along with a welcome breeze. Emily glanced up to see Frank silhouetted in the opening. He came down the stairs, his fair hair a nimbus of light, ducking to clear the threshold. He peered into an oversized brown portfolio. She recognized that covetous look. He'd scored.

"Hey, Frank," Emily said.

Startled, he looked up from the portfolio and squinted in her direction. "Emily?"

"What did you get?"

"What are you doing down here?" he said, closing the portfolio and fastening it shut. Emily recognized the dodge. Maybe he'd overpaid.

She stood. Or tried to, but lost her balance and staggered back. She dropped the bag and reached out for the utility table to steady herself. That's all it took. The table cracked and buckled. In slow motion, the piano frame that had been resting against it toppled sideways. Emily threw her arms over her head and crouched, cringing at the sound of more breakage, followed by a deafening version of the same discordant reverb she'd heard from upstairs.

When the dust settled, Emily looked up. Frank was staring in stunned silence. Finally he said, "Bloody hell. Are you okay?"

"I think so." Emily rose slowly to her feet. That's when she realized her flip-flop had come off and her bare foot was wedged firmly between the piano frame and what looked like a four-person church pew that had been lying on its back under the utility table. She tried to wiggle her foot loose but only succeeded in pinning her foot more tightly. "Ouch! Dammit." She looked across at Frank. He was picking through the broken pieces that she'd swept into the bag. "Frank, can you help me here? I'm stuck."

Frank's phone pinged. He slid it out of his pocket and looked at the readout, probably an alarm reminding him not to be late for the next yard sale. He smiled.

"Frank! Please? I can't—" Emily tried to inch her foot free, but the piano frame slipped again, slamming down onto the pew and her bare foot. Emily screamed in pain and yanked her foot free. The piano frame thudded onto the concrete floor, toppling a pile of boxes to a thundering cacophony.

"Ow, ow, ow." Emily collapsed in a heap, cradling her injured foot.

"Emmy!" Frank dropped the portfolio and rushed over, hooked her under the arms, and pulled her away from the piano frame and broken utility table. "Are you okay?"

No. Emily shook her head. Her foot throbbed.

"What were you doing down here, anyway?" he said.

"I was upstairs. I heard a crash and I came to see what happened."

A pause. "And what did . . . happen?" His gaze shifted from the discarded broom to the bag into which she'd swept the broken pieces to the breakage freshly scattered on the floor. Then back to Emily. Gently he examined her foot. Already it had turned angry black and red across the instep.

"It hurts like hell." She winced as she tried to flex her foot. At least it didn't seem as if any bones were broken.

Frank helped her to her feet. She set her injured foot on the floor and applied a little pressure. No pain shooting up her leg. "You need to get some ice on that right away," Frank said. He shoved aside the boxes on the steps to make room, then looped his arm around her waist and helped her to the stairs.

She leaned against him and climbed one step. Then another. "I heard a crash," Emily said. "I came down to make sure everything was okay. When I saw the mess, all I did was—"

"I know. Clean. Straighten," he said, helping her up another riser. "It's what you do. Just like my mother."

Emily stopped mid-step. Frank's mother was a perfectly nice woman, but in truth the only thing she and Emily had in common was Frank. However, at around this point in any argument, Frank dragged the poor woman into the discussion. The minute he'd left for college, his mother had taken it upon herself to straighten his room. His closet. His drawers. She'd thrown away his treasured comic books. *X-Men* #1. *Spider-Man. Miracleman.* She'd tossed his Voltron and He-Man and *Star Wars* action figures along with a pile of Transformers.

"Your mother—" Emily began.

"I know," Frank said with an indulgent smile. "She can't help herself."

"You're the one who can't help yourself," Emily shot back. "You dragged that . . . that . . . useless monster of a thing down here and left it propped up. Precariously. An accident waiting to happen." She turned and stared down at the piles of stuff that crowded the stairs and filled the basement. At the newly acquired portfolio that was still lying on the floor. "Who in their right mind needs this much crap? There's so much, and even you can't get to it. So what's the point? It's a sickness."

Frank looked stunned. "So now *I'm* sick?" He pushed past her into the laundry room and then turned back. "I'm fine. You're the one who's allergic . . ." His voice died.

Was he really dragging their fertility test results into an argument about his crap? Emily's eyes brimmed with tears as she managed the last few steps on her own and followed Frank into the kitchen. He opened the freezer, got out an ice cube tray, and slammed it into the sink. Some ice skittered across the floor. He grabbed a dish towel and scooped up a handful of cubes. He offered Emily the makeshift ice pack. She stared at it.

"Just so you know," Emily said, "I hate your crap. I hate all of it. I hate that you can't throw anything away. Or give any of it away. I hate that you can't leave other people's crap at their yard sales. And it makes me crazy knowing how much of it you've dragged into our attic. Into our garage. Into our basement. It feels like it's growing. Breeding!" She took a ragged breath. "Even if we're not."

3

FRANK REARED BACK as if he'd been struck. Emily was stunned, too. Those final words had burst out raw and uncensored. Frank dropped the ice pack on the kitchen table and stormed out of the house, slamming the back door behind him. Emily sank into a chair, picked up the ice pack, and pressed it to the side of her face. She held it there until the cold stung, then held it there some more.

Gingerly she lifted her leg and rested her foot on the seat of another kitchen chair. Her instep was bruised and swollen, but she could rotate her ankle. She rested the ice pack on the sorest spot. Then she leaned back and closed her eyes.

She shouldn't have torn into Frank like that. Because hating his crap was like hating his nose or his smile. And his frenzied collecting came as no surprise, not after eight years of marriage. But his crack about their fertility issues—*her* fertility issues, was how he framed it—had been mean and thoughtless. When they'd gotten the latest test results a few weeks ago, Frank had seemed relieved, maybe because there really was something wrong and it turned out not to be his fault. Emily was producing antibodies that were killing Frank's sperm. She'd been trying to get Frank to talk about what to do next, but he kept brushing her off. Too tired. Too busy. But not too busy to go to yard sales.

Maybe he'd been relieved, too, because, when it came to having a family, he wasn't as *all in* as he claimed to be. Or maybe it was their marriage that he wasn't that *all into*. That brought Emily to a full stop, and she choked up.

A half hour later, Emily was in her bedroom with the makeshift ice pack tied around her foot. As she finished sorting her closet, she ran through the roster of men she'd dated before Frank. There was Brad, the grad student who'd been late picking her up at the airport when she flew out to visit him at Berkeley. He'd been on a volleyball team and their end-of-season game had gone into overtime. Three hours of overtime. Richard, the lawyer who was sweet to her but insufferably rude to waitstaff and salespeople. Ed, an engineer who thought climate change was a sham and Ronald Reagan had been the Second Coming. Jim, who. . . . maybe it wasn't fair to count him. Their relationship had consisted almost entirely of steamy text messages and a photograph she wished she'd never seen.

Next to any of them, Frank was a prince. Yes, he had his shortcomings. But he remembered that she needed a salad spinner.

Her eyes misted over after she pulled her wedding dress—a short white sleeveless silk dress with a V-neck and a bunch of delicate (now crushed) pink silk flowers sewn onto the bodice—from the much-diminished clothing pile. She glanced across to her bureau, at a wedding picture of her wearing that dress with Frank beside her, strong and handsome and staring into her eyes with goofy affection. She could smell his aftershave.

Emily had known full well that Frank wasn't perfect when she'd married him, and she'd loved him anyway. Surely she was never going to wear that wedding dress again, but still she set it aside to hang back in the closet. Maybe one day they'd have a daughter and she could put it in a dress-up box.

A baby girl. Too bad Frank couldn't drive over to a yard sale and rustle up one of those. Emily swallowed the lump in her throat.

It was three o'clock when she took a final shot of the candle, which had burned down several inches. Blew it out and took another picture. She was telescoping the tripod when her phone pinged. Becca, punctual as always.

Meet you at the Park 'n' Ride in thirty.

Emily texted back.

Leaving in 5.

She shucked off her top and shorts and grabbed a freshly laundered pale blue collared T-shirt with their new company logo embroidered on one side, and a pair of matching cotton drawstring pants. Her admittedly dorky matching baseball cap was in her gear bag. She tried to slip on one of the blue sneakers that were part of their official ensemble, but her foot was too sore. No way could she wear them for the next few days at least. Instead, she put on a pair of roomy purple Crocs that she used for gardening. She took a test step and another one. They'd get her through the on-site consult that she and Becca did together before committing to work with a client.

She ducked into the bathroom and splashed cold water on her face. Brushed out her long hair and put it up in a ponytail. Then she went downstairs. Frank would return and find her gone. She left him a note—a frowny face with tears and below it a row of *x*'s and *o*'s.

Then she grabbed the canvas bag where she kept her gear, tucked her little purse and cell phone into it, and left the house.

Emily's white Honda Civic hatchback had been the last 2006 on the lot in December of that year, the model so basic that it didn't have automatic door locks. A month ago, she'd had the Freeze-Frame Clutter Kickers logo stenciled on the doors. The car started right up. It always did. For Emily, dependability far outranked flash. It was an easy ten-minute drive to the Park 'n' Ride on a Saturday afternoon, and when Emily arrived, there were plenty of empty spots. She pulled up alongside Becca's car, a white compact Kia whose door was also stenciled with their logo.

Becca lowered her car window. "Come on, let's roll."

Becca looked exactly the same as she had in elementary school, her Little Orphan Annie curls barely tamed. On through high school and college, she and Becca had been best friends, a pair of otherwise unaffiliated geeks whose friendship only grew from the days when they shared a trove of Barbie body parts and clothing and built a massive Barbie castle from cardboard boxes and tubes.

Emily grabbed her gear bag. She got out of her car, freezing for a moment as pain sparked across her instep. She locked her car and got into Becca's. Becca watched, pointedly waiting until Emily buckled up. In a former life as an ER nurse, Becca had seen more than her share of needlessly maimed victims of car accidents. She still had a scrubbed-clean, nursey feel about her, and the inside of her car was spotless and smelled of Pine-Sol. Her Clutter Kickers shirt and pants were freshly ironed.

"You okay?" Becca asked. "You look—"

"I'm fine." Emily really didn't want to talk to Becca about her fight with Frank. Or their fertility test results. Becca was married to one of the kindest men on the planet and she'd pumped out two perfectly adorable children without breaking a sweat. Emily wasn't proud of it, but at least she owned up to the jealous resentment she felt.

"And you're limping." Becca turned in her seat. "Is that a bruise?" She pointed to Emily's cheek.

Emily pulled down the sun visor and looked at the mirror attached to the back. There was a black smudge on her cheekbone. She licked her thumb and wiped it off. "Schmutz. I was down in the basement."

"I thought you were filming your closet."

"I was. But I was in the basement, too. Frank's piano guts assaulted my foot. You know, that thing inside a piano that looks like a harp? Weighs a ton? It wasn't his fault. Really."

"Really?"

Emily looked at her watch, though she knew what time it was. "Let's go. We're running late."

Emily was grateful that Becca let it go at that. They were out of the parking lot and on the highway when Emily said, "So tell me about this client."

"Ruth Murphy," Becca said. "Retired bookkeeper. Says she's friends with Mrs. Arnoldy."

Susan Arnoldy had been one of their first clients. A friend of Becca's mom, she'd rated just shy of *moderate* on the Hoarding Rating Scale. Becca and Emily had stacked and sorted a few hundred empty plastic containers in her kitchen. Poor Mrs. Arnoldy had broken down in tears when it came time to actually throw them away. What if she needed them?

Baby steps, Becca liked to remind their clients. The first ones were the hardest. But they were still waiting for Mrs. Arnoldy to call them to come back and help her tackle the rest of the house. Emily was surprised that she'd recommended them to her friend.

Fifteen minutes later Becca pulled up in front of Ruth Murphy's split-level home. Dandelions thrived in the front lawn, and the yews under her front window needed clipping. Ferocious clumps of black-eyed Susans bloomed on either side of the front steps. Emily put on her cap, threading her ponytail through the opening in the back. Then she got out of the car and followed Becca up the walk.

Becca rang the bell. *Young or old?* This was a game Emily used to play, going back to when she'd sold Girl Scout cookies door to door, trying to imagine the person who was about to greet her. Short, stout, and elderly, she decided.

Emily was two-for-three. With a white dandelion puff of hair, Mrs. Murphy had to be well past seventy and she came up to Emily's chin. But she was slender as a reed. She shook Emily's hand with a steely grip, then ushered them into a tidy living room filled with stuffy Victorian-style furniture—an upholstered settee and matching side chairs. The scalloped wood valances over the windows were pure 1950s, like the ones in the house that Emily's parents had sold before they moved to the Cape. It smelled as if the cookies laid out on a cut-glass platter on the coffee table were fresh-baked.

Emily looked around. This seemed like a house with a place for everything and everything in its place—what you'd expect of someone who made her living balancing accounts and keeping ledgers. What was there to organize?

She took a clipboard and pen from her bag and shot Becca a questioning look. Becca tipped her head toward a large leather recliner in the corner that was leaning back, its footrest raised

as if someone were still sitting in it. On the floor beside it sat a
pair of men's bedroom slippers and a drift of newspapers. On a
nearby end table sat an empty cut-glass tumbler and an ashtray
with a cigar stub. Emily sniffed. No cigar smell in the room.

Mrs. Murphy picked up a silver-framed photograph from on
top of an upright piano. The picture was of a young couple,
bride and groom, standing stiffly together as if they were perched
atop a wedding cake. The bride wore a high-necked silk gown
with mutton sleeves, the skirt falling to a graceful train behind
her. A cascade of roses rested in her arms. Alongside her stood a
much taller man, his thick dark hair parted and slicked down. He
wore a military uniform, epaulets on the shoulders and a narrow
leather strap across his chest. His cap was tucked under one arm
and his other arm was linked in hers.

"Me and Murph," Mrs. Murphy said. "Nineteen sixty. We
were married at Fort Bragg."

"He was handsome," Becca said.

"Bless his heart, he was that and more. Cunning devil one
minute, saint the next. I just don't know—" She pulled a Kleenex
from her sleeve and dabbed at her eyes. "It's been hard. Sometimes I feel so lost, I want to disappear."

Becca stepped over and touched Mrs. Murphy's arm. "When
did you lose him?"

Mrs. Murphy took a deep breath, unable for a moment to
speak. "A year ago. Massive heart attack. Just a few weeks after
he sold his dental practice. I told him not to retire." She reached
for another framed picture on the piano. The older man in the
picture was still handsome, his hair now a lush white pompadour
over defiantly dark eyebrows. Mrs. Murphy held the picture to
her chest for a few moments, then laid it facedown on the piano.
"Went, just like that." There was no sound when she snapped

her fingers. "Doctors said even if he'd been in the hospital when it happened, they couldn't have saved him."

"I'm so sorry for your loss," Becca said, as only she could, as if she genuinely shared Mrs. Murphy's grief over the death of this man she'd never met.

Emily sidled over to the pile of newspapers on the floor beside the lounge chair. The date of the one on top was July 14, 2018. More than a year ago. A Belleek vase on the mantel, white porcelain with shamrocks, was holding . . . what? Maybe they'd been roses, but now they were gray and mummified. The vase sat among what were most likely last year's Christmas cards.

"So," Mrs. Murphy said, taking a breath and straightening her back. "Murph's *things*." She smoothed her skirt. "I haven't been able to deal with any of it. Between the will and insurance, changing credit cards and bank accounts, seems like I'm constantly arguing with someone, trying to straighten things out. It wears you down, talking to bureaucrats whose goal is to get you off the phone as fast as possible." She heaved a sigh. "Well, at least that's mostly sorted. Now there's this. I've put it off and put it off, but it's time for me to deal with it. But there's so much stuff. I tried doing it myself, but I pick up one thing and try to decide what to do with it, and then another thing catches my eye and there's a memory . . ." She hiccuped. "It's exhausting. And where will it all go? We have no children, so . . ." Her voice trailed off. Emily could imagine herself in Mrs. Murphy's shoes—childless, widowed, and staring helplessly into the abyss that was Frank's basement. "So I called you. I thought, if only I had help, and I had some way to remember the things that were his. Know what I mean? The picture-taking seemed like just the ticket. Then I might be able to get through it. Or at least make a start."

"If you invite us in to help you," Becca said, "how and what we do will be entirely up to you. We can stop whenever you've had enough. Because this is your life. Your home. Your memories. Once we see what's here, we can give you a pretty good idea of how long it will take, from start to finish. But you make the rules. You feel as if you've had enough? All you have to do is say stop and we'll stop."

Mrs. Murphy took that in. She pursed her lips and nodded.

"So, let's have a look, shall we?" Becca shifted to her brisk, take-charge voice and Emily felt herself relax.

Mrs. Murphy led the way down a hallway, past a bedroom and a bath, to a closed door. She pushed it open, then stepped aside so Becca and Emily could go in first. The room smelled of dust, old paper, and, yes, a hint even now of cigar. At its center was a massive oak desk, its top piled with mail and a drift of auction catalogues. Sotheby's in Boston. T. E. Kalmus in Hyannis. The return address on an unopened envelope to Dr. Charles Murphy, DMD, was the American Dental Society.

"Okay if I take some pictures?" Emily asked.

"Be my guest," Mrs. Murphy said.

On the desk blotter sat a pad of lined paper, its top page half-written on in red pencil. On closer inspection, it was a list that began *FA LIBRARY* followed by *Twelve Months of Flowers, The Pinetum Britannicum,* and a dozen or so more titles. Looked as if Charles Murphy had been planning to go to the library when he died. A red pencil lay beside the pad, along with a coffee cup, the bottom coated with dried coffee. Emily took a few pictures. Then she lowered the camera and rocked back on her heels. The room was a perfect time capsule. She ran a finger across a bare corner of the desk. Dust-free, but still a time capsule.

"I never come in here. I keep the door closed because I can't bear . . ." Mrs. Murphy said.

"May I?" Becca asked, indicating the desk.

"Help yourself."

Becca opened the desk's file drawers. They were packed with folders and hanging files, each with a typed label. Emily started a list titled *Husband's Office*, writing down the categories of things they'd be sorting through. She took more pictures of the room, the desk, the bookcase, zooming in on the procession of carved wooden birds lined up, tail to beak, across a topmost shelf. Duck decoys. Long-legged wading birds. Smaller birds. Emily recognized a puffin and an owl.

Mrs. Murphy flipped a wall switch and a spotlight over the birds came on. Becca pulled over a chair and climbed from there onto the desk. She reached up and took down one of the birds, wiping it with the bottom of her shirt. She gazed at the bird for a moment before handing it to Emily. The pale gray bird with a long narrow beak was standing on one leg, its head pulled back as if it were about to spear a fish. Delicately carved, carefully painted, fitted out with brilliant paperweight-glass eyes, and signed on the underside, it had to be worth something to a collector.

Emily took pictures and handed the bird back to Becca. Then Becca climbed down and wrestled open a sliding closet door. Emily took a picture, counted the boxes and suitcases that were inside, and added them to her list. They'd have to be opened and at least visually inventoried. Her foot was starting to ache.

"There's more." Mrs. Murphy's hand fluttered as she gestured toward the window. "Murph loved boats. We have one in the yard."

Emily looked out. Sure enough, there in the backyard, alongside a freestanding garage, was a motorboat mounted on a trailer. Emily took a picture. "And in the garage?" she asked.

"Tools. Paints and varnishes and I don't know what all."

Emily's list had gotten so long she needed a second sheet. At the top, she wrote, *Hazardous waste.*

"We should have a quick look while we're here," Becca said.

"There's guns, too. Antiques. His gun safe's in the basement. And"—Mrs. Murphy fished a ring of keys from an ashtray on the desk and fingered through it—"there's this." She removed a key and handed it to Becca. Becca passed it to Emily. On the key, written in flaking red nail polish, was the number 217.

"I think it's to a storage unit," Mrs. Murphy said. "He must have paid a year in advance. The first bill I saw was this." She reached into her pocket and pulled out a folded sheet of paper. Her hands trembled as she unfolded it and held it out. "It came weeks ago."

Emily tucked the key into an inside pocket of her gear bag. "May I?" she asked, aiming her cell-phone camera at the bill. Mrs. Murphy nodded, and Emily took a picture. The bill was dated June and the amount due was for twelve months. It was from Inner Peace Storage. Emily was familiar with the outfit. They rented self-storage units in a nearby industrial park on the river and ran annoying radio ads.

"You paid the bill?" Emily asked.

"I did. Solved the mystery of what the key was for. Thank goodness I hadn't thrown it away."

"Do you know what he'd been storing there?" Becca asked.

"No idea whatsoever."

"We'll need to see what's in there before we can give you an accurate idea of what it will take to sort it out." *Sort.* Becca had been drilling Emily on using less offensive terms like *sort* and *straighten* instead of *clean* or *clear.* Even *declutter* could sound upsetting to someone who thrived in clutter, or someone like Mrs. Murphy for whom the clutter itself was freighted with emotional memories. "Do you want to come with us when we check this out?"

"I'd rather not, if it's all the same with you. I'm curious about what's in there, but I don't need to see for myself. You'll tell me, won't you?"

"Yes, of course. We'll check it out and then put together an estimate for you. We can have that done by . . ." Becca paused, waiting for Emily to fill in the blank.

"In a week?" Emily said.

"A week?" Mrs. Murphy moaned. "Can't you do it sooner than that? It took me forever to get up the nerve to call you. If I wait, I'm afraid I'll get cold feet."

"As soon as possible," Becca said, taking out her cell phone and thumbing through her calendar. "Let's see . . . Wednesday?"

Mrs. Murphy kneaded her hands together. "Couldn't you do it any sooner?"

Emily didn't think it would take that long to come up with an estimate that factored in what was in storage. "Sure. Assuming we're able to get into the storage unit, we'll try to email you an estimate Monday."

Mrs. Murphy beamed.

4

"MONDAY?" BECCA SAID. It was nearly half past five, and Emily was sitting in the passenger seat of Becca's car in front of Mrs. Murphy's house. "What were you thinking? We'd have to get over to that storage unit tomorrow."

Emily's foot hurt. She slipped off one of her Crocs, pulled her foot into her lap, and massaged it. "I thought you wanted *as soon as possible*."

"I know, I know that's what I said. But I didn't mean tomorrow. It's Sunday, and besides, I've got Makesh's family coming for brunch." Becca's husband had a large extended Indian family, brothers and sisters and their children, but it was his mother, the formidable Lakshmi, who set the bar high when it came to entertaining. "And Sophie has a piano recital. I promised her I'd do her hair and give her a manicure. If I don't, she'll have a fit and blame me when she screws up 'Für Elise.'"

Emily skimmed the list she'd already compiled. The workroom in the garage would be easy to inventory because Mr. Murphy had been a compulsive labeler. Roofing nails had their own container, as did bolts with their nuts attached, as did screws of various sizes. Each of the thirty or so antique rifles and pistols in the basement gun safe had been carefully labeled and documented, too.

"Based on what we've seen so far," Emily said, "this doesn't look like it's going to be too complicated. Ballpark three days to sort. Those carved birds could be valuable. I'll send photos over to Bill and Mary and see what they think." Bill and Mary owned an art and antiques gallery in Bridgewater and ran regular auctions. "It shouldn't be hard to find someone to evaluate the guns and tools. Which leaves the boat."

Becca said, "And whatever's in that storage unit. That's the wild card. No estimates until one of us gets in there and takes a good look at what's what. And if that means going in tomorrow, then it's got to be you. Though I hate for you to have to do it alone."

Emily pulled up the picture she'd taken of the storage bill. Units came in different sizes, and based on what Inner Peace was charging—$2,150 for a year's storage—this one was probably a medium-sized unit. "It's probably ten-by—"

"Let's not guess. Remember Mrs. Moore," Becca said.

They'd been seriously burned helping Nancy Moore downsize. She'd had a home and not one but four storage units loaded with brand-new purchases she'd made over at least a decade of buying from the Shopping Channel. The items that stuck in Emily's mind included a floor cleaner called the Whizz Mop (two of them), a pressure cooker that doubled as a steam iron, a massive juicer still in a box promising "whisper quiet nutrition," two treadmills, and a StairMaster. Plus enough handbags and scarves to stock a Marshalls. Mrs. Moore's daughter thought the picture-taking would help her mother let go, and it did. But the storage units turned out to be bigger than they'd expected and crammed fuller than anyone would have thought possible. When they billed Mrs. Moore for the unbudgeted hours, she refused to pay, and they had to eat the difference.

"Don't worry," Emily said. "I'll check it out tomorrow. Thoroughly. I'll write up an estimate for you to review." As she spoke she realized that tomorrow she was supposed to go to a PawSox game with Frank and his college buddies. She'd have to tell him that she couldn't go. After their fight, he'd assume her bagging it was some kind of passive-aggressive payback, And maybe it was. He'd been an asshole. But the truth was Emily never looked forward to hanging out with Frank's odious law partner, Ryan Melanson, and the rest of their gang, overgrown frat boys who reeked of self-confidence and greeted each other with high fives. By the third inning they'd be shit-faced and squinty-eyed.

Becca started the car but then sat there, staring at the house and chewing on her lower lip, her hands resting on the wheel. "Did it strike you as odd that Mrs. Murphy didn't seem all that curious about what was in that storage unit? I mean, wouldn't you want to know?"

Emily laughed. "Seriously? If it were Frank's storage unit? I'd pay double if you promised to nuke everything in it, sight unseen."

Becca didn't laugh. "Are you sure everything's okay?"

Emily forced a smile. "Don't worry. When it's not, you'll be the first to know."

Emily dreaded telling Frank that she had to bail on the ball game. On the drive back to the Park 'n' Ride, she decided it would be less fraught if she did it by phone. Becca let her off at her car. She got in, started the engine, and drummed her fingers on the dash while she waited for the AC to kick in. Then she dialed Frank's cell. He picked up after the fourth ring.

"Hey," he said.

"Hey," she said back.

She was trying to figure out what to say next when he broke the silence with "I got your note. Thanks."

Emily felt a rush of remorse. "I felt terrible after you left. I wasn't being fair."

"I don't get why you care what I collect. It's not in your face. If you'd just stay out—"

"I meant the fertility test results. We need to talk about it. We need to decide what to do, even if that means doing nothing."

She heard some shuffling on his end. "I know. I'm just not ready. I need to think about it," he said. Typical. He needed to *think*. She needed to *decide*. "I'm not sure."

"Not sure about what?"

"Kids."

"Isn't that why I stopped taking the pill? We always said—"

"No. *You* always said. I just listened."

That was a lie. Frank had even joked that he wanted to name his son Neuman after Alfred E.

"Well, I need for us to talk about it," Emily said. "If not now, then soon. The doctor said we have options. Right?"

"Okay, okay." It was the tone he took responding to what he perceived as a nag. "We'll talk. All right? Just not right now. How'd it go with the new client?" Changing the subject. But it gave her a lead-in.

"Actually, that's why I called. I wanted to let you know right away." She rushed on. "Turns out this is a big project, and I need to come back tomorrow to do some more prep." Emily tried to sound matter-of-fact but apologetic. "So I can't go to the game."

"Becca can't do it?" Frank sounded annoyed.

"She's tied up with family. All day and into the evening."

"She's tied up with family but you're not? Can't this woman just tell you what's in there?"

"She doesn't *know* what's in there. Her husband rented it—"

"And *she's* cleaning it out?" He snorted. "Typical."

The dig wasn't lost on Emily. "Her husband's dead."

That left a hole in the conversation.

"Anyway," Emily said, "we promised an estimate Monday, so I have to get in tomorrow and make an inventory. It'll take the better part of the day." This was a lie; she was pretty sure it wouldn't take more than a few hours. "Maybe you can find someone to use my ticket?"

"You know it's not about the ticket," Frank said. "I like having you there." Those games were a tradition dating back to before they were married. After a little pause, he asked, "How's your foot?"

It was swollen and throbbing, and needed to be iced. "It's better," she said.

"Glad to hear." After a pause, "I'm sorry you got hurt."

Emily felt vindicated. "I'm sorry I took your head off," she said. "It's just that . . ." It was just that his crap made her see red. Which she knew. Which was why she shouldn't have gone down into the basement in the first place. "Really, I'm sorry about missing the game."

That's when she realized he'd already disconnected the call.

5

FRANK'S Z4 WAS gone when Emily got home. A note on the kitchen counter read *DON'T WAIT UP, CLIENT MEETING.* Turnabout was fair play. At the bottom was a cartoon drawing of a bare foot with a heart-shaped frowny face drawn over the instep.

While she heated some leftover mac and cheese, Emily checked her email and the latest news headlines. After she ate, she went upstairs to her office, where she uploaded images for her closet-sorting video. She selected the ones she wanted to use, put them in order, and synced them to Scott Joplin's "Pineapple Rag." She ran the results, watching as her clothes took turns lying on the bed, then folding themselves or jumping into a garbage bag. She'd have to wait for the final image, her clothes arranged in a closet system of shelves and racks that she'd purchased but had yet to install.

Three hours after she'd started working on the video, she put together a title shot—her candle lit at full height, which she intended to bookend with the candle, shorter and blown out, at the end. That's when she heard the front door slam. "Frank? Is that you?" she hollered.

Moments later he stood in her office doorway. He looked tired and drained. "Long meeting?" Emily asked.

Frank nodded and dropped his briefcase on the floor.

She pushed away from her computer and stood. "You know I didn't mean to mess with your things."

"I know that," Frank said. "It wasn't your fault. I should have been more careful about how I left them." He pulled her into his arms and nuzzled her neck. He smelled of beer and cigar smoke. "I know I can be a jerk." Emily choked up, sideswiped by tears that filled her eyes. Frank snagged a tissue from the box on her desk and handed it to her. "Just not too much of a jerk, too much of the time. Right?" He sat in her desk chair and pulled her into his lap, turned on the gooseneck desk lamp, and aimed the light at her foot. "Let me see. Has it gone Technicolor?" He eased off her Croc and ran his fingertips gently over her bruised instep. Emily shivered with pleasure. "Can you wiggle your toes?"

Emily wiggled her toes. "I'm okay. Really. How was your meeting?"

"Productive." He smiled. "Ticked all the boxes. Want to hear the gory details?"

She didn't. "You smell like cigar. Celebrating?"

"I like the way you smell." He ran his hand up her leg. Emily shivered again. It had been a while since they'd made love in anything more than a perfunctory way. "But you're right." He sniffed his sleeve. "I smell of cigar smoke. And lousy Chinese food. I need a shower. But first, tell me more about your new client?"

Emily was surprised. Frank often asked about the stuff she was decluttering, but he rarely wanted to know about the person behind the clutter. "Mrs. Murphy? Poor dear. Her husband died a year ago and she still hasn't been able to throw away any of his things. She's even got the newspaper he was reading the day he died. But get this. Turns out he'd been renting a storage unit that she knew nothing about until the bill came."

Frank chuckled. "Don't get any ideas. I like my stuff where I can hang out with it."

"It did make me wonder. When you drop dead, am I going to discover that you've rented a bunch of storage units for everything you don't dare bring home?"

"Emily, come on. There's nothing I don't *dare* bring home. And what makes you think I'll be the first to croak?"

"If I go first," Emily said, "at least you can be sure I won't leave you a mess to deal with. Not even my corpse. You know I want to be cremated, right? Incinerate and scatter me anywhere."

"Do we need to talk about this right now?" It was another one of those topics that Frank didn't want to discuss and she wanted decided. He'd be in denial right up to the bitter end. Knowing how attached he was to corporeal things, Emily wouldn't be surprised if he'd opt to have himself stuffed, mounted, and posed permanently in his Z4. Wearing . . . ? She tried to imagine how he saw himself dressed for the hereafter. Corporate attorney? Yard sale denizen? Baseball fan?

"Stop trying not to laugh," he said. He stood slowly and she slid off his lap. "So how much of a mess did her husband leave her with?"

"I won't know until I check out the unit. That's what I promised to do tomorrow."

"Ah, right, tomorrow." He narrowed his eyes at her. "You know, you don't need to make up excuses not to go to our games. I thought you liked them. Makes no difference to me if you'd rather take a pass."

Was that a trick? Because Emily had always been under the impression that it did matter. Not only did he like her to go with him, he liked her to look good. At first she'd enjoyed the games. Looked forward to them. Liked going as Frank's girlfriend, one of the gang but tucked securely under his wing. Now it felt as if it took too long to drive down there, and then the game went on endlessly with what seemed like an entirely different roster of players each season. Plus his friends drank too much and they'd get handsy. Some of them.

She hesitated for a moment. "Actually, it's not my favorite thing."

"No big deal. I officially absolve you from having to attend this and all future games. There!" Frank grinned. "All you had to do was say so."

"If I change my mind—"

"I won't hold my breath."

"Tomorrow I really do have to work."

"I know." Frank sniffed his armpit. "And I really do need a shower." He picked up his briefcase and left the room. Minutes later, Emily heard the pipes thunk as the shower turned on.

She reran her closet-sorting video, made a few tweaks, and shut down her computer. Before she changed for bed, she dragged the bags of discarded clothing into the upstairs hall, went back, and shifted the neatly folded piles of clothing from the bed to the floor. The empty closet needed to be vacuumed.

She stretched her aching back and shoulders and envisioned the new rods and shelves and hanging drawers she'd bought. She hoped installing them would turn out to be as easy as the company's YouTube video promised.

"What are you doing still up?" Frank asked as he came into

the bedroom. His hair was wet and he was wearing his bathrobe. It was late. Nearly midnight.

"Second wind," Emily said.

He looked into her empty closet, then back at her, and gave
his head a little shake. He'd encouraged her new venture, but
she could tell from his expression that, for him at least, nothing
about it sparked joy.

6

SUNDAY

FRANK LEFT THE next morning wearing his Pawtucket Red Sox cap and Mookie Betts jersey, and carrying a cooler loaded with six-packs of Sam Adams. He couldn't take the beer into the park, but he and his buddies would be well lubricated by the time they left the parking lot. He really did seem fine with Emily not joining them.

Emily spent the better part of the morning preparing her new closet—taking down the old rods, unpacking new coated-wire shelves, rods, and assorted organizers, and marking spots on the wall where she needed to drill holes for drywall anchors. It was early afternoon by the time she was ready to head over to Inner Peace Storage.

She checked her gear bag to be sure she had the key to the storage unit along with all the supplies she might need. Clean rags and a roll of paper towels. Spray cleaner. Rubber gloves and dust masks. A label puncher along with rolls of plastic tape in five different colors. An extra camera. Later, once she and Becca started sorting and organizing, she'd need her tripod and portable lights.

It didn't take long to drive over to the sprawling complex of modular prefab units that squatted on the banks of Mariscotta

River. This part of town was still referred to as Upper Mills, even though the mill buildings had long ago fallen into disrepair and the dam had been taken down to allow fish to spawn. The storage complex was surrounded by a chain-link fence. Emily wondered if the color scheme at Inner Peace—the metal over-head doors to all the units were saffron-orange—was supposed to remind customers of the robes worn by Buddhist monks. To her, it felt like Halloween.

She parked in front of the office, a boxy, glassed-in room that was so compact it might have housed an ATM. Visible through the window was a deserted customer service counter. The hours painted on the door confirmed that the office wasn't staffed on Sundays, so Emily continued into the complex, making her way through the narrow alleys between units. When she found 217, she parked in front and got out. In the heat of the day, the mac-adam seemed to shimmer.

She approached the door of the Murphys' unit. A padlock secured the door's metal bolt. As with the key, the number 217 was painted on the padlock in red nail polish, most of it peeled away. It took not-so-gentle pressure to get the lock to snap open. She unhooked it, leaned down, and grabbed the door handle. Holding her breath, she started to raise the door.

The *beep-beep* of a horn stopped her. She turned. A golf cart, the same saffron color as the storage unit doors, pulled up along-side her. Security. The visor of a driver's cap shaded his eyes.

"Back again?" he said. She must have looked puzzled, be-cause he did a double take. "Sorry, I thought you were someone else. My mistake. Is this your unit?"

Just doing his job, Emily reminded herself as she beat back the impulse to tell him to butt out. She wiped away a trickle of sweat that was making its way down the side of her face. "The owner gave me the key." How had this security guard even known that she was here? She looked around and spotted a CCTV camera mounted at the roof line, one unit away. It was aimed down at her.

"Give you a hand with anything?" the security guard said, pushing back his cap and wiping his forehead with the heel of his hand.

"No, thanks. I'm good." She turned to face him. "You said someone was in and out of here? You sure it was this unit?"

"Yup. Right here. Seen her a few times, actually. Not my business, of course."

Her? Before Emily could ask what the woman looked like or how recently she'd been here, the driver took off.

She raised the door of the storage unit. The interior was in shadow. A blast of hot air drove her back and she gagged on the smell—mildew and general rot. She returned to her car to get a face mask from her gear bag.

Back at the storage unit, face mask strapped in place, Emily felt for a light switch and flipped it. Overhead, fluorescent lights flickered on. The readout on a thermostat hanging beside the light switch was blank. So much for the climate control that Inner Peace liked to advertise.

The space was narrow and about twice as deep as it was wide. Lining both sides were floor-to-ceiling metal shelves. Emily moved down the center path, noting that most of the shelves were stacked with books and boxes. Some were loaded with document tubes. As she'd observed with Mr. Murphy's workshop, everything was sorted with the kind of precision that Emily's mother, a retired librarian, would have relished. Books were shelved one-deep. Boxes and tubes were labeled.

Emily took a quick break, stepping outside into slightly less oppressive heat. She lowered her face mask and took a few deep breaths. Then she put the mask back on and went in again to look more closely.

On one shelf sat a set of leather-bound books, the spines embossed in gold. *Les Misérables.* Volumes I–V. The lower part of the book spines looked as if they'd been dipped in white powder. Beside them was a pair of taller books, their spines so blackened that their embossed titles were illegible. When Emily tried to pull one of them from the shelf, its spine broke, releasing a cloud of what were probably mold spores. In her hands, the book felt fragile, although the gold coat of arms embossed on the red-leather front cover still looked fresh where it had been protected by the adjacent book. She peeked at the title page, trying not to crack the spine.

Hakluyt's Voyages. Beneath that, it read, *Anno 1599.*

Emily took photos of the spine, the cover, and the title page, where the paper was foxed and sprinkled with black dots. She and Becca would need a book dealer to advise them on whether this was a reprint, and whether in this condition it was even worth saving.

As she slid the fragile book back into its spot, she knocked over a gadget that had been hanging from the shelf's edge. She picked it up. It looked like a pager with a blank readout. Looking more closely, she saw it had a label: GOTECH HYGROMETER. She slipped out her phone and googled the words. Apparently it measured temperature and humidity and sent an alert when its parameters were breached. When it was charged. This one was as dead as the person it would have alerted.

Emily stepped outside again for a few quick breaths of fresh air, then ventured to the far end of the unit. Across the back was a sturdy wooden workbench. Behind it, shelves were loaded with glues and adhesives, cleaning supplies, and paintbrushes. The lid on a bottle of rubber cement was coated with dust.

Emily took a series of pictures of the interior from various angles, and close-ups of some of the most badly damaged books. Then she turned her attention to the rows of containers that lined the shelves. She raised the lid of a medium-sized plastic bin that was labeled DOORKNOBS. As promised, it was filled with them. Crystal octagons, one of them a deep amethyst. Brass, embossed with the raised image of a hand holding a torch encircled by the words BOARD OF EDUCATION. White porcelain, still mounted to a rusted keyhole plate. This was not junk. It was a collector's collection. She lifted the lid of an adjacent cardboard shoebox. Inside was a vintage thermostat, mounted in a brass cage with lovely filigree work. Wires dangled out the back.

Emily replaced the lids. Mrs. Murphy's Murph and Emily's Frank would have been soul mates. She could imagine their poker game: *I'll see your 1936 thermostat and raise you a World War I copper fan.*

Emily counted the books on a length of shelving (twenty-six), counted the number of shelves loaded with books (twenty-four), and multiplied. Around six hundred. Next, she counted boxes: thirty, ranging in size from shoeboxes to liquor boxes. Judging by the labels, they contained all manner of building hardware.

Then she turned her attention to the document storage tubes. Some were no more than a foot long, others as long as three feet. There were at least sixty of them. She pulled out a tube at random. The end had been chewed away. No climate control, *and* rodents.

Emily was about to open the tube when she noticed, at the far end of the shelf, an anomalous, unlabeled black hatbox with the New York City skyline around it in yellow. She tucked the document tube under her arm and pulled the hatbox from the shelf. It was light—not filled with hardware. The edge of the lid had come unglued.

Just then her phone chirped. Becca. Juggling the hatbox and the document tube, she stepped outside and removed the mask to take the call.

"Where are you?" Becca sounded breathless. In the background, Emily could hear a piano laboring.

"The Murphys' storage unit. How's 'Für Elise'?"

Becca ignored the question. "Listen. I'm glad I caught you. I just talked to a potential client. She said she called last week but no one got back to her. I don't know how we missed that. She asked if we could go over and see her. Now." Becca paused. "I told her no. We don't work Sundays and we don't work nights. She said there were extenuating circumstances."

"What extenuating circumstances?"

"Reading between the lines, I think it's about her husband. Right now he's out of the house. I told her no. Sorry. I mean, we can't turn on a dime. Then, after I hung up, I get a call." Becca lowered her voice, "*This is Ryan Melanson the third.*" It was a pretty good imitation of Frank's law partner's resonant bass. "He was calling on that woman's behalf, begging us to reconsider. He says she lives in Mandarin Cliffs and she'll pay double whatever we usually charge, and that he personally vouched for us."

"*Ryan* recommended us?" Emily was shocked, because she and Ryan Melanson had barely spoken since the last time she and Frank had had Ryan and his then-wife over to dinner. Emily had been in the kitchen chopping onions when she smelled Ryan's whiskey-scented breath and felt his hand cup her behind.

She'd whirled around and jabbed the knife point into his belly, nicking the fabric of his black silk shirt, and told him to back off or she'd rip off his testicles. Surely even thick-skinned Ryan would know that his personal recommendation wouldn't cut any ice with her.

Maybe Becca's desperate caller was a new woman in Ryan's life. Or perhaps an old flame. He'd had a bonfire of those. Whoever she was, it sounded as if she shared his sense of entitlement. On the other hand, she and Becca did need more clients. Just the other day, Frank had suggested that they market their services to a wealthier clientele. Post ads on the community bulletin board at their nearest Whole Foods. Wealthy clients could be more demanding, but they'd be less likely to balk when it came time to pay.

"She'll pay double?" Emily said.

"Exactly. Plus, *bird in the hand*. So I thought I'd better run it by you before I left it at no."

With its fancy homes and winding lanes, Mandarin Cliffs might as well have been another universe, but it wasn't all that far from Emily's neighborhood. And a house in Mandarin Cliffs was likely to be air-conditioned, Emily thought as she wiped her face and neck with her shirttail. "Well, we didn't say *when* on Monday we'd get back to Mrs. Murphy."

"Right. You could finish up the storage unit in the morning and head over to Mandarin Cliffs now. Okay?" It was ten after five and Emily was, at most, twenty minutes from Mandarin Cliffs. Taking Emily's silence for *yes*, Becca added, "I'll call her back and let her know. And I'll text you her name and address. You're the best."

"I guess," Emily said. The one good thing about teaching had been that once she'd finished grading papers, she'd had complete control of her off-hours. "I hope this doesn't turn into a regular thing."

"It won't if we don't let it," Becca said. "Before you go, what's it look like there?"

"It looks like . . ." Emily stepped to the doorway of the storage unit and looked in. Hot air no longer pulsed out. "Old books. Vintage hardware. And—" Just then she lost her grip on the document tube that she'd tucked under her arm. When she tried to catch it, her cell phone clattered to the concrete floor. Before she knew it, the hatbox had tumbled, too, spilling papers and cards.

Emily grabbed her phone. Not broken, thank goodness. "I'll tell you one thing," she said to Becca, "this won't be straightforward. Mr. Murphy was paying for climate control and he wasn't getting it. Looks like rodents have been having a banquet in here, too. Whatever else, Mrs. Murphy should bring in an insurance appraiser before we clear this out, and possibly an attorney, too." Squeezing the phone between her shoulder and ear, she stooped and began to gather the pieces of paper that had spilled from the hatbox.

Becca said, "We need to include coordinating that in our estimate."

But Emily almost missed the suggestion. The slip of paper in her hand was a bookplate engraved with an image of a table laden with books. Below the picture were the words *MIDDLEBURY COLLEGE LIBRARY*. And below that, *GIFT OF SILAS M. PEARSON 1910*.

"Talk to you later," Becca said. In the background Emily heard what sounded like Sophie coming down hard on piano keys. The call disconnected. A few moments later Emily's phone pinged with a text.

Quinn Newell 55 Ardmore Ln

Emily picked up another slip of paper. This one was card stock, yellowed with age. Typewritten at the top, it said, *This book should be returned to the Library on or before the last date stamped below.* The date stamped was *NOV-1 '79*.

She shuffled through the rest of the papers. Library book pockets. Bookplates. Due-date slips. There were hundreds of them . . . in a storage unit that contained hundreds of old books.

7

EMILY STUFFED THE cards and bookplates back into the hatbox, set it on a shelf, turned off the light, and pulled the door to the storage unit closed. It took several tries to force the padlock to snap shut. As she backed away, she stumbled over the document tube she'd been holding when Becca called. She picked it up and went to return it, but when she tried to unlock the padlock again, it wouldn't give. She didn't want to break the key, so she gave up and made a mental note to bring a can of WD-40 with her when she returned.

She put the key in her pants pocket and tossed the document tube on the passenger seat. Stuffed her face mask back into her gear bag in the trunk. Standing behind her car, hidden from the CCTV camera, she stripped off her top, bunched it up, and used it to wipe the sweat from her face and neck. At the bottom of her gear bag was a fresh blue Clutter Kickers polo shirt. She slipped it on.

On her way to Mandarin Cliffs, Emily mulled over what she'd found in the storage unit. Of one thing she was fairly certain: Mr. Murphy was not a hoarder. He was a serious collector, a connoisseur who kept track of his treasures. She fully expected to find a detailed inventory hidden somewhere in his office or maybe in the storage unit, assuming it hadn't rotted away.

But the hatbox full of library slips raised the question. Had Mr. Murphy legitimately purchased his books or were they on "permanent loan"? And if the books were questionable, what about the documents in those tubes?

Stopped at a red light, Emily gave a furtive glance across to her passenger seat where she had one of Mr. Murphy's document tubes right there in the car with her. What happened when a client's clutter consisted of *potentially* stolen goods? It was an issue that Becca and Emily wouldn't have chosen to touch with a ten-foot pole.

The car behind her beeped, a reminder that their new client was waiting. Emily pushed the tube to the floor and nudged it under the seat. Tonight, at home, she'd try to figure out what exactly they were dealing with.

The entrance to the not-quite-gated (surrounded by fancy iron fence with an open entryway) enclave of Mandarin Cliffs was marked by a gold-embossed sign mounted in a boulder in a small oriental-style garden with a miniature waterfall. The street, its houses set back on generous lots rife with blooming hydrangeas, curved and forked and forked again. Quinn Newell's house was at the far end of a cul-de-sac. Prime property in a primo neighborhood.

It was nearly six o'clock when Emily parked and got out of her car. She took in the house. Make that *château*, clad in beige stucco and figured stone. Its grand entrance featured massive double doors, flanked by rectangular columns that—Emily stepped back as she looked up—stretched all the way to the roof. A tower room in the front corner had windows all around. The house dwarfed its neighbors. Mandarin Cliffs was, after all, still New England, where conspicuous consumption was considered wretched excess. These people must not be New Englanders.

Emily found two peppermint Altoids in the bottom of her purse. She scraped off the fuzz and popped them in her mouth. Then she ran her fingers through her hair and smoothed her T-shirt. She wished she'd worn something less . . . servile. Though wasn't she providing a service not all that less menial than cleaning toilets and mowing lawns? Slapping her name on a business card and calling herself a *professional organizer* didn't make her work any less sweaty.

If Becca had been here, she'd have given Emily a dope slap. What was it about other people's wealth that was so toxic to Emily's self-esteem? Now, that was something that needed to be shaken out, smoothed, assessed, and tossed away. Emily reminded herself that what she liked about her new career was that success was tangible. No test was needed.

She grabbed her gear bag from the car and went up to the front door. Pressed the heel of her hand firmly against the doorbell and waited, standing straight, chest out.

Young or old? Quinn was one of those names that had recently become popular, along with Sophie and Olivia. From the house, and from the fact that Ryan Melanson III had referred this client to them, Emily expected Quinn to be manicured, blond, and impeccably dressed.

Wrong on all counts. The woman who came to the door was a thirty-something brunette, her shoulder-length hair held back loosely with a banana clip. The clothes—black yoga pants with a black racerback tank—were not impressive, though they were probably Lululemon. If she was one of Ryan's conquests, she was an outlier in terms of looks. Not that she wasn't attractive, she just wasn't flashy. Well within the bounds of average. Maybe the money made the difference.

Emily winced. It was bitchy and unfair of her to judge. She knew nothing about this woman, and had only experienced Ryan at his most reptilian.

The woman blinked at Emily bleary-eyed, as if she'd just woken up. "Are you from Clutter Fuckers?"

Something about the way the word rolled off the woman's tongue cracked Emily up. "Clutter *Kickers*," she managed to say.

"Oh dear." The woman put her hand to her forehead and squinted at Emily. "I'm so sorry. What did I call it?"

"Never mind. Here." Emily fished a business card from her bag. "Freeze-Frame Clutter Kickers. You must be Ms. Newell."

"Quinn," the woman said, studying the card. Bangs shadowed her wan-looking eyes. "Thank you so much for coming. I know it's not the most convenient time."

Ya think? "No problem. You talked to my partner. I was doing an assessment for another client not all that far away." Emily gave Quinn what she hoped was a sincere smile.

"Well, it's kind of you to say that. I'm afraid I had a bit of a meltdown on the phone. But I'm not a nut or a princess, I swear."

No, Quinn Newell did not strike Emily as a nut. The not-a-princess part she was less sure about. For sure, she was a bit jittery. High? Emily took in the vast entryway. That sweet smell wasn't weed. More likely potpourri. But she knew better than to ask the obvious question: Why the fire drill? She'd watched Becca work with new clients often enough to know that answers would emerge. Attacking people head-on with *why* questions could drive them into a protective crouch. Instead, she said, "So you know Ryan Melanson?"

"We're"—Quinn hesitated—"friends." She rushed on with, "He speaks highly of you. Says you're trustworthy. Dependable. Quite a straight arrow." Quinn spoke without a hint of irony.

"He works with my husband," Emily said. She wasn't about to get into her own history with Ryan. She looked around. "Well, this is quite a house."

"No kidding," Quinn said with a smile. "My husband's taste. Actually, his ex's. Three guesses where he met that one. Vegas!" She snickered. "Actually, that's not true. I don't know where he met her. I don't actually care. But I like to tell people that, because she was a dancer and her design aesthetic is pure Vegas."

Emily would have pegged it more as Versailles. The two-story foyer—it felt larger than the rotunda of the courthouse where Emily had served jury duty last year—dwarfed its spare furnishings. The floor was a patchwork of Chinese Oriental carpets in pastels and cream. Against the wall stood an elegant, oversized Biedermeier-style chest of drawers and a settee with striped satin upholstery. And, of course, there was a grand staircase.

The walls, on the other hand, were hung haphazardly with prints and posters, along with old advertising signs and the occasional African or Alaskan mask. The mishmash of centuries and cultures and tastes created a pleasant visual cacophony.

Quinn must have followed Emily's gaze, because she said, "Furniture's not my taste, either. And that stuff on the walls?" She shrugged and shook her head. "Those belong to my husband.

Wally's big into vintage advertising. In fact, that's where he is right now, at an auction of the stuff. Went all the way to Hyannis, if you can believe that."

A brightly colored sign for laundry detergent, the paint flaking at the edges to reveal bits of rust, hung crooked at the bottom of the grand stairs. Emily couldn't stop herself from going over to straighten it. When she did, she realized it was covering a fist-sized hole in the wall. She glanced back at Quinn. At what was surely a bruise under her eye.

Emily was startled by a creaking sound overhead. Was someone else in the house? Quinn looked up, on the alert, too. A *pad-pad-pad* soon revealed itself to be a fat calico cat that sauntered down the stairs and rubbed the side of its head against Emily's leg. Emily reached down to pet the cat. It arched its back, paused for a moment, then slithered over to Quinn, who ignored it. Maybe the calico was the first wife's cat.

Quinn said, "Wally's a pack rat. You wouldn't believe the stuff he's got down in the basement."

Actually, I would. Emily was sure she hadn't said it out loud, but still Quinn gave her a close look and asked, "Don't tell me, you're married to one, too?"

Emily felt her face grow hot. *Empathize but don't overshare.* That was Becca's maxim. Her role was to listen and take notes. Be supportive and professional. *It's not group therapy.*

"Does your husband know you're consulting us?" Emily said, feeling an uneasy twinge. How ugly would it get if he returned unexpectedly and found Emily here?

"I told him, but does he *know*?" Quinn laughed. "That's practically an existential question, because he's not the world's best listener."

"I ask because it's one of our rules. I can't help you declutter someone else's stuff. My partner should have explained that to you on the phone."

"She did. And don't worry, it's not. I wouldn't dare touch any of his stuff. There'd be hell to pay. Come on out to the garage. I'll show you what I need your help dealing with."

8

EMILY FOLLOWED QUINN through an airy open kitchen. On the pink-granite counter sat a massive copper-and-brass espresso machine. Several pizza boxes lay in the recycle bin. Vintage tin cans were lined up along the tops of the bleached-wood cabinets. On the wall, a clock with a black cat, its tail the pendulum that ticked and tocked side to side, was an advertisement for something called Black Cat shoe polish. Stuck to a bulletin board were about a dozen business cards. Emily foraged in her bag for another Freeze-Frame Clutter Kickers business card. "Mind if I pin this up for you?"

"Sure," Quinn said. "Thanks."

Emily used an orphaned pushpin to post her business card alongside a class calendar for the women's fitness center in East Hartwell. Morning vinyasa yoga classes were circled in red.

Quinn opened the refrigerator and took out a bottle of prosecco. She grabbed a pair of balloon-shaped wineglasses that were hanging upside down from an overhead rack, filled them with prosecco, and offered one to Emily.

Emily hesitated.

"What, you don't like prosecco?"

"It's not that," Emily said. Actually, Emily and Frank drank prosecco whenever they had something to celebrate. It was cheap, reliable, and it was also Emily's beverage of choice on the rare occasion when she threw herself a pity party.

"You're not supposed to drink on the job?" Quinn said with a sly smile.

No drinking on the job was another of Becca and Emily's rules. Plus, that was an enormous glass Quinn was waving about, and prosecco went straight to Emily's head. Especially on an empty stomach. Her stomach gurgled, reminding her that lunch had been hours ago.

"You probably aren't supposed to work weekends or after five, either. And yet here you are." Quinn held out a glass to Emily. "Come on. In for a penny, in for a pound."

Emily couldn't help smiling. *In for a penny* . . . that was an expression her mother often trotted out when she tempted Emily with a six-hundred-calorie slice of her world-class cheese pie. Emily dropped her gear bag on the terra-cotta tile floor and took the glass.

Quinn raised her own glass in a toast. "Cheers!"

Emily held up her glass. The bubbles glistened. "What are we celebrating?"

"Me. Calling Clutter"—Quinn's gaze rested on Emily's T-shirt—"Kickers for help. Finally." She took a sip and waited for Emily to do the same. The wine was ice-cold and not too dry. "Here's to taking care of business." She clinked Emily's glass, drank some more, and carried her glass and the bottle out the kitchen door and into a garage. Emily took one more small sip of prosecco, then picked up her gear bag and followed Quinn.

The garage, like the rest of the house, was oversized. It had four bays. Nearest to the kitchen door was an empty bay where Emily presumed the absent Wally parked his Ferrari, or whatever muscle car he drove. In the next spot sat a sporty red Miata convertible. Probably Quinn's. Marking the boundary between these two bays was a row of orange traffic cones.

"Those cones?" Quinn said. "He's afraid I'm going to sideswipe his precious car. What does your husband drive?"

"A BMW Z4," Emily said

"I knew it. And he'd die before he'd let someone else drive it. Am I right?"

Of course she was right.

The remaining two bays in the garage were a jumble of densely packed furniture, storage boxes, and assorted junk. "See all that?" Quinn said. "I lived in a studio apartment and that's pretty much all I owned before I moved in with Wally." She hit a button that raised both of the garage's double doors. "When I moved in, he promised he'd make room for my things. I figured, no biggie. It's not like we're short of space. Guess I didn't know him as well as I thought I did, because here we are, three years later, and my junk's still sitting in the garage and the house is still *his* house. And you know what? I don't even care anymore." She shook her head, splashing some wine on the floor. "I gave up my job. My name. Why not give it all up?"

"That sucks," Emily said. It was no small thing, giving up your own home to move in with someone. Then to have your possessions quarantined? At least Frank had never begrudged Emily her own space and, for the most part, kept his crap out of it.

"You know, people see the big house." Quinn's eyes brimmed with tears. "The fancy car. And they think, wow, she's got everything."

Emily felt a flash of guilt, because that was exactly what she had thought. She took a swallow of wine. "You must have been in love with him."

Quinn chewed on her lower lip. "I suppose so. Kind of." In a whisper, "But if I got a do-over?" Quinn gave a bitter laugh. "I was thirty-five, my biological clock is ticking, I wanted to be married in the worst way. Guess that's what I got." She turned her gaze toward the house. "I should never have married Wally, but I did. I have no illusions about the bargain I've made. Most days I get up and do my thing. It's okay."

Emily could have said the same thing about her own marriage. She and Frank let each other do their own thing. And her biological clock was set to run out.

"But this," Quinn went on, gesturing to the piles of her belongings. "It's so disrespectful, don't you think? Makes me feel like a worthless piece of shit."

"Quinn, you're not your things." The minute Emily said that, she realized it wasn't true. To a very real extent, people could be defined by the things they kept, each one a choice, even if it was not a conscious one. Emily was her sock drawer, both before and after. Mr. Murphy was his decaying books and decorative hardware. Frank was his piano guts.

As if on cue, Emily's foot throbbed. She reached down to rub it, and when she straightened, Quinn was looking across at her. She had a pale intensity about her, repressed rage that Emily sometimes saw when she unexpectedly caught her own reflection in a mirror.

Emily shivered and took another drink. Quinn topped off Emily's glass and her own.

"Seriously," Quinn said, "how would you like to be married to a guy who goes to auctions and flea markets and brings home"—she grimaced—"would you believe, prosthetic limbs? He's got a complete collection. Arms. Legs. Lefts. Rights. Even some fingers. So creepy."

"Mine's into rotting church pews," Emily said. "And horror comics."

"Autographed Dwight D. Eisenhower bobblehead dolls," Quinn said. "Preserved piranha fish and morpho butterflies."

"*Star Wars* action figures." Emily raised her glass. "Original! Still in their boxes!"

Quinn said, "And his idea of a romantic evening? Binge-watching *Antiques Roadshow*." She lifted her own glass.

"Yours, too?" Emily clinked and took another drink. "At least your husband's stuff's right out in the open. He's not hiding it from you."

"How do I know what he's got hidden?" Quinn tilted her head back and emptied her glass. Wiped her arm across her mouth. "Yours has a secret stash?"

"Define *secret*." Did the basement count as a *secret stash* if Frank thought Emily would never go down there? "I know where it is, but I try not to look. Today I met a widow whose husband left her a jam-packed storage unit that she knew nothing about until the rental bill showed up a year after he died." She reached into her pants pocket, pulled out the key, and flashed it at Quinn. "Turns out it's packed to the gills with old books and prints."

"Shhh." Quinn put her finger to her lips. "Please don't tell Wally."

"And you know what storage company he's been using? *Inner Peace* Storage. Poor thing, she was far more serene before she knew about that storage unit. And when she finds out what's in it, she'll be a complete wreck."

"What's wrong with their old books and prints?" Quinn asked, leaning close.

Emily stopped herself from answering. The wine was talking. She wished she could put the words back in her mouth as she tried to slip the key back into her pocket. But she missed, and the key dropped onto the concrete floor. When she bent to pick it up, blood rushed to her head. As she staggered sideways, she managed to kick the key under a chest of drawers.

Quinn put out a hand and Emily grabbed it to steady herself. When the dizziness passed and Emily straightened, Quinn scooped up the key for her and dropped it into Emily's gear bag.

Emily set her wineglass on the floor. "Okay. Well, then," she said, trying to collect herself. Becca would have been apoplectic if she'd witnessed this performance. Emily focused her attention on the mounds in the garage. "If it's okay with you, I'll take a few pictures. That will help us estimate how long it will take. And you'll need to think about whether you really want to dump all of it. You don't get a day-after do-over."

"I'm not going to need one," Quinn said firmly. "Now that I'm ready to deal with this, I want to be done with it."

Emily assessed the pile. This would be eminently manageable, especially if Quinn really was committed to getting rid of everything. But Emily had been at this long enough to know that nothing turned out to be as simple as it seemed at first blush. She fired off four quick shots from outside the garage. She had only a limited view of what was there. Shoeboxes filled with CDs were within reaching distance. Stuffed animals—Care Bears, each a different pastel—were stuck in a cardboard liquor box on one of the bureaus.

"I see you still have your Care Bears," Emily said. When they were kids, Emily and Becca had each had her own set. Months ago, Emily had laundered and sun-dried hers, then packed them in a box. Leaving them on her front steps for charity donation pickup, she'd felt as if she were abandoning beloved pets. She'd convinced herself that she had to part with her own sentimental clutter in order to start her new career. Now she was sorry she hadn't at least kept her favorite, turquoise Wish Bear, with its belly badge a yellow shooting star.

"Care Bears are just the tip of the iceberg." Quinn reached into the pile for a large brown Bloomingdale's bag. She opened it and pulled out a hooded red T-shirt with BOSTON emblazoned in white letters down the sleeve. Emily recognized it as a BU Terriers basketball T-shirt.

"You went to BU?" Emily asked.

"I did," Quinn said. "Undergrad."

Frank and Emily had met at BU when they were in graduate school, she in education, he in law. He'd had a T-shirt just like the one that Quinn was holding up as Exhibit A of useless sentiment. Emily had slept in the shirt when she'd stayed at the apartment that Frank shared with Ryan, long before the pair had started their own law firm. The place had been a squalid firetrap, four flights up in the Fens. Emily wondered what had happened to the shirt.

Emily picked up her wineglass. She knew she shouldn't have more to drink, but she wanted to swallow the bittersweet memory.

"But this shirt wasn't mine." Quinn held it up to her face, closed her eyes, and inhaled. "Or Wally's." Another BU boyfriend? No wonder Quinn's husband hadn't wanted it in his house.

"Was T-shirt man the one that got away?" Emily asked, wondering if it had been Ryan.

"Not exactly," Quinn said, her cheeks coloring slightly. "But Wally knows the shirt's not his. He goes off the rails, crazy jealous, if I mention any of my old boyfriends. It's silly, really."

Out of the blue Emily remembered the photo album she'd put together, pictures of herself and her high school sweetheart. Such a genuinely nice guy, he'd made her adolescence tolerable. She kept the album where she knew Frank wouldn't look, in a box with her mother's china. He'd never have understood why she kept those photos. She didn't really understand herself.

Emily set her glass back down and held her cell phone high over her head. Aiming the camera down into the scrum, she took a picture, then checked the viewfinder, enlarging the image to see what was there. Was that a papasan chair? Quintessential dorm furniture. Easy to get into, nearly impossible to get out of. She'd once had one, its cushion upholstered in gold corduroy. Lying across this chair's wicker frame was a rolled-up area rug.

"You think I'd be able to sell some of this?" Quinn asked. "Not that we need the money."

There was no point in sugarcoating it. Emily indicated a pair of pre–World War II mahogany chests of drawers, cousins to the one she'd inherited from her own grandmother. "That's sturdy and nice-looking, and thirty years ago you might have found a buyer. But these days, it's what people refer to as"—she drew air quotes—"'brown furniture.' Frankly, it's hard to give away. But there'd be a ready buyer for that kitchen set if you put it out at a yard sale." She pointed to a 1950s kitchen table and matching chairs with their aluminum tubing and yellow-vinyl seats.

"Oh goody. A yard sale! And let's not invite Wally." Quinn laughed.

"Or you could donate. There's a ton of charities and you'd get a tax deduction. I can find one that will pick up."

"What I really should do is stuff all of my old shit down Wally's goddamned—" Quinn broke off and stood perfectly still for a few moments. The bruise on her face had turned livid in the harsh light. Then she put her head back and drank from the bottle. Swiped her mouth with the back of her hand. "Think there are any charities that will come over and pick *him* up? Or maybe he's just another worthless piece of—what did you call it?—brown furniture. Maybe I should just chuck him off the roof instead."

Emily had picked up her glass and just taken another sip of prosecco herself when something about the matter-of-fact way that Quinn said *chuck him off the roof* struck her as hilarious. She laughed so hard, wine came fizzing out her nose. She clapped her hand over her face and doubled over.

"Or slip poison mushrooms into his lasagna," Quinn went on. "Or accidentally back over him." She held up her hands as if she were holding on to a steering wheel and looked over her shoulder. "*Rrrmm.* Oops! My bad."

Emily imagined the piano frame falling from their bedroom window onto Frank's head as he dragged a church pew in through their bulkhead door. She laughed and raised her glass. "To *'til death do us part.*"

"To accidents waiting to happen." Quinn raised the bottle. Then slowly lowered it. Her look turned somber. "Or maybe it's safer to hire a hit man, a complete stranger, and be done with it?" She gave Emily an appraising look. "So, could you?"

"Could I what?" Emily said, though she knew exactly what Quinn was asking. Of course, she could never kill anyone, and certainly not Frank. So maybe it was the wine, or the boyfriend's T-shirt, or the vision of that piano frame dropping from a second-story window that kept her from saying so.

"I'll bet you would. In a heartbeat." Quinn winked. "If you thought you could get away with it."

9

EMILY SPENT THE next hour in a wine-infused haze. She took more photographs of the piles in the garage and scribbled some nearly indecipherable notes, including a list of the few items in the garage that Quinn wanted to keep and her preferences about how to dispose of the rest.

Finally, Emily quoted Quinn a fee for their organizing services, inflating her guesstimate by 50 percent. To double it felt like price gouging. She gave Quinn a PayPal account to which she could transfer a $500 deposit. "If you decide to move forward."

"Well, of course I'm going to move forward," Quinn said. She gave Emily an awkward hug. "I feel really good about this. I just know I can trust you completely. Ryan was right." Her smile seemed utterly genuine.

Emily was jotting down the best times for Emily or Becca to return—when Quinn's husband wouldn't be there, of course—when Quinn slipped her cell phone from her pocket and looked at the readout. "Not mine. That must have been yours."

Emily got out her phone. Sure enough, she'd missed a text from Frank.

Em, could you stop at JC & bring me coffee? :-x

"Your partner?" Quinn asked.

"My husband."

"The prince?"

Emily laughed. "Did I call him that?"

"Reading between the lines."

"He wants me to pick him up a coffee on the way home. I've got just enough time to stop in the Square."

"They say jump, we say how high," Quinn said.

"It's not like that. Really." Frank was usually the one who picked up a coffee for *her*. He even tried to get to the coffee shop before they ran out of her favorite cider donuts dusted with cinnamon sugar.

"Whatever," Quinn said, giving Emily a skeptical look.

Emily had just enough time to do a quick pee and still make it to the Java Connection before it closed. As she was leaving, Quinn offered her a black plastic controller. "Here's the remote that opens the garage door. Take it. You'll be able to get in and out when I'm not here."

Emily hesitated. "Let's wait until after we have a signed agreement." Even then, she doubted that she'd want to come back when Quinn wasn't here. She didn't want to run into Wally.

"No worries. It's a spare. Keep it for now and give it back when we're done." Quinn dropped the controller into Emily's gear bag and walked Emily out to her car.

Emily knew she'd have to find a way to keep Quinn from steamrolling her. Right now she was too woozy to push back.

As Emily started her car, the double doors to the Newells' garage slid shut and the piles of old furniture and stuffed toys disappeared from view. She pulled away from the curb. Any of the items piled in that garage would have stuck out like a sore thumb in the interior of the Newells' grand house, loaded as it was with antique and designer furniture, Persian rugs, and a carefully curated selection of vintage advertising. Emily's and Frank's tastes weren't quite as strikingly different, or so she told herself. She could appreciate the Art Deco, machine-age design of a vintage electric fan. Even if it was useless and far from kid-friendly, it was a thing of beauty. It was an entire collection of them that left her cold.

Feeling the effects of too much wine, Emily bit her lower lip to anchor her attention as she turned onto the main road. She opened the car windows to let in some fresh air. She and Frank had always had their differences. But was his acquisitiveness pathological hoarding? Was her aversion to chaos obsessive nitpicking? Would she end up, years from now, bound to a man she'd once loved but with whom she no longer shared much in common? *'Til death us do part* would be a very long time, and maybe that was okay. Case in point: her parents. Lila Laubenstein had been a librarian whose passions were books, art, theater, and more books. A retired cop, Bert loved golf chased with a six-pack, a football game, and more golf. When he wasn't teeing off and she wasn't volunteering at the library at their senior center, they spent their days at opposite ends of a two-bedroom condo watching two different TVs. Hers would be tuned to *The View*, while he had on Fox News. Emily herself was the one thing they had in common.

Without a child to bring them together, would Emily's and Frank's differences become irreconcilable? Would they still *spark joy* for each other? Because trying to "fold" Frank, tidy him up, and trim his rough edges would prove futile. She'd fallen in love with his smile and sharp intellect. He was solid and handsome, even if he drove her around the bend with his auctions and yard sales. At least he wasn't addicted to Fox News and he didn't screw around. And he didn't punch her or tell her what she couldn't bring into their house. Only what she couldn't take *out* of it.

Emily pulled up in front of the lone car parked in front of the Java Connection. The neighboring sandwich shop and insurance office were closed. The Java Connection was a recent addition to what residents referred to as the Square, though the actual Square was now a parking lot. The coffee shop took up half of what had once been a hardware store that closed when Home Depot opened a half mile away. Its plate-glass windows dated back to the sixties. A sign hanging in the front door read WELCOME. And below that, RESTROOM FOR CUSTOMERS ONLY.

As Emily got out of her car, she called Frank. "I'm here," she said when he answered. "What do you want me to get you?"

"Thanks, doll," he said. "Americano with an extra shot of espresso."

"Decaf?"

"God, no. Sacrilege."

Emily pocketed her phone and pushed through the door of the coffee shop. The interior was chrome and brick and barn board, the walls hung with vintage coffee posters that would have been right at home in Walter Newell's collection, had they been originals. The tables were empty and a single customer stood at the front register. The top shelf of the glass cabinet that usually held the cinnamon-sugar cider donuts was empty. Of course there wouldn't be any left at this time of day, and if there had been, they'd have turned hard as hockey pucks.

Emily was approaching the counter when the man already there wheeled around and crashed into her. His coffee splashed all over. "I'm so sorry," Emily said, even though it wasn't her fault. "I didn't realize—"

"Christ Almighty," said the man. He wore a baseball cap and aviator glasses with yellow lenses, and he had a well-tended beard and mustache. He looked down at his coffee-stained yellow polo shirt and now-lidless venti, then bent still farther to see the coffee (he took it black, Emily noticed) pooling in the toe well of his butterscotch leather loafers.

Under his breath, he spat, "Stupid cow."

Emily recoiled. But before she could come up with an equally hateful epithet, he'd brushed past her. She watched him stride out the door and walk past her car. Then, making eye contact with her through the front window of the coffee shop, he over-handed his coffee cup against the back of her car.

Prick. Asshole. Too late, apt retorts came to her.

The barista, a young woman with a rich mocha complexion and long dark hair that was parted down the middle, was already at Emily's side with a roll of paper towels. It was only then that Emily realized coffee had splattered all over her shirt and pants as well. As she patted her arms dry, she heard the screech of tires from outside. She looked out the window. The man and his car were gone.

"Charming fellow," Emily said. She handed the barista the coffee-soaked paper towels. "Thank you."

"You are sure you are not hurt?" The barista—on closer inspection she was not all that young—gave Emily a sympathetic look. She wore oversized gold hoop earrings and pronounced "sure" *eh-sure*, adding a syllable, the way Emily's Spanish-speaking students often had. Her name badge read ANA.

"I hope he's not one of your regular customers," Emily said.

Ana dropped a fresh wad of paper towels on the floor and bent to spread them around to sop up the spill. "I never seen him before." She wore a bracelet of colored macaroni strung together. A mom.

"Needs to seriously chill out," Emily said.

"You think?" Ana laughed. She scooped up the towels and stood. "So, what can I get you?"

An Americano with an extra shot, Emily told her. While Ana filled her order, a kid who couldn't have been more than sixteen came out from the back, turned the sign in the front door from OPEN to CLOSED, and started to mop the floor.

"On the house," Ana said when Emily tried to pay.

"No. Seriously," Emily said, offering a ten-dollar bill.

"Absolutely not. And I am so sorry."

"Not your fault." Emily stuffed the money into the tip jar and went out to her car. Coffee was splashed across her rear window and had run rivulets through the grime coating the white trunk lid.

Furious as well as shaken, Emily unlocked her car and got in. She hoped that asshole's fancy shoes were well and truly ruined.

10

ON THE SHORT ride home, the smell of coffee evaporating off her clothing made Emily nauseous. She turned onto her street and drove slowly down the block. Just once, it would be nice if Frank left the outside lights on for her. She pulled into the driveway and got out of the car, hurried to the back door and felt for the lock.

Once inside, she made her way to Frank's office. The door was ajar. She pulled it open. A single lamp was on in the corner. Frank sat at his desk, his face lit by his computer screen. She crept up behind him. Startled, he jumped in his chair and nearly knocked the coffee from her hand.

"You're back," he said, snapping his laptop shut.

"What are you up to?"

"Working." He pushed his chair away from the desk and swiveled to face her. He was wearing boxers and an undershirt.

"At this hour?"

"Okay. Sussed me out. I'm working, but I'm also bidding. Online auction ends in a half hour and I need to stay sharp." Emily didn't want to know what he was bidding on; she just hoped it was small and flat. She held out the coffee. He took it, lifted the lid, and sniffed. "Thanks."

"How was the game?" she asked.

"We won. Barfield had four hits, cleared the bases in the seventh. What about you? You said you had to work, but I didn't expect you back this late."

He looked up at her with that million-dollar smile of his, his look turning askance. "Looks like you're wearing some of this." He blew on the coffee and took another sip. "What happened?"

"Asshole ran into me at the coffee shop." All that remained was a fleeting impression of a big man with a trim dark beard, tinted glasses, and an angry scowl. *Stupid cow.* It was telling that he'd picked that particularly demeaning insult. "Spilled his coffee and blamed me."

"That sounds unpleasant."

"It was." She looked down at her shirt and pants. "It'll come out in the wash."

Frank settled back in his chair. "So tell me, other than that, how was your day?"

She perched on the edge of a two-drawer file cabinet. "I checked out that storage unit. Then I took a quick run over to meet a new client. Someone Ryan sent our way."

"Really?" Frank guffawed. "See, he's not such a bad sort. Probably trying to worm his way back into your good graces."

"He knew better than to call me. He phoned Becca and begged us to go see the woman right away."

"I wondered what he was up to. He took a call and left the game early. What's her name?"

"Quinn. Quinn Newell."

Frank thought for a moment. "Must be a new one."

"She lives in Mandarin Cliffs."

Frank's eyebrows rose. He rubbed his fingers against his thumb.

"Looks like it," Emily said. "Fabulous house. Married to a creep."

"A dead creep?"

The comment made her squirm. "No, it's the other client, the one with the storage unit, who's a widow. Becca and I should be able to help both of them, though I'm really not sure why the woman in Mandarin Cliffs feels like she needs our help at all. It's not like she's a hoarder. Because we know firsthand what *that* looks like."

Ignoring the dig, Frank said, "Sometimes people have a hard time letting things go." Maybe he *had* been listening to her when she filled him in on her clients and their possessions. "At least Mrs. Mandarin Cliffs will pay you what you're worth."

"You guessed it. Ryan suggested that we could charge double our usual rate."

"You're worth double. Working Sunday night? Are nights and weekends going to become the new normal?"

"Hey, I don't tell you when to work and what to bill your clients."

"Point taken." He gathered up the papers strewn across his desk.

"A new case?"

"Homeowner's suing over a smoke detector that she says short-circuited and caused her house to catch fire. She's not asking for a big payout. Just expenses. But it could open the door to a class action, so they're taking no chances." He took a drink of coffee. "Never thought I'd be reading circuit schematics and fault trees. Know what's the most common cause of smoke detector failure?" He smirked. "Dirt. People don't clean them." He turned away from her and opened his laptop.

Emily felt sympathy for the homeowner. Frank would probably annihilate her on the witness stand as he made the case against her housekeeping and for the company that manufactured the device. Once upon a time, he'd have been on her side, David dueling Goliath. Turned out, the satisfaction of winning for the underdog went only so far when you were making a paltry $50K a year. Though Frank didn't seem to miss it, he claimed working for the public defender had been great experience, standing up for people who more often than not had gotten themselves in trouble out of ignorance or impulsiveness, one ill-considered decision leading to another and another. Emily wondered if she and Becca weren't doing exactly that now, helping Mrs. Murphy get rid of her husband's trove when already there were red flags about how exactly he'd acquired it.

"Question," she said. "Purely hypothetical. As a former defense attorney."

"Uh-oh." Frank closed his laptop.

"Suppose I help someone declutter their house and it turns out that the clutter they're getting rid of isn't theirs."

The furrows between his eyebrows deepened. "Explain."

"Just suppose that I suspect it's, I don't know, items that he or she borrowed—"

"Borrowed?" He sounded incredulous.

"Hypothetically."

Frank cracked a smile. "In other words, hypothetically stole."

"Like I said, I'm not sure. Do I have an obligation to report my suspicions to the police?"

Frank thought for a few moments. This was one of her favorite things about him. When you asked a question about the law, he didn't shoot from the hip.

"Well, it's not a crime to witness a crime," he said at last. "And it sounds as if we're not talking child abuse or murder, in which case you'd be obligated to report your suspicions. So no. You have no *legal* obligation to report a suspected theft. You're in the clear unless you actually help the person get away with it. That's aiding and abetting, and depending on the crime, you could be charged. But for just knowing it's there and suspecting that it's stolen? That doesn't put you in jeopardy."

That was a relief. "What if I then help this client sell the stuff that I suspect may be stolen?"

"Then . . . well, now it gets more serious. You could be charged with fencing stolen property if the police have evidence that you knew it was stolen. Which is by no means a slam dunk." He paused and looked across at her. "What kind of value are we talking about? Hundreds of dollars or thousands?"

"Does it matter?"

"It matters."

"Worst-case?"

"Emily, I don't like where this is going. You really think what's in there could be stolen?" He seemed taken aback. "Worst-case, it's a felony to be involved in the disposal of stolen goods worth two hundred fifty dollars or more. You could go to jail."

Going to jail was not among the goals Emily and Becca had scoped out for themselves when they'd started their business. "Don't worry yet. I have no idea what it's worth or how he got it. So far, all I've done is look at some of the stuff."

"What kind of stuff is it?"

"Books. Doorknobs."

"Doorknobs?" Frank's face lit up.

"Boxes of them. You'd go nuts. And . . ." She hesitated. Was she betraying client confidentiality by sharing with him what she'd found?

"This is Mandarin Cliffs?"

"No. Our other client. The widow with the dead husband's storage unit."

"Well, for the time being, be careful not to remove anything. Taking possession—"

"Shit," Emily said under her breath, remembering the document tube.

"You took something?" Frank said. He sounded astonished.

"I didn't mean to," Emily said. "I've got it in the car."

"And it's valuable?"

"I have no idea. Maybe. I should run it back right now. I've got the key—" She tried to remember where she'd put the padlock key. She checked her pants pockets before remembering that it had fallen on the floor of Quinn's garage. Quinn had picked it up and dropped it in her gear bag. "I'll drive—"

"Drive? I don't think so. You get stopped, I doubt you'd pass a Breathalyzer."

"You can tell?"

"It's pretty obvious. Besides, it's late. No one's going to arrest you for holding on to it overnight."

Emily didn't need convincing. She was exhausted and still feeling queasy.

"And keep in mind," Frank added, "I'm being pretty cautious with my legal advice. If what's in that storage unit was acquired aboveboard and legally, you're good to go. If not, and if it's worth a significant amount of money, then you need to protect yourself. That's why you have insurance. And lucky you, you also have free in-house counsel. If it comes to that." Frank took another drink of coffee. "Thanks for this. I've got a few more hours before I can turn in. You get in bed."

"Don't forget about the auction," Emily said.

"I won't." He opened his computer and glanced at the screen. "When it's over, I'll come up and tuck you in."

Upstairs, Emily peeled off her coffee-stained T-shirt and pants and left them on the bathroom floor. She pulled on a nightgown and began to brush her teeth. She thought about the storage unit and its contents. There were plenty of reasons a man might not want his wife to know about his collections. It depended on their relationship, and Emily knew nothing about the Murphys' marriage. She hoped that Mrs. Murphy's husband had acquired his treasures legitimately. But if he had, why keep them hidden?

She rinsed her mouth and splashed cold water on her face. Her tired eyes stared back at her from the mirror. She got in bed, trying not to notice her closet. Even more unsettling than a cluttered closet was one that was in the midst of becoming uncluttered. And speaking of unfinished business, she needed to alert Becca.

She got out her phone and started typing a text:

Need to talk. Murphy's storage unit is

What was it? Emily settled on

complicated. Call if you're up.

She waited for the notification TEXT DELIVERED. But nothing came. Becca must have her phone turned off. Probably for the night. Emily texted again.

Call me first thing.

She was about to shut down her phone when a text message pinged. Not Becca. Emily didn't recognize the number, but it was her local area code.

PAYPAL: Mission Accomplished! xxx ooo

So, what do you think? How soon? Please please please.

Cheers! 😈

That sounded like Quinn Newell. She must have deposited the advance payment into the Clutter Kickers account, wrapped it in hugs, and kept right on drinking. This was not the start of a professional relationship. But what had Emily expected when she'd undoubtedly overshared?

Emily closed her eyes and tried to block out exactly how many gory details of her personal life she'd revealed.

Emily texted back what she hoped sounded like a formal response:

As discussed, looking forward to working with you. More next week. Emily L. Harlow (Freeze-Frame Clutter Kickers)

"Here," Frank said from the doorway. He was carrying her favorite mug, gray ceramic with purple irises painted on. "Non-alcoholic."

The smell of hot cocoa wafted over. Emily set her phone on the bedside table. Frank hadn't made cocoa for her in ages, maybe not since a blizzard a few winters ago after they'd shoveled three feet of snow from their driveway and scooped it from where the wind had packed it around their cars' engine blocks.

Why did one look at Frank's crap make her forget how sweet and thoughtful he could be?

"Did you eat dinner?" Frank asked.

She hadn't, which was why the wine had gone right to her head. Frank handed her the mug. "Drink. It will help you fall asleep," he said.

Emily blew on it and took a sip. Then another. Did cocoa really help you sleep? Or was it another one of those things that people believed but turned out to be a canard? After all, wasn't chocolate loaded with caffeine? Or was it like too much red wine—knocked you out and two hours later you were wide awake? Or maybe cocoa and chocolate were different things, chemically speaking. Or—

She stopped herself. Her brain was in overdrive, pinging from one inane thought to the next. She relaxed and inhaled. "Thank you. This is just what I needed," she said.

Frank picked up her cell phone. "Your battery's nearly dead. Want me to plug it in for you?"

"Thanks." Emily sank back into the pillows. "My charger's . . ." Where had she left it? "I think it's in my gear bag. Could be in the kitchen or maybe in the car."

Frank kissed her on the top of her head, turned out the lights, and left the room.

She took another drink and inhaled deeply. She closed her eyes, trying not to think about all the loose ends left from a day of surprises. Middlebury College bookplate. Board of Education doorknob. The tube that had to go back to the storage unit ASAP.

Her head jerked forward. She took one last sip and set the mug on the table. Her mouth tasted of cocoa grit. She really should get up and brush her teeth and rinse out the mug. But she didn't have the energy.

She closed her eyes. Her phone's LOW BATTERY message flickered in her head, along with a pair of devil emoticons. Plug herself in. That was what she needed to do. But she didn't have a plug, and the outlet was . . .

MONDAY

IT SEEMED LIKE only moments later the sun was shining in through the bedroom windows and Emily blinked awake. She'd forgotten to close the blinds. It was after nine, and Frank's side of the bed was rumpled but empty. She never slept this late. Her cell phone was on the bedside table, plugged in. She powered it on.

She tried to sit up but managed only to prop herself up on her elbows. It felt as if a fifty-pound weight shifted in her skull. She hadn't had a hangover this bad since college.

In the bathroom, she sat doubled over on the toilet, trying not to think about throwing up. When she was able to get up—slowly—she splashed cold water on her face and neck. Brushed her teeth. Then she knocked back a couple of aspirin and forced herself into the shower. Under the pulsing showerhead, her mind cleared.

She wrapped herself in a towel and padded out to her bureau. It still came as a surprise to find her underwear neatly rolled in the drawer. No more having to forage through to find what she wanted; now it was like plucking a chocolate donut from a tray of glazed. Such a simple thing. It might not spark joy, but it did spark serenity. Her foot was still too sore to lace it into a sneaker, so she put on her Crocs again.

When she got downstairs, she saw that Frank had gone to work. He'd left her a pot of coffee, but all she could stomach was weak tea. She toasted a slice of bread, but managed to chew and swallow only half of it. Frank's warning about the risks of handling stolen property made her anxious to get over to the storage facility and return the tube ASAP. She took a can of WD-40 from under the kitchen sink for the lock and left the house. Fifteen minutes later, she arrived at Inner Peace Storage.

She parked in front of Mrs. Murphy's unit and grabbed the document tube from under the passenger seat. Black mildew coated one end of the tube and Emily swiped it a few times against her pants leg. Since she'd started Clutter Kickers she had a much higher tolerance for mildew. As she gave the tube one final swipe, the plastic end cap came loose and fell on the floor of the car. Emily was putting the cap back on when she read the tube's handwritten label: *WILLIAM ALEXANDER MAP OF THE NORTHEAST.*

Why not at least have a look at what was inside before she put it back? She slid the document out and smoothed it across the steering wheel. The map was about a foot by a foot and a half. The paper was thick, more parchment than newsprint, and slightly yellowed. The words *New France* were written in an elegant cursive hand across the topmost landmass. Below that, *New Scotland.* And over a body of water, *Golfe of Canada.* An ornate compass occupied the lower corner.

Emily was no expert, but it certainly looked old. It was an engraving or an etching, though Emily didn't know the difference. With no tears or foxing, it was in pristine condition. She used her phone to google the words on the label. Back came a link to an auction house that, in 2012, had offered what looked like the identical map. According to the description, it was published in

London in 1624. In "excellent condition," it had a value estimate of . . . Emily blinked . . . *$12,000*. If the map in front of her was worth that much, and if it turned out to have been on permanent unofficial *loan*, she and Becca were catapulted into felony territory.

Carefully Emily rolled up the map and slipped it into the tube, anxious to put it back on the shelf where she'd found it. She got out of the car and approached the storage unit, feeling around in her gear bag for the key. When she didn't find it, she sat on the ground and dumped out the contents of the bag. The can of WD-40 rolled away as she pawed through her supplies. Finally she found the key snagged in the lining. But when she went to use it, the padlock she distinctly remembered hanging on the door was gone. The padlock in its place was round, not square; brass, not silvery; and it had no nail-polish number painted on.

For a moment she wondered if she'd come to the wrong unit. She stepped back—216 to the left, 218 to the right. Someone had been here since yesterday and changed the lock.

As Emily stood considering what to do next, one of the security carts came toward her. She could flag down the guard and report a changed lock. She'd have to explain that she wasn't the owner, that the owner was dead, and she was working for his wife who'd inherited the storage bills. She imagined his reaction. Eyebrows raised, he'd probably ask for some kind of proof that she had the right to be here, but she had no signed statement saying that she was acting on Mrs. Murphy's behalf or, for that matter, anything in writing that said that Mrs. Murphy was the beneficiary of the property in this particular unit.

As the security cart crept by at a glacial pace, Emily shoveled her belongings back into her bag. She retrieved the can of

WD-40 and put it in, too. A sideways glance confirmed that this was the same guard she'd seen before. He nodded at her and Emily nodded back. Her shoulders tightened as she waited for the cart to pass.

What in the hell was she supposed to do now? She couldn't open the padlock and finish her inventory. Plus she was now stuck in possession of a possibly antique map that could be worth thousands of dollars.

Emily got back in her car, tossed her gear bag and the document tube in the backseat, banged the heel of her hand on the steering wheel, and called Becca.

"There you are!" Becca said. "I was just about to call you. What's going on? What do you mean, it's 'complicated'?"

Emily said, "I mean it's possible that the books in that storage unit are from libraries."

"Libraries," Becca said. "*Borrowed* from libraries?"

"Best-case."

"Yikes."

"Exactly. At least I took a ton of pictures, so when we get back in we should be able to tell if anything's—"

"Wait a minute. I thought you were already in."

"I was. Last night. But I couldn't get in again this morning. Someone's changed the lock."

"Someone? But who? How? Mrs. Murphy said there was just the one key."

"She didn't even know the storage unit existed until that bill arrived. Someone else could have a key. One of the security guards told me yesterday that he'd seen a woman going in and out of that unit."

"Mrs. Murphy?"

"Not likely. He thought it might have been me."

Silence from Becca. Then a groan. "Mrs. Murphy's going to have a fit. But the sooner she knows, the better. Can you meet me over there?"

"You're done with family?"

"They'll survive an hour without me." In the background, Emily could hear a dog howl. "My sister-in-law and my aunt are still here. Between them, they can watch the beasts. I'll call Mrs. Murphy and tell her something has come up and we need to see her right away."

Emily breathed a sigh of relief. She was so glad she wasn't in this alone. "Thank you."

"For what?"

"For being calm and competent. For not coming unglued when things don't go according to plan."

"Nothing ever does. When we get back in there, we're going to need someone who knows their way around books to give us advice about what we're dealing with. Normally I'd call in a book dealer. But it sounds like we need an informal, confidential take on what we've gotten ourselves into first. From someone we know. Personally."

Of course, Becca was suggesting Emily's mother. For years, Lila Laubenstein had managed special collections for the library at Auburn Design School. She'd know how to handle the William Alexander map. How to tell if it was an original or a reproduction. She could also tell at a glance if repairs to Mr. Murphy's many damaged books were even feasible, and whether they were library copies.

As soon as Emily finished talking to Becca, she called her mother. Lila Laubenstein answered on the second ring with a bright, "Hello, dear. Is everything all right?" Lila was acutely attuned to changes in routine, and a Monday morning call from Emily was unusual.

"We need your expertise," Emily said.

"We?"

"Becca and I. For a client."

"Of course you do." Emily heard her father's rumbling bass in the background. "It's Emmy," her mother said. Then, to Emily, "Your father says hello." More rumbling. "All right, all right. I'll take the phone outside." Back to Emily. "Your father's doing his crossword, and you know how he gets."

All too well. A creature of habit, Bert Laubenstein would be settled in his easy chair with his morning coffee, immersed in three newspapers. He'd go from sports section to comics, and on to puzzles, timing how long it took him to complete them. Crosswords, sudokus, acrostics. He was in a decades-long race against himself. Lila never did puzzles, but she was an enabler. In doctors' offices, she tore the puzzles out of the magazines and brought them back for Bert.

"There," Lila said a minute later. "I'm on the balcony. It's a beautiful day. The fog's burned off. And you're asking for help. What more could a mother ask?" She cackled. "Which of my many areas of expertise are we talking about?"

"We're helping a woman deal with a collection she inherited from her husband. Some of the books and prints are in rough condition. Mold. Mildew. We're trying to figure out if they're salvageable, and how many of them are library copies."

"That shouldn't be hard to tell. Libraries clearly mark their discarded books. Crooked book dealers know how to hide the evidence, but usually I can tell."

"I know. That's why I called you. There's also a lot of documents. They're mostly stored in tubes and I think they're in good shape." Emily hesitated, then said, "One of them is a map. I googled it and found one that looks the same online. At auction, it was estimated to bring twelve thousand dollars."

"Twelve *thousand?* No library worth its salt would discard a twelve-thousand-dollar map. Did you look for a library stamp? It could be embossed or printed, probably near the edge of the page."

Emily opened the tube and slipped the map out again. Sure enough, overlapping the lower right margin there was an oval stamped in black ink. Inside the oval, it read PROPERTY OF BLAINE FREE LIBRARY. "Blaine Free Library," Emily said.

"The Blaine," Lila said. "That's in Maine. Hang on. Let me get to my computer." Emily heard their balcony door slide open and shut. She imagined her mother crossing her living room and continuing down a hallway to the guest bedroom that doubled as her office. A minute later, typing. Then, "Right. Private library set up in the thirties. A couple of Richardson buildings with a collection of fine books and prints. And it's got a trust to fund it in perpetuity as a library for locals. I'll bet it's a lovely place to work. No politics."

"There's always politics, anytime there's more than two of you," Emily said.

"Since when did you get so smart?"

"Google this," Emily said. "See if you can find what I did." She read her mother the label: "*William Alexander Map of the Northeast.*"

Emily heard Lila's keyboard clicking. "That map . . . oh my." She was silent for so long Emily wondered what she was thinking. Before she could ask, Lila said, "I'd have to see it to know for sure, but it looks like it's a page from a four-volume collection of illustrated travel stories. *The Pilgrimage*. Published in 1625. I wouldn't be at all surprised if the one you found on-line realized a good deal more than twelve thousand dollars. Of course, the map's been reproduced, but if it's the real deal . . ." More clicking, then Lila said, "I'm in the Blaine catalogue. Their special collections. Here it is, a four-volume set. According to them, the book that map should be in is on their shelf."

"So, the question is—" Emily began.

"—does theirs have a page missing. We'd have to go there and take a look."

"Of course. And that's just the first document I've looked at. There's dozens more. Will you come up and give us a hand?"

"Emmy, let your fingers do the walking. Boston's full of anti-quarian book experts. I'm sure there are people who'd be happy to consult, especially if your client is thinking about selling."

"You're as knowledgeable as anyone. And Mrs. Murphy will like you. She'll trust you."

"Well, I appreciate the vote of confidence, but my eyesight's not what it used to be, and my back—"

"Bullshit."

"Don't swear."

"Hogwash."

"Well . . ."

"Admit it, you'd love to get in there and be the first to see what's what."

"Mold? Mildew?"

"I have an endless supply of breathing masks."

"Swell."

"You'll come, won't you?"

Lila laughed. "You know you had me at *old books*. But I've got bridge this afternoon."

"Tomorrow, then. That works. Thank you. I'll make up the bed in the guest room."

"Please give Frank a heads-up. Tell him I'm looking forward to seeing him." She ended the call with her distinctive laugh.

12

"WELL, I WAS not expecting you ladies back so soon," Mrs. Murphy said an hour later. She seemed only mildly puzzled by Emily and Becca's return, more preoccupied with not having tea sandwiches to offer them than with the reason for this unexpected visit. Emily was still feeling the effects of the night before and was just as glad there wasn't any food.

From the living room décor, you'd never know that the man of the house had collected fine old books and prints. There was just one small bookcase, its shelves filled with paperbacks, mostly romance novels and mysteries. The artwork, such as it was, consisted of plaques printed with cheery aphorisms like CHERISH YESTERDAY, LIVE TODAY, DREAM TOMORROW. And LIVE WELL, LAUGH OFTEN, LOVE MUCH. The likely source for these was a Christmas Tree Shop, not an antiques dealer.

Becca said, "We wanted you to know what we found in your husband's storage unit."

"Goodness. I hope nothing gruesome," Mrs. Murphy said with an uneasy laugh, "or embarrassing."

"Nothing like that," Becca said. She looked across at Emily.

"I got into the storage unit yesterday," Emily said. "It's packed with all kinds of stuff. Books. Prints. Doorknobs."

That made Mrs. Murphy smile. "Murph loved old hardware. His father was in construction." She glanced across at her husband's picture on the piano. Seeing it again, Emily was struck by how distinguished-looking Mr. Murphy had been, with his thick white hair and dark eyes, more like the son of a matinee idol than a builder. "He used to talk about how whenever Big Charlie worked on an old house, he'd bring home thingamabobs, like doorknobs and hinges. I remember he brought home a garden statue of the Virgin Mary. They called it Our Lady of the Bathtub. He wanted to put it in their backyard, but Kathleen said absolutely not. Once he brought home a stained glass window. That one, she let him install in their front door. But most of what he brought home he kept in his workshop." Her eyes filled with tears. "I had no idea Murph kept any of it, but then, I didn't care for it and it never occurred to me to ask."

It sounded altogether plausible that Murph had moved his father's thingamabobs directly into storage. He certainly hadn't installed choice antique hardware in his own house. The pulls on the kitchen doors and cabinets were ordinary stainless steel.

"There's quite a collection of books," Emily said, taking out her cell phone and showing Mrs. Murphy some of the pictures she'd taken. "Their condition's iffy. Climate control seems to have failed. Mold and moisture do a number on paper. But there's also document tubes like this one." She showed Mrs. Murphy the one she'd taken with her that contained the "Map of the Northeast." She opened it, slipped out the map, and unrolled it. "See, it's in excellent condition."

Mrs. Murphy just sat there looking perplexed. "Of course, I

knew Murph had a thing about old books and maps. But I had no idea he collected them."

Emily didn't add, *Or that he kept them in a secret storage unit.*

"The hardware won't be hard to sell," Emily said. "Folks who restore old buildings will be lining up to take it off your hands. Some of the books may be salvageable. And there may be significant value in the documents. But provenance is an issue."

"Provenance?" Mrs. Murphy sat forward, examining the map more carefully. She looked across at Emily.

"How your husband acquired them. Who owned them before." Emily pointed at the library stamp in the map's lower margin. "That stamp. It's the Blaine Library's."

Mrs. Murphy's gaze shifted and her eyes widened. "In Portland?"

Emily nodded.

"Murph and I were there. Several times, if I remember correctly. He loved to visit libraries."

Emily hated what she had to say next, but plunged ahead. "I'm sorry to have to tell you this, but the book that this map comes from is still listed in their collection."

Mrs. Murphy blinked. Her brow furled as she tilted her head and stared at the map. It took a few moments for the implication to dawn on her. "Surely he bought it from the library. Or from a reputable dealer. I can't believe . . . My husband would never . . ."

"This could be the only one like this," Emily said. "But I did also find a box full of bookplates and due-date cards that have been removed from library books."

Mrs. Murphy straightened. "Are you suggesting that my husband stole from libraries?"

"I'm saying that provenance is an issue," Emily said. "Who

knows, maybe the books were discards. Maybe the map belongs to someone else and your husband was just storing it. Figuring it all out will take time. Which brings us to another issue." Emily paused. "When I tried to get back into the storage unit this morning, someone had come in overnight and changed the lock."

"Changed the lock?" Mrs. Murphy looked confused. She looked back and forth from Becca to Emily.

Becca said evenly, "Do you have any idea who might have done that?"

"How in blue blazes would I know?" Mrs. Murphy sucked in her cheeks and shook her head. "I've never even been there. And now you tell me it's full of library books and stolen maps, and someone broke in."

"We're not sure any of it's stolen, or that anyone broke in," Becca said, looking to Emily to continue.

Emily said, "The thing is, a security guard who was there told me that he's seen someone opening up the unit from time to time."

"That would have been Murph, of course," Mrs. Murphy said.

"Recently. In the last few months. And he said it was a woman."

Mrs. Murphy swallowed hard. "A woman?" She started to say something else and stopped. Settled herself. "Exactly what are you suggesting? That my Charlie was a common thief? And on top of that, he was up to some kind of mischief with some . . . bimbo?"

"No one's suggesting—" Emily began.

"You most certainly are." After a frosty silence, Mrs. Murphy added, "He couldn't. He wouldn't."

"This must be confusing and upsetting." Becca gave Mrs. Murphy her most sympathetic smile. "You say you knew nothing about the storage unit until you saw the bill. So it's possible, isn't it, that

those books and prints in there aren't your husband's? Maybe
he was storing someone else's things. A brother or sister—"

"Murph was an only child," Mrs. Murphy said.

Emily said, "Or someone he worked with?"

Mrs. Murphy folded her arms and looked stone-faced ahead.
"He was retired."

"A friend?" Becca tried.

"One of *our* friends? I doubt that very much." Mrs. Murphy
clamped her lips together and shook her head.

"The fact remains that yesterday," Becca said, "after we left
the unit locked up, someone came along and changed the padlock. And now we can't get back in."

Mrs. Murphy didn't seem to be listening. Her eyes were fixed
in front of her on the middle distance. Her gaze turned angry
and shifted, pinning Becca. "How do I know this lock business
isn't just a cover for some kind of shenanigan? How do I know
Charlie's things are even still in there? It doesn't make much
sense otherwise, now, does it?" Her chin quivered.

Emily was speechless. No one had ever doubted their integrity. But before she could respond, Becca said calmly, "I can see
why you might think that. I agree with you, it doesn't make a lot
of sense. I can only assure you that we haven't taken anything
and we haven't done anything that you didn't specifically ask us
to do. We're here now because we need to know what you'd like
our next steps to be."

"What do I want you to do now?" Mrs. Murphy swept the
map onto the floor. Emily scrambled after it. Mrs. Murphy sat
on the edge of the settee kneading one hand over the other as
Emily rolled up the map and slipped it into its tube. "He could
have explained," she said. "He'd know what to do next." She got
up and stood facing her husband's reclining recliner. "But un-

fortunately I can't ask him what in the name of God he thought he was up to with this storage unit of his. Why he needed books and maps and whatnot. And why he needed to hide them from me." She took a tissue and blew her nose. "And why he canceled his doctor's appointment the day before he died. Said he had indigestion. Indigestion?" She dabbed at her eyes with a tissue. "I can't ask him because one minute he's here and the next minute he's gone." She sank into the recliner, her shoulders hunched, her body deflated. "Oh, Charlie. This can't be happening. It's not fair. It's really not fair. What am I supposed to do now?" She gave Becca a plaintive look. "You tell me, what am I supposed to do now?"

13

"POOR THING. MY heart goes out to her," Becca said later as she and Emily stood on the sidewalk in front of Mrs. Murphy's house. "She's grieving, of course. Stuck in denial for over a year. Anger's supposed to come next. I think even she realizes that, at some level, all this rage is a step forward. Maybe that's why she didn't end up telling us to take a hike."

Emily opened her car door and tossed the document tube across to the passenger seat. She'd been surprised, too, that at the end of their meeting, Mrs. Murphy wanted to continue to work with them. She was already talking about investigating what was in the storage unit and returning anything that hadn't been acquired on the up-and-up. Before they'd left, Mrs. Murphy placed a call to Inner Peace Storage. She barely managed to explain the situation before breaking down again.

Becca had taken over. She told the manager that, by the way, climate control in the unit had failed some time ago. "There's mold and mildew. Very toxic. Disastrous for the valuable books and prints that were being stored there. Not exactly the conditions that your advertising promises." That sped up the discussion.

In the end, the manager had promised to investigate and arrange for a time when they could meet him there, as soon as possible, and he'd break open the unit. It might even be as soon as tomorrow.

Becca's gaze shifted to the Murphys' untidy front lawn. "What is it about men and their secrets?" she said. "Don't you think you'd know if Frank had a jam-packed storage unit hidden somewhere?"

Emily laughed. Why would Frank need a storage unit, with the way he'd been expanding his "collection" into their basement, attic, and garage?

"A lot of people keep secrets from their spouses," Becca said. "Little ones. Big ones."

If Frank did have a secret storage space, then Emily, like Mrs. Murphy, would have no way of knowing about it. She and Frank kept their finances separate. Frank's personal bills went to his law office. And for all the overtime Frank spent there and all the sporting events he attended or watched on TV with his buddies, he could easily have had an entire second life.

"No one expects to drop dead," Becca said. "Indigestion the day before? That was probably the start of a heart attack."

"Still," Emily said, "it would be nice if he'd cleaned up after himself before he checked out. He's left her with a big mess to figure out." She started to get into her car.

"Hang on," Becca said. She looked at her watch. "I need to get back. By now the kiddos are probably painting the kitchen walls with peanut butter. But give me a quick update on our other new client. How'd it go?"

"Quinn Newell," Emily said.

"Tell me her husband doesn't collect doorknobs."

No, Quinn Newell's problem was that she'd collected a selfish bastard of a husband. "He's a collector, all right. Vintage advertising. But what she wants to declutter is a garage filled with stuffed animals and forties furniture."

"*His* stuffed animals?"

"Hers. When she married him, he wouldn't let her move her things into *his* house. Three years later, she's ready to kiss them goodbye."

Becca blinked, absorbing that. "Sounds like she should kiss *him* goodbye."

"That thought occurred to me. But as you're fond of saying, we're not marriage counselors," Emily said.

"Or divorce attorneys," Becca said. "So you think the husband could be a problem."

The hole in the wall. Quinn's bruised face. That queasy feeling Emily had had the night before returned. "I think it was a big deal for her to call for our help. I'd rather be there when he's not."

"Sheesh," Becca said under her breath. "And I was so optimistic. Cleaning out a garage sounded like a tidy little project, one with a beginning and an end."

"And it is, basically, except for the load of emotions to unpack in the middle," Emily said.

"That goes without saying. Though you'd think a storage unit would have been manageable, too. It's not even connected to a house." Becca shrugged back at Mrs. Murphy's house and Emily turned to look. The corner of a curtain in the front window dropped. "And this husband's out of the picture."

At home later that afternoon, Emily got to work on her closet, drilling holes for drywall anchors and installing brackets for shelving and rods. She took pictures as she went along. It was mindless work, so satisfying at the end when she vacuumed the closet floor, stood back, and took in the results. Its orderly emptiness was calming.

It took her another hour to put away her clothes. Summer clothes hung separate from winter. Tops hung on a rack above pants and skirts. Emily even indulged in sorting by color, only because (she told herself) it photographed better. When she was finally done, she went to her office to upload the pictures. She was finishing when she heard Frank come in. A few moments later he was at her office door. "How's the trial going?" she asked.

"The trial. Right." A pause. "It hasn't started yet. We offered to settle. They're considering. What about you? Did you return whatever it was that you took from that storage unit?"

"I tried to, but someone changed the lock. And it turns out a map I inadvertently took out of there could be worth thousands."

Frank's jaw dropped. "Thousands?"

"Mom thinks it's a page from a book. Possibly stolen from a library. So now, of course, I'm worried about what's in the rest of those tubes. Mom's coming up to take a look. She'll be staying with us for a few days, at least until we get this thing sorted."

Frank's usual response to one of her mother's impending visits was a heartfelt groan. Instead, he looked relieved. "Smart plan," he said. "She knows all about old maps and libraries. And it will make her feel useful."

Emily cringed. She was glad her mother couldn't hear Frank's patronizing comment. Before she could process his change of heart, their landline rang. Most of the calls on that phone were robocalls from energy companies wanting them to switch, or, more recently, a pseudo-IRS agent threatening to jail them if they didn't pay up. Still, old habits died hard. Emily went into the kitchen, where the answering machine kicked on and her recorded voice played: "Sorry we can't take your call, you know what to do." A click. Then silence. Or, no, there was a sound. Breathing.

Then, "Emily? Are you there?" The quavery voice sounded familiar. "I need to talk to you. It's Wally. I—"

Frank watched from the doorway as Emily picked up the handset. "Quinn?" she said.

"Emily? Thank God you're there."

"What is it?" Emily said, though she was not eager to get drawn into another of Quinn Newell's fire drills.

"Wally didn't come home last night. I didn't realize until I got up this morning. I waited and I waited, and he still hasn't shown up. I tried to call his cell. No answer. His office. He's not there."

Frank gave Emily a questioning look. She mouthed, *Mandarin Cliffs*.

"Maybe the auction ran late and he decided to stay over," Emily said. "Did you call the auction house?"

"I did. Know what they told me? Last night's auction ended at six. Why would Wally lie to me about that?"

Emily refrained from offering some of the more obvious answers to that. "Maybe something happened and he couldn't call you. Like a car accident."

"That's what I thought. So I called every hospital I could find between here and Hyannis."

"Has he ever done this before? Stayed out overnight without telling you?"

"He always calls."

"Did you try calling his friends?"

"I tried everyone I could think of . . . everyone I know. Nobody's heard from him. I was about to call the police when I remembered what you and I talked about last night."

Last night. Emily felt her face flush.

"We were just kidding around. Right?" Quinn went on.

Emily held the receiver away from her ear and stared at it. Quinn couldn't be serious. When she listened again, there was silence on the other end. Then, "Uh-oh."

"Uh-oh what?" Emily said.

"What?" Frank said.

"A police car just pulled up in front of my house." Quinn's voice was a whisper.

Emily put her hand over the mouthpiece. She told Frank, "Her husband didn't come home last night and the police just pulled up in front of her house."

Frank asked, "What does she expect you to do about it?" at the same time as Quinn said, "Oh . . . my . . . God."

Emily shushed Frank. He moved alongside her and she angled the receiver so he could hear.

"Two police officers." Quinn's voice was faint. "They're getting out of their cruiser. They're walking up to the door." A doorbell chimed. "Should I answer?" She didn't wait for Emily's response, which was just as well, because Emily didn't know what to say. "Go away, go away, go away," Quinn whispered. "Shit. There's the bell again." A pause. "Now one of them's going around back."

Emily listened, her heart in her throat. The last thing she heard before the line went dead was what sounded like banging on a door.

Emily tried calling back but the call went directly to voice mail. She hung up, shaken.

Frank said, "So this is someone you met exactly once? Why is she calling you?"

Because they'd bonded? Because Quinn had shared her fantasy

of what life would be like without her husband, and then he'd disappeared?

"She sounds more than slightly neurotic," Frank said.

"Wouldn't you be upset? Her husband's missing and the police show up on her doorstep?"

Frank gave a dismissive wave. "Hysteria is not a good strategy when you're dealing with police. Speaking as a former criminal defense attorney. You want to help her? I know you do. She shouldn't be alone."

Emily didn't need to be convinced, not with Quinn's *We were just kidding around, right?* echoing in her head. Quinn hadn't called her because Emily was her new best friend.

"I could go over there, but I'm not sure I'd be much help," Emily said. "I've never had to deal with the police."

Frank gave her a long, hard look. "Do you want me to come with you?"

Relief flooded through her. "Would you?"

"She needs to know that I can't represent her. I don't deal with police or missing husbands or—"

"But you'd know what to do if it comes to that. You could connect her with the right attorney. I'm sure she'll just be grateful to have someone there who's got some idea what's going on." Emily grabbed her bag and got out her car keys.

"Let's get over there," Frank said. He took the keys from Emily. "They're probably asking questions that she shouldn't be answering right now."

14

EMILY HATED IT when Frank drove her car, but once he'd settled behind the wheel, she couldn't very well pry him loose. Soon she was clutching the armrest as Frank accelerated down the street, downshifted around a corner, ran a yellow light, and blew past a twenty-five-mile-an-hour speed limit sign. Traffic was snarled, as usual, in the Square. Still, Frank passed a slow-moving car on the right and honked at a parked car that tried to pull out in front of him. In a lull when they were waiting at a red light, Emily managed to text Quinn, saying she was on her way.

Once they were out of the Square, Frank put on another burst of speed. At last the car swerved around a corner and into Mandarin Cliffs and slowed as Emily directed him to Quinn Newell's house.

No police cars were parked out front.

"They must have come and gone," Frank said.

"Maybe her husband's back"—Emily checked her phone—"and she just hasn't had a chance to let me know." She got out of the car. A blanket of moist heat assaulted her.

Frank got out, shaded his eyes, and gazed across at the house. "This is quite a heap. Hope he got her to sign a prenup."

He could be such an asshole. And typical Frank, he assumed it was the husband's money. What made it more annoying was that he was probably right. "Are you here to help or to snark?" Emily asked. "Because if you say something like that when we're in there with her, I'll kneecap you."

She started across the perfectly manicured front lawn. When she reached the front door, she rang the bell. "Quinn!"

When there was no answer, she turned to tell Frank that she was going to go around back. That's when she realized Frank was still at the curb, crouched behind her car and examining . . . something. She returned to see what. A broken taillight.

"What happened?" He squinted across at her. "You back into something?"

"Not that I remember."

He ran his hand across the car's rear bumper. "Then it looks like something backed into—"

"Emily?" They both turned around at the querulous voice. Quinn stood at the front door, holding the calico cat.

"What's her name again?" Frank said under his breath as they approached the house.

"Newell," Emily whispered back. "Quinn Newell."

Close up, Emily could see that Quinn looked exhausted, her face puffy, cheeks white. The bruise was slightly faded but still livid. Her yoga pants and top might have been the same ones she'd been wearing Sunday night.

"What happened?" Emily said. "Where are the police?"

Quinn just stood there, staring at Frank like he was curdled milk. "Who is this?"

"My husband," Emily said.

"This is Frank?" Quinn seemed surprised.

"Huh?" Frank said, and shot Emily a questioning look.

"Don't freak," Quinn told him. "Emily and I talked about you. I just imagined . . . well, something different. Never mind."

Emily felt the prick of embarrassment. She couldn't remember exactly what she'd told Quinn about Frank, but she was sure it hadn't been flattering.

"Frank Harlow," Frank said, flashing his smile. "Emily thought you might need legal advice." He offered Quinn his hand.

"Legal advice," Quinn said, eyeing his hand but not shaking it.

"Dealing with the police and all," Frank said. "Not something most of us have to do every day. I'm sorry to hear about your husband."

"He's missing. Not dead." Quinn shifted her gaze to Emily as she nuzzled the cat. "Right?" The cat squirmed from her arms, twisted in midair, dropped on all four feet with a thud on the threshold, and slinked back into the house.

"You still haven't heard from him? " Emily said.

Quinn shook her head.

"Emily asked if I'd come along to see if I could help," Frank said. That wasn't exactly how it had happened, but Emily let it pass.

Quinn gazed down at Frank's still-extended hand. She shook it. "I'm sorry. I must seem rude and ungrateful. I'm just so upset by all this. I really appreciate you coming. Both of you. Come in." She led them into the house and through to the kitchen. She turned back. "Coffee?"

Coffee? It was just the kind of thing women did, offered a refreshment to guests when life had been upended, a pathetic call back to normal. Emily was about to say no thanks when Frank said, "Sure. That would be great."

Quinn pulled out the refrigerator's freezer drawer, got out a bag of coffee, and kicked the drawer shut. Hands shaking, she tried to scoop a measure of coffee into the top of the gleaming espresso machine, but a cascade of beans flooded the counter. She slammed the bag on the counter, scattering more beans. Stamped her foot. "Shit shit shit shit." She clapped her hands on the sides of her head and stood there, rigid.

Emily put her arm around Quinn. "You don't have to play hostess," she said. She felt Quinn slowly go limp against her as Frank gathered the beans on the counter and scraped them back into the bag. Unhooked a hand vac from the wall and vacuumed up the beans that had fallen on the floor.

"Sit," Emily said, pulling out a stool from under the counter. "Tell us what happened."

Quinn grabbed a tissue from the counter and blew her nose. She perched on the stool, looking wan and spent. Emily noticed a business card on the counter. *East Hartwell Police Department.* From a lieutenant detective. She picked it up and showed it to Frank. Then she waited for Quinn to collect herself.

"There were two of them," Quinn said.

"Police officers?" Frank asked.

Quinn nodded.

"Detectives?"

"Cops. Detectives. Is there a difference?"

Frank seemed taken aback. He closed the bag of coffee beans and put it in the refrigerator. "So you had reported your husband missing?"

"No. I was going to. And then they just showed up. They were looking for Wally, too."

"Why?"

"They said they were investigating a car accident. Last night." Quinn choked up. "No one was hurt, but it was a hit-and-run."

"Really?" Frank said. "And you told them . . . ?"

Emily could envision Frank operating like this in a courtroom, questioning a witness on the stand. Trying to get the information he wanted without seeming to lead, even when it was his own client and he was taking them through an orchestrated set of questions they'd rehearsed.

"I explained to them that he went to an auction yesterday and didn't come home. They wanted to see his car, but I told them it wasn't here. They asked if they could look in the garage."

"And?" Frank asked.

"What was I supposed to do?" Quinn said, straightening and scowling at Frank. "Tell them to get lost? The car's not here, so why not let them look? I didn't want them to think I was lying."

"It's a felony to lie to the police, but here's the thing," Frank said. "They can lie to you. They make things up to get you to reveal—"

"Reveal what? So you *don't* think they came here to investigate a hit-and-run?"

"I believe that's the reason they gave you, but I have no idea what they really came for, and neither do you," Frank said. "Alls I'm saying is cops can lie to you, but you can't lie to the cops. Which is why we often advise people not to say anything."

"Well, I didn't have your sage advice. I told them the truth. Wally's car's not here. He didn't come home last night. I told them I hadn't reported him missing because . . ." She picked at a loose thread in her leggings. "Well, because he sometimes gets back very late. I told them I was about to call the police when they showed up. Right after I talked to Emily." Her voice turned shrill. "And that's the God's honest truth."

"All right, all right." Frank put up his hands. "You don't need to convince me. What else did they say?"

"That someone would get back to me."

"You can count on that. Please, take my advice," Frank said, his voice bullying. "When they come back asking questions, take a time-out until you have someone with you. It's like when you get bad news from a doctor. You need someone with you to hear and translate and be your witness." Quinn folded her arms and closed her eyes, and Frank softened his tone. "You're going to be stressed. It's only natural. But don't talk to them alone. Call a friend or, better still, an attorney. Because—"

A tear trickled down Quinn's cheek.

"Enough!" Emily said. "Just stop. Can't you see she's upset enough without your haranguing her?" She turned to Quinn. "You have to excuse Frank. He spent time—or should I say *served* time—working as a public defender. He's used to viewing the justice system as lose-lose for the average citizen. Always adversarial. Always worst-case."

"Sometimes," Frank said, "you think everything is fine and it turns out to be worst-case, and you've basically dug yourself a hole and climbed into it."

Just then a phone rang, a marimba playing a minor scale. It wasn't Emily's—her ringtone was crickets. Quinn slipped from her stool and picked up a cell phone from the counter. She glanced at the readout. Swallowed. "It's them again." She gave Frank a frightened look. "East Hartwell PD."

The phone rang once more before Quinn thumbed to answer it and put it to her ear. "Hello?" A pause. "Yes, that's me." A longer pause as she turned to face the wall. "Uh-huh. Okay . . . um-hmm . . ." She carried the phone into the next room.

"I'm sorry if I came on too strong," Frank said to Emily. "People can be so oblivious, especially when they're upset. She needs to know what she's up against."

"You can't blame her for being upset." Emily drifted toward the doorway, trying in vain to overhear Quinn's conversation.

"Believe me, I get that. I'm just not sure she understands how the real world—" Frank broke off when Quinn came back into the kitchen.

She was clutching the phone and she'd gone even paler. "They found Wally's car."

15

FRANK LOOKED STUNNED. "Just his car?" he asked Quinn. Emily winced. He could be colossally insensitive.

"They found it," Quinn said, "in the commuter parking lot at the town wharf. They're going to start looking for him." She sounded like an automaton. "They want me to bring them—" She clasped her hand over her mouth and took a moment, then swallowed and squared her shoulders. "They want a photograph and something with his scent." She looked around, as if what she needed were close at hand.

"Maybe something he recently wore?" Emily suggested.

"Yes. Of course. That would be the thing." But still Quinn stood there, frozen.

"And a recent photograph?" Frank said, tipping his head toward Emily.

"Upstairs?" Emily said. "Or maybe in his office?"

Emily followed as Quinn drifted out of the kitchen, through a narrow pantry, through the dining room, and on to a wood-paneled study in the back of the house. This had to be Wally's man cave. The Chesterfield sofa was tufted cordovan leather. Overhead lighting was hidden in a red-glass hanging dome with

Budweiser written in gold letters across the rim. A wide flat-screen TV hung on one wall, while the other walls were hung with framed magazine covers. *MAD. National Lampoon. Cracked. Creepy.*

Quinn picked up a framed photo from the corner of a sleek blond mid-century modern desk. The picture looked like a selfie of Quinn and her husband, standing on a windy beach with waves breaking in the background. Quinn paused for a moment, staring at the photo. She inhaled a ragged breath, then removed the back of the frame and handed the snapshot to Emily.

So this was Walter Newell. He had dense dark hair that curled around his face, a mustache, and a goatee. He squinted at the camera and grinned. Quinn, tucked into his side, rested her head on his chest.

"I need to explain," Quinn said, turning to face Emily. "I didn't, you know, *mean* any of those things I said the other night. Because I'd never. Ever. You didn't think—?"

"Of course not. It was the wine. I said things I didn't mean, either. We were just being . . ." Emily searched for the right word. *Silly* wasn't quite right. Because how silly was it, to dream up ways to get rid of your husband?

Quinn didn't wait for Emily to finish the thought. "Okay, great. I just wanted to be sure we're on the same page here. Because if something terrible has happened to Wally, something bad, like one of those things we talked about?" She gave Emily a long, hard look. "I wouldn't want you to think—"

"It was just talk," Emily said. Of course it was. Why would Quinn think otherwise? "Right?"

"And it was just between us."

Emily got it. Quinn didn't want her sharing what they'd talked about with the police. "Right."

Quinn gave a weak smile. "Of course. That's what I knew

you'd say. Ryan swore up and down that you were absolutely trustworthy, but I've just met you the once, and I had to ask. And I didn't want to ask in front of Fred."

"Frank."

"Whatever."

Emily followed Quinn upstairs to the master suite at the far end of the upstairs hall. It was enormous, of course. The bed was unmade, piled high with pillows. Quinn picked up one of them, held it to her face, and inhaled. Her eyes misted over for a moment before she threw the pillow back down.

The air conditioning hummed. The sour smell might have been coming from a cut-glass vase filled with red roses, their heads dropped as if in prayer, the water a greenish cloud. Quinn opened a door and entered a walk-in closet, though *closet* was a misnomer. You could easily have moved a twin bed and a bureau in there and called it a bedroom. As it was, the built-ins put Emily's own new closet system to shame. One wall boasted a stack of clear-fronted drawers next to double-decked racks for shirts and jackets. The other two walls of the closet contained two rows of hanging rods for pants and more shirts. Emily stared in awe at the neatly organized racks of men's shoes. High-top black leather sneakers. Cordovan oxfords. Laced boat shoes. Walter Newell probably had more pairs of shoes than Emily had socks.

Quinn moved to the back of the closet and tilted open a built-in clothes hamper. "Something with his scent," she said, sifting through laundry. She lifted an undershirt from the basket. "This should work."

Emily followed her back downstairs. In the kitchen, Quinn slid her husband's undershirt into a large freezer bag. She added the photograph and zipped the bag shut.

"Please, take my advice," Frank said. "Don't be alone when you talk to the police. You don't know what their agenda is."

"Their agenda," Quinn said, tossing the freezer bag on the kitchen counter and folding her arms, "is to find Wally."

Frank screwed up his face, like he did when he was annoyed. "Right now that seems likely," he said. "But it's smart to have someone with you. How could it hurt?"

Quinn looked back at him. "And who would that someone be? You?"

Frank shot Emily a subtle eye roll. Yes, she agreed, Quinn was biting the hand that was trying to feed her.

Frank said, "I can. If you like. But—"

Before he could finish, Quinn said, "Emily? Could you come with me?"

"You'd be better off with an attorney," Emily said.

"I'm better off with a *trusted* friend," Quinn shot back.

"You sure you're okay going with her?" Frank said as he stood with Emily in front of the house, waiting for Quinn to back her car out of the garage. "Because you seem, I don't know, distracted."

Freaked out was more like it. She barely knew Quinn, but in the short time they'd spent together she'd felt a connection. They were both in flawed marriages. And for all of Emily's complaints about Frank, if he'd disappeared one night and the police had found his car abandoned the next morning, she'd have fallen apart.

Emily said, "She needs someone for emotional support. Not just to protect her from the police."

Frank put his arm around her and squeezed. "You're a good

person. Promise me you'll call if things get weird. Even if you're not sure but it feels sketchy, call. And remember, she doesn't have to answer any of their questions. Keep reminding her of that."

Emily eased herself free of his arm. The garage door opened and she heard a car engine turn over. Red taillights and then backup lights came into view as Quinn pulled her car out of the garage.

Emily stood behind her own car, waiting for Quinn to pull up alongside. Frank touched her car's broken taillight. She was surprised that she hadn't noticed that before. Not when she was at the Park 'n' Ride with Becca. Not when she got home last night. Not when she'd driven to the storage unit that morning. And it wasn't just a broken taillight; there was also a dent on the rear bumper and a stain. She touched it and dried flakes came off on her fingertips. She sniffed. It had a coffee smell. Emily wiped her hand on her pants.

Frank took one look at Quinn's Miata and rolled his eyes at Emily. As if he were in any position to comment on someone else's sports car. He opened the passenger door and Emily got in. Quinn handed her the plastic bag with the undershirt and photograph before she accelerated out of there. As the car leapt forward, Emily's seat belt tightened across her lap and neck. She yanked at it, but it locked in place, cinching her even more tightly.

"I know, that thing's annoying," Quinn said. "Don't tug. Just ease it out. It's like one of those finger toys. The harder you pull, the tighter you're trapped."

A finger toy. That was the perfect analogy for how Emily was becoming ensnared in Quinn's drama. Emily relaxed, and sure enough, the seat belt loosened.

Quinn drove up the street, past the entrance to Mandarin

Cliffs. Before she pulled onto the main street, she turned to Emily. "If they ask where we were last night, I was with you."

"Of course. You were."

"From six on. You didn't leave until late."

Emily gave Quinn a sideways look. Quinn was gripping the steering wheel, tendons strained in her neck.

Quinn added, "Because we're in this together."

In what together? Emily's seat belt tightened, cutting into her neck again. She shifted her position and hooked her arm inside the seat belt strap, working it loose.

"And just so you know," Quinn said, "I talked to Wally yesterday before I talked to your partner. He said he'd be getting home late and I thought, you know—" She choked up and smacked the steering wheel with the heel of her hand. "All I could think was that at long last I had a little window of opportunity, so I called you guys. I thought . . ."

Quinn went on, her voice rising, but Emily wasn't listening. Walter Newell hadn't come home last night, but his car had been involved in a hit-and-run. Emily's car had been struck by a hit-and-run driver. Seemed like an odd coincidence.

16

THE EAST HARTWELL police station dominated one corner of a busy intersection opposite a brightly lit Burger King and was catty-corner to a dark veterans' cemetery. Emily's stomach rumbled as the smell of burgers and fries wafted over. It was past dinner-time, she hadn't eaten, and she wasn't about to eat anytime soon.

Quinn had stopped talking a few minutes before they arrived. The sky was black, too humid and overcast to see stars. The parking lot, in contrast, was brightly lit, with spotlights worthy of a sports stadium. Quinn pulled into a visitor parking spot and sat, chewing her lower lip, her knuckles white. She turned and gave Emily a tight smile before getting out of the car. Theirs was the only non-police car in the lot.

The police station looked old, its granite steps worn smooth leading up to a pair of grand pillars that flanked the front doors. But the façade was the only part of the original station that had been preserved. Beyond the doorway—Emily followed Quinn inside, blinking away the glare—the interior featured featureless white vinyl flooring and white walls, harshly lit by overhead fluorescent lighting set into a drop ceiling.

A uniformed officer sat at a desk behind the counter that

divided the room. He was an older man with sagging jowls that quivered as he chewed a wad of gum and poked an index finger at a computer keyboard.

Quinn inhaled deeply and approached him. "Sir?"

The officer looked up. "Ma'am." He took in both of them without a flicker of interest.

"We're here to see Sergeant . . . Wait a minute, I wrote it down." Quinn rummaged through her purse. She came up with a scrap of paper. "Stanley."

"And you are?"

"Quinn Newell."

"And Emily Harlow," Emily said.

"IDs, please."

Quinn fished out her driver's license and handed it to him. Emily did the same. The officer raised an eyebrow and picked up the phone. While they waited, he spoke into the handset in a rumbling undertone. He must have gotten a green light, because he hung up and rotated a ledger book toward them. After both Emily and Quinn signed, he gave them each a blank name tag and waited while they wrote their names and pressed on the labels. Emily felt like a piece of evidence, tagged and catalogued.

"Ladies." The deep voice came from a police officer who'd entered from behind the desk officer. "Mrs. Newell?"

"That's me," Quinn said in a whispery soft voice. She seemed to shrink under the short, stocky uniformed officer's gaze.

"And?" He tilted his head in Emily's direction.

"This is Emily . . ." Quinn's voice trailed off and Emily realized she'd forgotten her last name.

"Emily Harlow," Emily said, hoping she sounded confident.

"Sergeant Brian Stanley," the officer said with a nod. "I spoke with you on the phone."

"You found my husband's car? And asked me to bring these."
Quinn offered him the plastic bag with the photograph and the
undershirt.

He glanced at the bag and then handed it to the desk officer.
Then he raised the hinged end of the countertop and ushered
them through. "We have the car downstairs," he said. Quinn
shot Emily a tense look. "Let's go take a look."

Emily hooked Quinn's arm and followed Stanley down two
flights of stairs. The smell of car tires and cigarette smoke grew
as they descended. The basement was a vast parking garage
that stretched the length of the building. Their footsteps echoed
on the concrete as they continued past parked police cruisers,
SUVs, and vans. Past taped-off boundaries surrounding cars
that surely hadn't come in under their own steam. One was
a Honda, approximately the same vintage as Emily's, its back
end accordion-pleated into the body of the car. A steering wheel
poked through the shattered windshield, as if a Humvee had
run into the back of it full-tilt. Fatal, had to have been. Emily
had to look away.

In the farthest corner of the basement garage sat a silver sedan. The car was barely damaged. It had overlapping chrome
O's on the front grill—an Audi. The passenger-side headlight
was cracked and the front fender scraped. There were no plates.

"Oh God," Quinn said, dropping Emily's arm. "That looks
like his car."

"It was left overnight in the parking lot at the town wharf,"
Stanley said. "That lot empties out after the trains stop running.
It matches a car that was reported involved in a hit-and-run."

"Was there . . . Did you find . . ." Quinn began, but she couldn't
finish. She cleared her throat. "My husband didn't come home
last night. I've been so worried something happened."

"That's the only damage," Stanley said, pointing to the front. "We were hoping you could confirm that it's your husband's."

"May I look inside?" Quinn asked.

Stanley said, "Go ahead. But please don't touch anything."

Stanley lifted the tape barrier and Quinn slipped under it. Stanley followed. He snapped on a latex glove and opened the driver's-side door. The smell of leather and musk wafted out as Quinn stooped to look inside. Past her, Emily could see that the upholstery in the car was black leather, tufted like the breast-plate of a Ninja turtle, and the steering wheel was clad in black leather with red trim.

Quinn bit her knuckle. Her shoulders shook and she started to cry. "It's his," she rasped.

"I'm sorry, ma'am. We'll find him," Stanley said. He closed the car door and raised the tape for Quinn to step out.

A blue plastic tarp was spread out on the floor next to the car. On it was a black flashlight and a snow scraper. A flare kit and jumper cables. A pile of papers with an Audi owner's guide on top. A gallon container of windshield fluid. A lug wrench. And a pair of aviator glasses with yellow lenses.

Could this have been the car she'd parked in front of at the coffee shop last night? It might have been a silver Audi. In the Java Connection the driver had been backlit and she'd been dis-tracted by the spilled coffee. All she remembered clearly was a mustache and a close-cropped beard, along with a baseball cap and glasses—yellow-tinted aviator glasses, just like the ones lying on the blue tarp.

"Mrs. Newell, when did you last see your husband?" Stanley asked.

Quinn was now standing beside Emily again. She grabbed Emily's hand and squeezed, though at that moment Emily could have used bracing, too. "Yesterday. He left the house at around noon. Or maybe one. I wasn't paying attention. I knew he'd been looking at an auction listing and planned to bid on some of the items."

"Auction." Stanley slipped a pad from his pocket and jotted a note.

"Later he texted me to say he'd be back late and not to wait up." Quinn rummaged in her purse for her cell phone. She thumbed through, then turned the screen to face Stanley. "Here's his text message."

"Do you mind?" Stanley said, taking the phone from her. He used his own phone to take a picture of her screen, then made another note. "And he sent this text to you from the auction?"

"That's where he says he is. Can't you people tell?"

"Depends on how he had his phone set up." Stanley shook his head. "Everyone thinks police departments have the kinds of resources they see on TV. Where was the auction?"

"Somewhere down the Cape."

"Hyannis," Emily piped up, remembering Quinn telling her that.

"Right. That's it," Quinn said, seeming flustered.

"Do you know what auction house?"

"Stone Mills Auction Gallery. I called them. They couldn't tell me a thing."

"So he was meeting someone there," Stanley said as he wrote.

"Was he?" Quinn said. "I wouldn't know about the people he hangs out with when he's at his auctions. I never go with him. Not my thing."

"Not . . . your . . . thing." Stanley repeated the words as he wrote them down. Then he looked across at Quinn, his head tilted. "And after he texted, what did you do?"

"What did *I* do?" Quinn gave Emily a tight-lipped smile. Her expression said, *Here we go.* "Nothing. I stayed home."

"Is there anyone who can vouch for you?"

Quinn pointed to Emily.

Emily said, "Right. We were together."

Stanley looked at Emily as if registering her presence for the first time. Eyed her name badge. "Miss Harlow?"

"Mrs." Emily was glad that she was married to a lawyer who'd somewhat prepared her for this interrogation. "I'm a professional organizer."

Quinn added, "She's helping me downsize."

"And you arrived at what time?" Stanley asked.

Emily looked at Quinn. "Around six?"

"Right," Quinn said. "I called her when I knew Wally would be tied up."

That caught Stanley's attention. "And why was that?" he said.

"You don't need to answer—" Emily began, but Quinn plowed ahead with, "He doesn't like strangers in the house. I wanted her to come when he wasn't there." Her look challenged Sergeant Stanley to question that.

Stanley scratched his head and gazed at Emily. "And you stayed until when?"

Quinn answered. "I turned on the TV after she left and the ten o'clock news was on."

Emily squirmed. Quinn was stretching it. If Emily had left Quinn's house that late, the coffee shop would have been closed by the time she got there.

"And you got home at . . ." Stanley looked at Emily.

"I didn't notice the time." That was the truth. "It had to have been past ten." The truth again. "I live in East Hartwell, it's a short drive."

Stanley nodded. Reviewed his notes. "So you ladies were there together for, what, four hours? From six until after ten? Then what?"

"Like I said, I watched what was left of the ten o'clock news," Quinn said. "Then I went to sleep."

"Sleep." Stanley straightened his shoulders and narrowed his eyes at Quinn. "You didn't feel like you needed to stay awake? Wait for your husband to come back?"

"No." Quinn took a step back. "Not really. He told me not to wait up."

"You've been married for how long?"

Quinn swallowed. "Three years."

"So this wasn't the first time your husband had called to say he was getting home late and not to wait up?"

"That's why I wasn't worried," Quinn said, a hint of defiance in her voice. "I thought he'd gone out with his buddies after the auction. He does that sometimes. To celebrate. Especially if he makes a kill." Stanley gave her a surprised look. "That's what he calls it when he scores a good buy."

"Well, here's what I'm trying to work out," Stanley said. "Our dispatch gets a call Sunday night at nine fifty-five. Hit-and-run in the Square. The description of the car matches your husband's, and this car has the dent to prove it.

"But that night, traffic was tied up coming back from the Cape. Summer Sunday. Accident on the Bourne Bridge and another one on the Sagamore. Perfect storm. Hyannis to Boston, no matter what route you took, it would have taken at least three and a half hours. He'd have to have left Hyannis by six-thirty in order to be back here by ten."

Quinn stood there blinking. "All I know is, he said he'd be late. Don't wait up." She shook her phone at him. "You saw his text."

"You watched the ten o'clock news? What station?"

"I . . . I wasn't paying attention," Quinn said.

Stanley came back at Quinn, challenging her to remember what had been on the newscast, but Emily barely listened. She was imagining herself in Quinn's place, being grilled about exactly what had happened the night before. What had she and Quinn talked about? Exactly how much wine had they each had to drink?

"Seriously?" Stanley said as he stood there, calmly stroking his chin and staring at Quinn. Quinn had gone rigid with rage. "What did you think when you got up the next morning and your husband wasn't there?"

Frank would have strongly advised Quinn not to respond. "I sleep late," she said. "All right? He's usually up. When he wasn't downstairs and his car wasn't there, I assumed he'd gone to work. I didn't realize he was missing until I tried to reach him at work and they told me he hadn't come in."

Stanley just stood there for a few moments, his gaze shifting from Quinn to Emily to the car, and back to Quinn. "So, let me repeat the timeline back to you." He looked down at his notes. "From six o'clock on, you two ladies were together."

"Six o'clock on," Quinn said.

"Right. Exactly," Emily said.

"And you left at around ten?" He looked to Emily for confirmation.

Any minute, he'd drill down and ask Emily exactly where she'd gone after she left Quinn's house. She couldn't pretend that she hadn't stopped in the Square for coffee or that her unpleasant encounter with a man who could have been Walter Newell hadn't happened. She tried to imagine Frank's advice—beyond *Don't lie*, probably something on the order of *Pull a Hail Mary*.

Instead of answering Stanley's question, Emily said, "I'm re-ally sorry, you're going to have to excuse me. I desperately need to use the ladies' room. Do you mind? Just tell me where it is and I'll come right back."

Quinn shot her a terrified look that said, *Don't leave me alone.* Emily mouthed the word *Sorry.*

Stanley looked annoyed. "Up one flight." He pointed to a door at the opposite end of the floor. "Turn right. Down the cor-ridor. It'll come up on your right." He looked at his watch. "Why don't you meet us in the lobby when you're done?"

Emily resisted the urge to break into a run as she made her way across to the stairwell. She heard Stanley ask Quinn, "Were you and your husband having any kind of problems?"

"I . . . we . . . What are you trying to get me to say?" Quinn's voice spiraled up. Emily felt guilty about leaving Quinn alone with Stanley, but she had to get out of there before she found herself in his cross hairs.

"I'm just trying to ascertain—" The rest of Stanley's words were cut off as the door to the stairwell closed behind Emily.

17

EMILY CHECKED UNDER the doors to the two stalls in the women's room. No feet. She took out her phone. Four bars. It was nearly ten o'clock. She called Frank. *Pick up, pick up, pick up.*

He answered on the fourth ring. "Where are you?" he said.

"I'm still at the police station."

"Have they found him?"

"No. I need—" Emily froze at the sound of footsteps in the hall.

"Emily, if they—"

"Shhh. Stop. Just listen." Emily cupped her hand over the phone and lowered her voice. "Quinn's husband's car. It was in a hit-and-run at about ten o'clock last night in the Square."

"Isn't that where you . . ." Frank said. "Wait a minute. Are you saying he's the jerk you spilled coffee on last night at the coffee shop?"

"He spilled coffee on me," Emily corrected.

"But how is that even possible?"

"Quite a coincidence, huh?"

"Maybe." A long pause. "Or maybe not. What if he was in the house? Heard you take my call and knew where you were going?"

It was possible. Maybe that creaking she'd heard from overhead wasn't the cat. If Walter Newell had been upstairs listening to Emily and Quinn bitch and moan about their husbands, he'd have been well and truly pissed. "Do I tell the police that I went to the coffee shop after I left Quinn's house?"

Frank didn't answer right away. "Did you tell the police that you *didn't* stop for coffee?"

"I said I went home. I didn't mention anything about the coffee stop."

Silence on the other end.

"Frank?"

"I'm thinking."

Emily knew Frank was analyzing and weighing the options. But she needed an answer. What if Stanley came back at her with more questions? "If I don't tell them now and they find out later, won't that be worse?"

"Emmy, stop acting like you're guilty. You didn't do anything. You haven't lied. You've just—"

"Withheld information that I know full well could be pertinent."

"Really? They already know his car was in the Square because someone reported the hit-and-run. What does it add to their investigation? Unless . . ."

"Unless what?"

"Unless it's your car that he hit."

Emily shuddered, remembering the moment when the man from the coffee shop had locked eyes with hers from outside and pitched his coffee cup at her car. How his tires had screeched as he drove off. "What if he did? And what happens when the police discover—"

"*If* they discover."

"But my car. My taillight."

"Easily fixed. I'll take care of it."

"Now?" Could he really just snap his fingers and make it go away?

"I know a guy who owes me." Frank's voice sounded so reassuring. "Emmy, you know as well as I do that you had absolutely nothing to do with this man's disappearance. So why waste the detective's time?"

That made sense. But still, the *good girl* in her wanted to come clean. "But what if I saw something that could help the police find him?" Like . . . had the man from the coffee shop been carrying one coffee or two? Had there been anyone waiting for him in his parked car? *If* she'd noticed, that could have helped. But she hadn't.

"Emmy, for once think about what's in your own best interest." Frank sounded exasperated. This was his *I know how the world works and you don't* tone. "It will only open up a can of worms if . . . well, if, worst-case, that woman's husband never comes home and she says something that makes them suspect that you had something to do with his disappearance."

Emily swallowed hard. "Why would they think that?"

"Do I need to spell it out? He spills his coffee on you. Dents your car. Anyone would be ticked off. Heck, if it were me I'd have been itching for a fight."

"But I'd never—"

"I know normally you'd never. But you were drunk."

"Not *that* drunk."

"I'm not saying that's what happened. Just showing you what can happen when you go offering information to the police. If you were here right now I'd bop you on the head with that sportsmanship trophy you won at Girl Scout camp. Promise me you won't go back and spill your guts to that police officer. They'll hold you for questioning, and who knows what will happen after that? I worked with the criminal justice system for years. I've seen how quickly things can go south."

Later, as Emily and Quinn sat in Quinn's Miata in the police station parking lot, Quinn said, "Thanks for being here for me, Emmy."

Emmy? Only family called her that. Emily was somehow both annoyed and flattered by the familiarity of it. "Sorry I had to leave you alone with that detective," Emily said.

"I'm sure you had your reasons." Quinn closed her eyes in a long blink. "I just can't believe this is happening. That really *is* Wally's car. Which means—" She shook her head. "I don't know what it means. I don't want to think about what it means. How can someone be here one minute and not here the next?"

Emily had heard virtually the same question from Mrs. Murphy, and once again she was at a loss for words.

Quinn said, "The parking lot where the police found Wally's car, do you know where it is?"

"The town landing?" Sure, Emily knew. Every fall, they held a neighborhood yard sale there that Frank never missed.

"Is it far?"

"A mile, maybe a mile and a half."

Quinn shifted to face Emily. "Would you mind terribly," she said, using a little-girl voice, "if we stopped there on the way back? I need to see the place. *Feel* it. Does that sound crazy?" The wince Emily felt must have shown, because Quinn went on to say, "I know, I know. You're probably desperate to get home. The thing is, I don't think I can manage it alone. Last favor, I promise." Wasn't it enough that Emily hadn't contradicted the half-truths Quinn had sold the police? "I know you probably just want to get rid of me."

Quinn didn't wait for Emily's answer. She started the car and pulled out of the parking lot. "It's this way, right? You'll tell me where to turn, won't you?"

Ridding herself of Quinn really was like trying to remove a finger toy. The woman's sense of entitlement was bolstered by a practiced helplessness. But the landing was on the way back. Just a quick detour. Emily texted Frank to let him know she'd be another twenty minutes or so. She was about to put the phone away when it chirped. Becca. By then they'd reached the side street that led down to the boat basin and the light-rail station.

"Turn here," Emily said, and let Becca's call go to voice mail.

The commuter lot was half-empty. An outbound train must have just left, because a few cars were pulling out as Quinn pulled in. A lone woman stood on the platform, waiting for an inbound train. Quinn parked and got out.

Emily remained in the car and listened to Becca's message. "Can you meet me and Mrs. Murphy at the storage place tomorrow morning at ten? They're going to break open the unit for her."

Emily texted back a quick okay and sent a second message, to her mother, asking if she'd be able to drive up early the next day. Then she got out of the car and joined Quinn under a streetlight at a railing that separated the parking area from the river.

Quinn folded her arms and hunched her shoulders. A stiff breeze whipped her dark hair away from her face as she stared past the cattails and loosestrife, past the deep shadows into the inky darkness beyond the water's edge. Across the river on the opposite bank, Emily recognized the warren of storage units with saffron-colored doors that were lit up a short distance downstream. Inner Peace Storage. She hadn't realized the storage facility was so close to the town wharf.

Quinn said, "I thought I'd feel him here. Feel *something*. But I don't." She turned and scanned the commuter lot. "Where do you think they found his car?"

Emily followed Quinn through the lot, from one pool of light to the next, and onto the boat ramp at the far end. There was no lighting there, and it took a few moments for Emily's eyes to adjust. Boats were lined up nearby and kayaks were chained like bikes to a rack.

Quinn ventured down the boat ramp and crouched. The sky was dark. No moon. No stars. An empty plastic water bottle bobbed at the water's edge. A length of twisted nylon rope was trapped in the weeds. Quinn picked up a pebble and overhanded it into the water. Bits of light glinted where it splashed down. Quinn was reaching for another pebble when Emily noticed a white card caught in the weeds. It was blank except for a large **37** printed in bold type. It could have been a bidder card. Walter Newell had been to an auction.

"Quinn," Emily said. Quinn launched the pebble and then squinted up at Emily. Emily pointed to the card. "Do you see that?"

It took Quinn a moment to spot what Emily was pointing to. She reached for the card and plucked it from the weeds. "Oh my God," she said as she stared at it. Turned it over and over. Then held it to her chest and started to sob. Emily stood beside her, feeling helpless. She didn't even have a Kleenex on her to offer. With a screech of its brakes, a train pulled into the station.

Quinn let Emily walk her to a bench. Quinn wiped away tears with the heel of her hand. Water lapped against the shore, and what had to be one of the last inbound commuter trains of the night bleated as it left the station, leaving behind an empty platform.

As they sat there, Quinn talked about Wally. How they'd met at a ball game. How tongue-tied she'd felt when she'd met his wealthy parents. Their over-the-top wedding, paid for by the groom's family, at a five-star hotel. How the priest who'd married them had been drunk and kept calling her Queenie, and Wally liked to tease her by continuing to call her that. Their honeymoon, a posh Caribbean cruise.

Every so often Quinn paused to check her phone for messages.

Quinn's first inkling that this might not be the union she'd dreamed of was when Wally spent hours in the ship's casino, gambling and drinking and gorging on the all-you-can-eat buffet. When their honeymoon ended and she moved into his house, she was blindsided when he wouldn't let her move in anything but her clothes and toiletries. She'd told herself that, given time, he'd loosen up, but three years later, he'd only become more controlling.

"He was insane about it," Quinn said. "Completely insane. Every once in a while I'd bring something into the house, just to see if he noticed. He did. Every damned time." She bit the words off. "It's like my stuff was contaminated."

Emily felt a twinge of guilt. In her marriage, she played the spouse trying to keep her partner's beloved junk from invading their mutual living spaces. But surely she was nowhere near as toxic about it as Walter Newell had been. And Frank's collecting? Quinn was a piker by comparison.

Just before mosquitoes drove them from the riverbank, Quinn checked her phone for messages one more time. There were none.

❧

It was late when Quinn dropped Emily at her house. On the kitchen counter, Frank had left her a note. *GETTING YOUR CAR FIXED. PIZZA IN THE FRIDGE.*

Thank you, thank you, she said to herself. For the car. For the pizza. She warmed the slices he'd left her. As the microwave hummed, the kitchen filled with the irresistible smell. Standing at the sink, she wolfed down a slice. Salt. Fat. Heaven.

She grabbed the second slice, along with a napkin this time, and took it to the table to eat. An icy Coke would have been perfect, but she'd stopped buying soft drinks when Frank got so addicted to diet soda that they were buying it by the case and their dentist said his teeth were dissolving. She got up and went to the sink, ran some water into her cupped palm, and drank it.

The house felt empty and silent. Emily went upstairs and changed into a cotton nightgown, opened the bedroom windows as wide as possible, and turned on both the attic fan and the TV. Red Sox against the Dodgers in Los Angeles were tied at 1–1 in extra innings.

Usually a televised baseball game put her right to sleep. But tonight she kept listening for Frank. Thinking about Quinn *not* staying up and waiting for Wally to come home the night before.

Between innings, she kicked off the top sheet and closed her eyes. An announcer droned, "Do not take Cialis if you take nitrates for chest pain . . ." It felt as if it had been days ago that she'd hurried off to Inner Peace Storage to return that map, only to find herself locked out. Could it have been only earlier today that she and Becca had given Mrs. Murphy the disquieting news that someone had changed the lock? And once that fire had been put out, Quinn had called with the news that the police were on her doorstep.

At least Frank was getting Emily's car fixed. A manager

would break open the storage unit tomorrow. And her mother was coming to give her expert opinion of exactly what Mr. Murphy had been up to with his so-called collecting.

But for every question that was being resolved, Emily had another that remained a mystery. Where was Walter Newell? Had he been the man she'd run into at the Java Connection? Why had he abandoned his car at the town wharf?

Wheels within wheels, she thought as she watched the Red Sox first baseman strike out.

TUESDAY

OVERNIGHT THE HUMIDITY rose, and by the time Emily got up on Tuesday morning, she felt as if she'd been sleeping on wet sheets. The sun was hidden behind a haze of dark clouds, and the temperature was already in the eighties. Too bad a meeting with the manager of Inner Peace Storage required at least a work uniform. She ironed pants and a matching Polo shirt, wishing she could wear a loose shift instead. Her foot felt better, the swelling down, but it seemed wiser to stick with Crocs for one more day.

When she got downstairs, it was nearly nine. Lila was already there, sitting at the kitchen table across from Frank, each of them reading a section of the paper and holding it up like a barrier. Lila's rolling suitcase and purse the size of a saddlebag sat on the floor by the back door. In the month since Emily had last seen her, her mother had dyed her hair red and cut it short and spiky. As she'd told Emily countless times, the problem with getting older was that women over sixty were treated as if they were invisible. At sixty-five, between the hair, a short silk caftan in swirling shades of pink and purple, and the layers of bangle bracelets that jangled whenever she gestured, Lila showed the world just how determined she was not to disappear. She also seemed impervious to the heat and humidity.

"You made it," Emily said, giving her mother an air kiss. "How was traffic?"

"I left at six." Lila got up and poured Emily a cup of coffee.

"And?" Emily took the cup and sipped. Weak. She could tell Lila had made it. Frank made coffee so strong you'd think a spoon could stand in it.

"Just the usual congestion, crossing the bridge. Would you believe, people actually commute from the Cape? Then a mess up here at the merge."

Which meant—Emily glanced at the kitchen clock—Lila had probably been here for at least an hour. Alone. With Frank.

"Your car's back," Frank said, putting down the paper and rising to his feet.

"Your car?" Lila said.

Emily and Lila followed Frank out to the curb where her car was parked. Emily walked all the way around it. The rear taillight had been replaced, the dent in the back erased, the spill washed away. Good as new. You'd have to get out a magnifying glass to see—

"Oh dear," Lila said. "What happened?"

"Where?" Frank said.

"There," Lila said, bracelets jingling as she pointed a lacquered nail at the back of the car. Spot-on. She looked at Emily over the top of her rhinestone-rimmed glasses. "It's obvious, isn't it?" She ran her hand over the offending area. "There's a dimple. And the paint's thicker here." She backed away, squinting. "Plus, one taillight's a lot cleaner than the other." She looked at

Emily. "Might not be as noticeable if you got your car washed occasionally, dear."

Emily exchanged eye rolls with Frank. "A few dents add to the charm of an old car, don't you think?" she said, looking pointedly at her mother's ancient Volvo, which was parked a little farther up the street. The chrome trim on its front and rear bumpers was pockmarked from Lila's technique of parallel parking. She'd back up until she tapped the car behind her, inch forward until she tapped the car in front. Only sometimes, it was more than a tap.

"What I think," Lila said, hands on her hips, "is that you should always put your best foot forward. Especially when you're in a service industry. And an amateur repair makes you look like you don't care. It's like a business card with a typo." Lila looked up as thunder rumbled in the distance. "We're going to need umbrellas."

"No worries," Emily said as she walked around to the back of her car and crouched within arm's length of the repair. "I've got umbrellas in the trunk." Of course she knew where the car had been damaged, but would she have noticed if she didn't? Probably not. Which, in a nutshell, was the difference between Emily and her mother. That was the reason Lila had been so good at her job, and the whole reason Emily wanted her to have a look at Mr. Murphy's collection.

"You're right," Emily said. "I should get my car washed more often. And it is definitely going to rain. " She checked her watch. "We should get going soon. We need to be at the storage place in thirty minutes."

While Emily drove, her mother *tsk*ed her way through the pictures of the storage unit that Emily had on her cell phone. "This is going to be painful. The condition of those books." She shook her head. "And what about those tubes?"

"That one I talked to you about? It's in the back." Emily pointed over her shoulder. "See what you think."

Lila undid her seat belt, turned in her seat, and reached for the tube. She settled back and examined the label. "I should probably be wearing gloves."

"In the backseat, too. In the bag that's on the floor."

Lila hauled the bag forward, rummaged around. "What's this?" she asked, showing Emily the baby-blue stun gun.

"It's a stun gun. Frank makes me carry it for self-defense."

"*Makes* you?"

"Figure of speech."

"I should hope so. I didn't raise you to . . ." Her voice died out as Lila examined the stun gun. "Looks dead to me. If you're going to carry one, you should at least keep it charged."

How did she even know? "Please just put it back in the bag," Emily said. She needed her mother, but she could only defend herself about so many things.

Thankfully, Lila dropped the subject. She rummaged around some more in Emily's gear bag until she found a pair of latex gloves. She put them on, then popped the plastic lid off one end of the tube. Peered into the tube, then upended it. The map slid out.

Lila gently flattened the paper across her lap. "New France, New Scotland, Golfe of Canada." She whispered the words like an incantation as she ran gloved fingertips over the compass and a windblown Neptune with his trident that occupied the lower corner.

"Do you think it's original?" Emily asked.

Lila leaned close to the paper and sniffed. "I'd need to look at it with a magnifier, but the paper seems right." She ran her fingers across the top of the page. "Of course, it could be giclée."

"What's that?"

"A really fine print copy. Digital technology. It's so good that you can't see the dots, and if it's printed on period paper, well, it can fool even an expert. But this?" She ran her fingertips around the margins. "It appears to have been printed from a plate. There's a pressmark." She held the map up to the light and rotated it a quarter turn at a time, examining each of the edges. "And it's been removed from a bound book. See how only this edge is rough, where the others are sharp?"

"I'll take your word for it," Emily said as she drove past the turnoff for the town wharf. A drop of rain plopped on the windshield. "You're saying it's been torn out?"

"Carefully. By someone who knew what they were doing. If I had to guess, I'd say they used wet string. Placing a piece in the gutter margin weakens the paper. Leave it there for a few minutes, and you can make a clean tear. It's quiet, doesn't require bulky tools, and leaves barely a trace. Slip the document up a coat sleeve, and Bob's your uncle." Lila held up the map. "This is a beauty. Really old. Historically significant. You can see why someone would want it, assuming it's original, of course." She sighed. "And the Blaine doesn't even know they're missing it."

19

BECCA AND MRS. Murphy were waiting at the storage unit when Emily and Lila pulled up. Before getting out, Emily slid the map into its tube. As soon as the storage bin was open, she'd put it back. She popped the trunk and got out an umbrella for herself and one for Lila.

Mrs. Murphy narrowed her eyes as they approached, and Emily wondered if she thought Lila might have been the woman the security guard had recently seen going in and out of her husband's storage unit. She looked puzzled when Lila hugged Becca.

"Mrs. Murphy, this is Lila Laubenstein," Emily said. "She's my mother, and she knows everything there is to know about books and prints."

"Not everything," Lila said. "But I've been around for a while and paying attention."

"Your mother?" Mrs. Murphy asked, her face relaxing into a smile. She shook Lila's hand. As different as they looked— Mrs. Murphy all in black like an Italian widow, her white hair and unvarnished face accepting her age; Lila in bright plumage, fighting it all the way—Emily realized that they were probably about the same vintage.

"My mother was a librarian," Emily said.

"*Is* a librarian," Lila said. She smiled at Mrs. Murphy. "You can take the girl out of the library, but it's not something you stop being, even after you've officially retired, and I haven't been retired all that long." Her smile faded as she thought for a moment. "Well, maybe it has been a while. I worked in special collections."

"Really?" Mrs. Murphy asked. "Where?"

"The Auburn Design School. It's in—"

"I know where it is," Mrs. Murphy said. "Murph and I visited. Beautiful Kahn building."

Lila's face lit up. "One of his first truly modern designs."

Emily glanced at Lila, her radar up. It occurred to her that there could easily be material from the Auburn Design School Library in the storage unit.

"We visited just about every library he designed," Mrs. Murphy went on. "Also the McKims. The Richardsons. We're going to Seattle to see the main library. We *were* going, at any rate."

"Rem Koolhaas," Lila said. "Brilliant architect."

"I've heard it's an amazing building, inside and out. Murph used to say—" Her voice broke. After a moment she cleared her throat.

"I'm sorry," Lila said. "Really I am."

Mrs. Murphy sniffed and gave a wan smile. "I think my husband would have liked to be an architect. Unfortunately he grew up in a family that didn't nourish artistic talent. He made a good living as a dentist. But it was a job, not a passion."

"I wonder, have you been to the Ames—" Lila began.

"In Easton?" Mrs. Murphy said. "Of course. Another magnificent Richardson. And so beautifully maintained. And I'm sure you know the Richardson in downtown Quincy?"

Lila put a hand over her heart. "The La Farge windows."

"Oh my, yes."

Opposites meeting on common ground, Emily thought. Becca shot her a surprised look. *Go figure.*

Then Lila asked, "Have you gotten to the Blaine?" Emily's ears pricked up.

But before Mrs. Murphy could answer, a security cart pulled up and a man got out. Not the security guard Emily had spoken with before—this man was young, trim, and looked bored. He wore khakis and a saffron-colored golf shirt with a name badge that read MANAGER. From the floor of the cart he picked up a clipboard, then turned to face the four of them. "Ruth Murphy?"

"That's me," Mrs. Murphy said.

"Ma'am. Can I see some identification?"

Mrs. Murphy, who was wearing a shoulder bag across her body, found her driver's license and showed it to the manager.

"Thank you. All I need is your signature, authorizing us to remove the lock." He gave her the clipboard and a pen. Mrs. Murphy signed.

The manager tossed the clipboard onto the seat of the cart and lifted an enormous bolt cutter from the floor in the back. Its pincer jaws were as big as a catcher's mitt, its handles steeply separated. He approached the storage unit's closed door, bent over, and inspected the padlock. He angled the bolt cutter so it hooked the shackle, set his feet apart, and grunted as he pressed the handles together. There was a loud crunch as the metal caved. He wiggled the bolt cutter free, unhooked the shackle, and opened the hasp.

Emily held her breath as he reached down for the door handle. She glanced at Mrs. Murphy, who stood squinting from the concrete apron just outside the unit, her hand over her mouth as if dreading whatever was about to be revealed.

The manager raised the overhead door, reached inside, and flipped on the light.

Emily had been afraid they'd find the interior partly or completely cleared out, but everything looked more or less as she remembered. A wooden workbench loaded with supplies stretched across the far wall. On both sides were floor-to-ceiling shelves loaded with books and document tubes and boxes.

But as she exhaled and took a breath, she realized that something *was* different. There'd been a sour smell before. Mold and mildew. But the stink that now wafted from the interior was far worse. Putrid. Maybe because of the heat? Or perhaps an animal had gotten trapped inside? She put her hand over her mouth and nose.

The manager must have smelled it, too, because he scowled and took a few steps back. "What are you storing in here?" He turned to face Mrs. Murphy. "Plants and animals aren't allowed. Nothing wet or—" He sniffed again. "No food. No fertilizer."

"Fertilizer?" Mrs. Murphy said, drawing herself up. "You haven't the slightest idea what you're talking about, young man."

Emily said, "Maybe it's because the climate control isn't working. From the looks of the book collection, it hasn't been working for quite some time."

The manager examined the thermostat on the wall by the

door. Raised his hand and felt a vent in the ceiling. Scowled. "I'll look into it and get back to you. Right away." The speed with which he got in his cart and rode off made Emily wonder how long it would be before Mrs. Murphy actually heard from him.

Mrs. Murphy hung back with Becca as Emily stepped into the unit, with Lila behind her. Emily put the document tube on a shelf with other tubes and looked around for the source of the odor. Meanwhile, Lila moved slowly down one side of shelving, pulling down an occasional book, gently examining it, putting it back.

Taking shallow breaths, Emily pulled down the hatbox she'd looked in earlier. She gave it to Lila, who opened the lid. Lila's frown deepened as she leafed through the library book pockets and due-date cards that filled it to the brim.

Emily got out her phone, intending to compare the photos she'd taken with what was in front of her, when she noticed a red baseball cap on the floor near the workbench. She stooped to pick it up.

Under the workbench was a rolled-up area rug with burlap backing. She hadn't noticed it on her earlier visit. It was lying in a shallow puddle of water that hadn't been there earlier, either. Was the place leaking, too? Emily inched closer.

Standing at the workbench, Lila whispered, "This is quite a set of supplies he's got. Bleach pens and gum erasers and sandpaper. Alcohol. An iron."

"Mom." Emily interrupted Lila's inventory. "Look." She pointed to the rolled-up rug under the workbench. Her attention was riveted on what was poking out from one end of it. The fingers of a pale hand. Sticking out the other end were the toes of a pair of sneakers.

Lila bent over, took one look, and backed away.

Emily set the baseball cap on the workbench and picked up a document tube. She poked it at one of the sneakered feet. Stiff. She reached in and touched the fingers. They were cold and clammy.

Lila already had her phone out. "Hello, police?"

20

"WE FIND A dead body and you're sorting library cards," Emily said under her breath to Lila. They were waiting in the little office at Inner Peace Storage. Lila held the open hatbox in her lap and was organizing the cards, clipping groups of them together with paper clips she'd appropriated from the office desk. Becca and Mrs. Murphy stood, talking quietly and looking out through the porthole Becca had cleared in the fogged-over window. Two police cruisers had already arrived, but all Emily could see from the office was the light from their beacons reflecting in the moist air. The facility manager had gone back to the storage unit with the police, and the women had been told to wait in the office until they came back.

There was a flash, a loud crack of thunder, and sheets of wind-driven rain pelted the glass.

"What else can I do?" Lila whispered back. She added a card to a clipped group. "This is my way of coping. Stay busy. Focus on minutiae. You know the old saying, don't worry about the mule, just load the wagon. If I were at home and something upset me, I'd be cleaning out my junk drawer." She gave Emily a defiant frown. "Where do you think you get it from? Don't judge."

It was too late for that. Emily went over to a water dispenser in the corner and helped herself to a cup of water. She drank, trying to clear from her head the noxious, cloying smell of a body that had been left for who knew how many hours in a hot storage unit that lacked even basic ventilation. When she returned to Lila, she whispered, "You think the collection is stolen?"

"*Shhh.* Don't know yet," Lila whispered back. "I'm getting things organized, preparing for later when we contact these libraries." Lowering her voice still further, Lila added, "Once Ruth understands what she's got, that's what I expect she'll want to do."

Ruth. Already her mother was on a first-name basis with Mrs. Murphy. Emily was glad she'd asked her mother to help out.

Headlights lit up the water-streaked windows as a white emergency van drove past, heading in the direction of Mr. Murphy's storage unit. Emily had no idea how long it took for a body to stiffen up, but the person rolled up in the rug could have been dead for quite some time. Had the body been there on Sunday? Was it possible that she simply hadn't noticed it? The thought made her skin crawl.

She took out her phone and thumbed through the photos she'd taken inside the storage unit on Sunday. Found one of the workbench. She enlarged it and lightened the exposure, confirming, to her relief, that underneath there'd been no puddle of water, no rolled-up rug, no baseball cap.

"What's happening? What are they doing out there?" Mrs. Murphy said. "How long are they going to keep us here?"

The police officer who'd arrived first—Emily hadn't recognized him from her visit yesterday to the police station—had said that he couldn't give them a time frame, but that someone would be back to talk to each of them. Emily wondered if she should call Frank. He'd be apoplectic if she didn't. Her thumb was hovering over his name when a man entered the office. He was not wearing a uniform, but a laminated ID badge with the insignia of the Hartwell police hung from his neck. He was square-jawed and stern, and his mere presence made Emily feel as if she should stand. She shut off her phone and pocketed it. Lila stuffed the cards she'd been sorting back into the hatbox and closed the lid.

Mrs. Murphy marched right up to the man. Her puff of hair came up to his chin. "Please, can't you explain to us who that person is, and what he is doing in my husband's storage unit?" Emily had to admire her spirit, though it was pretty clear that the poor person rolled in the carpet was no longer *doing* any-thing.

"Ma'am. That's just what we're trying to find out." The man's gaze traveled across the four of them. "I'm Detective Lieutenant Moran." He pulled a pad from his pants pocket and flipped it open. "And you are?"

"Ruth Murphy," Mrs. Murphy said.

"You say that's your husband's storage unit."

"Mine now. He died," Mrs. Murphy said, her chin quivering, daring him to contradict her.

Lila stood beside Mrs. Murphy and linked arms. "Mr. Mur-phy died about a year ago," Lila explained. "We're here to help her clear out the unit."

"And you are?" Moran asked.

"Lila Laubenstein," Lila said.

"Emily Harlow," Emily said.

Moran looked from Emily, to Lila, and then back to Emily. "Mother and daughter," Lila said.

Then he looked from Emily to Becca, no doubt taking in their matching outfits. "I'm Rebecca Jain," Becca said. "Emily and I are business partners. We're professional organizers."

"Thank you," Moran said. "Which of you found the body?"

No one answered right away. Finally Emily said, "I guess I did. We all noticed the smell, but we didn't realize what it was until I looked under the table. The puddle of water caught my attention."

"When were any of you inside the unit before today?" Moran asked.

That would be Emily. Again. "I was here on Sunday. Alone," she admitted.

"Did anyone see you?"

"A security guard came by. I'm sure he'll remember."

"And then you came back today."

"Actually, I came back yesterday."

"Yesterday?" Moran looked surprised.

"But I couldn't get in. Someone—"

Mrs. Murphy interrupted. "I *had* a key. I gave it to her. It worked and then it didn't."

"Not exactly," Emily said calmly, though at that moment she could have strangled Mrs. Murphy. "The key you gave me worked the first time I was here. But not when I came back the next day." Enunciating her words, Emily added, "Someone had changed the lock."

"And from the looks of it, they did a good bit more," Lila said under her breath.

"Apparently," Moran said. "So you came back this morning? All of you."

Becca said, "The manager needed Mrs. Murphy's signature giving him permission to break the lock. Which he did."

"Do you still have the broken lock?" Moran asked.

Of course that would be important, Emily realized. Because whoever dumped the body in the storage unit would have handled it. "The manager must have taken it with him. Honestly, I don't remember." She looked to Becca, who shook her head.

"He took it with him," Lila said. "I'm sure he did."

"Thank you. We'll locate it." Moran smiled at Lila like she was star pupil. "So let me see if I understand. Sunday, Mrs. Harlow was here. She unlocks the unit. Looks around. Leaves. When she returns the next day, the lock's been changed."

"Right," Emily said.

"And you're certain that you locked up when you left here Sunday."

"Positive."

"What time was that? "

"Around five-thirty." Emily realized that she was covering the same ground that she'd gone over yesterday when she'd accompanied Quinn to the police station to identify her husband's missing car.

Moran asked, "And when you were here Sunday, did you notice anything else unusual?"

Emily said, "Do you mean, was there a man's body under that table? No." She got out her phone and showed him pictures she'd taken, pausing on the one of the workbench.

Moran narrowed his gaze. "What makes you think it's a man's body?"

The only sound in the office was the patter of raindrops. Emily said, "The little bit that I could see. The shoes. The fingers. The baseball cap. I just assumed."

Mrs. Murphy gave a nervous laugh, then clapped her hand over her mouth.

"I wonder if any of you recognize him." Moran put away his

pad and took out a cell phone. He held it out so each of them in turn could see a photo of the man. His face was bloated, skin the color of clay. His eyes were closed. He had dark, close-cropped hair, and a mustache and beard.

"I don't know him," Lila said.

"Nor do I," added Mrs. Murphy.

Becca said, "I don't recognize him, either."

Emily didn't say anything. She could feel everyone's eyes on her. Walter Newell had dark hair and a mustache and beard like this guy, but that was hardly enough to say it was him.

"Take your time," Moran said. "Death can alter a person's appearance."

Emily tried to visualize the picture that Quinn had brought to the police, or the man she'd run into at the coffee shop. "There was no identification on him?" she asked.

Moran didn't answer. He opened the door to the office and beckoned her outside. Emily hesitated, unsure whether to follow. She turned to her mother, but for once her mother had no advice. Emily braced herself and followed Moran.

Outside, the rain had turned to a fine mist and it felt as if the sun was trying to break through. Moran tilted his head and looked down at her. "You recognize him, don't you?"

"No," Emily said, the denial coming too fast. "But I know who he might be."

21

DETECTIVE MORAN'S CAR looked like your average black full-sized sedan, but inside it was equipped with a computer and scanner, and a metal grille separated the front seat from the back. Moran had let Mrs. Murphy and Becca and Lila leave, and driven Emily to the open storage unit, where he parked, then got out of the car and walked off, leaving her in the car alone. Emily tried to let herself out, but there was only a metal plate where a door handle should have been. "Hey!" she shouted. She could just make out Moran inside the unit, talking to someone in a dark uniform. Pointing in her direction.

Emily found the window control on the armrest and tried pushing it. Pulling it. But the window didn't budge. She banged on the glass. Leaned with all her strength against the door. There was no getting out.

She tried to stay calm as she got out her phone but she fumbled, entering her password wrong twice before getting in. Finally she managed to call Frank. The call was connecting when Moran pulled open the car door and Emily tumbled out into spitting rain, dropping her phone on the ground.

Moran picked up her phone, wiped it on his pants leg, and

glanced at it before handing it back to her. Emily could hear Frank's voice message, *Can't take your call right now.* She touched the red circle to end the call. For now she was on her own.

"Sorry. That took longer than I expected," Moran said. "Are you okay?" He reached into the front seat for an umbrella, raised it, and held it over her. "I needed to make sure I could bring you in."

Emily took a breath and steadied herself. Her heart hammered as she walked past what turned out to be a coroner's van, backed up to the door of the unit. Moran raised yellow crime-scene tape, but only let Emily come inside just past it.

That smell again. Emily gagged.

"Just give us a minute," Moran said to two technicians working inside the unit. The two men stood and stepped away from the body of a man lying on his back on a thick plastic tarp.

Emily forced herself to look. The man was tall and muscular. The face was pale, not gray like Moran's photograph, and down one side was a deep red stain.

She felt Moran watching her, waiting for her to react. She said, "I don't recognize this man. I don't know him."

"But?" Moran said. He folded his arms and waited.

"But he could be the husband of one of my clients. That man—the husband—he went to an auction Sunday night and he's been missing ever since. The East Hartwell police found his car in the commuter lot at the town wharf."

"The wharf," Moran said, turning his gaze in that direction.

Emily added, "Yesterday I went to the police station with his wife to identify the car. Like I said, I'm not sure if this is him. I saw the picture his wife gave the police. The hair seems right."

One of the technicians handed Moran a plastic bag. Looked like there was a wallet inside, open to a driver's license. Moran looked at it.

"Walter Newell?" Emily said.

Moran nodded.

Detective Moran took out his phone and placed a call. He turned his back to Emily and spoke quietly. Emily caught some of it. "Walter Newell . . . *N-E-W-E-L-L* . . . Wife reported . . . Where?" His tone was decidedly pissed as his gaze shifted toward East Hartwell's town wharf. "What did they find? . . . Anything else I should know?" The last laced with sarcasm.

As Moran talked, the technicians wheeled a gurney to the edge of the storage unit. They folded the plastic tarp around Walter Newell's body like a cocoon, then lifted it up and onto the gurney. Moments later, they'd loaded him into the coroner's van.

Quinn's husband was dead. Quinn would be devastated. Grief-stricken and no doubt guilt-ridden, what with all her talk about the many creative ways she'd have liked to dispose of him. And Emily had gone along, laughing, imagining various ways she might go about dispatching Frank. She cringed at the memory, because what was happening now was no joke.

"How well do you know his wife?" Moran asked.

"She's our client. Like Mrs. Murphy. We were going to help her declutter."

"She has a storage unit?"

"A garage. We're helping her get rid of the things she no longer needs."

Moran nodded. "Given what you do, I'd imagine your clients

confide in you. Isn't there usually something in their life, beyond the clutter, that they're trying to fix or at least get past?"

"You're right. Decluttering can help people with issues that have nothing to do with the actual stuff that's filling up their living space. Our discussions can get quite personal. But I take the confidence that my clients place in my discretion very seriously."

Moran wrinkled his brow in annoyance. "Walter Newell was murdered, Mrs. Harlow. Anything that you can tell us about him could help us find his killer."

"I don't know anything about him," Emily said. She thought of Frank's lawyerly advice and chose her next words carefully. "Walter Newell was not my friend. I've never been introduced to him. I met his wife, in a professional capacity."

"Really," Moran said. The back doors to the coroner's van slammed shut and he turned to watch it drive off. Then he raised the crime-scene tape again, gesturing for Emily to precede him out. The rain had stopped. "So why do you think his body was dumped in a storage unit that you happened to be clearing out?"

It was a good question, one she'd been asking herself. "Do you think he was killed here?" she asked, avoiding having to come up with an answer.

Moran's gaze dropped to the rug Walter Newell had been rolled up in. A technician was wrapping it in plastic. "We'll know that soon enough. But as far as how he got here . . ." The sun broke through as he pointed to a CCTV camera mounted to the roof of the unit beside the Murphys'. "As soon as we view the footage, I expect we'll have an answer to that, too."

22

DETECTIVE MORAN DROVE Emily back to the Inner Peace office. The sun had come out and the pavement was steaming. "I'd appreciate it if you'd come to the police station and give a written statement," he said after he opened the car door for her. "Today. While the details are fresh in your mind."

How long would it be before she could shake that nauseating smell or stop seeing Walter Newell's pale face, stained as if someone had smeared the side of it with Mercurochrome?

"I'll go now and get it over with," Emily said.

Emily got into her car. Moments later, a police cruiser drove past. No lights flashing. No rush now. Emily followed it, driving slowly toward the exit.

The surveillance footage would confirm what Emily had told the police. That she'd arrived and opened the unit on Sunday. Left after a few hours. With any luck she'd been hidden by her car when she'd changed her shirt. It would show her trying to get back in the next day.

But in between, what? Because overnight, someone else had opened the unit, dragged in a dead body rolled up in a wet area rug, shoved it under the workbench, and then left the unit fastened with a new padlock.

She reached the street entrance. A uniformed officer moved aside orange cones that temporarily blocked the way. Just beyond was parked a van with a satellite dish mounted on top. BOSTON 35 was written in fat red and white block letters on the side.

Emily gripped the wheel and accelerated past. She hoped against hope that they weren't already broadcasting the story. She could imagine the headline: "Body Found in Self-Storage." That would get people's attention, immediately conjuring the severed head from *Silence of the Lambs.*

Quinn would be waiting at home for some word of what had happened to her husband. Continuing to check her phone. Hoping for a call from a friend or a hospital or Wally himself. Emily shuddered to think that Quinn could learn of her husband's death from a news crawl.

Maybe Emily could reach her and break the news. Then at least she'd be somewhat prepared when the police showed up on her doorstep. If Frank had been found dead, Emily would have been grateful for that small buffer, a window of privacy in which to absorb the shock.

Emily pulled over to the curb, slipped her phone from her pocket, and called. Quinn picked up after a single ring. "Hello? Emily?" She sounded breathless.

Emily swallowed hard. How to begin?

"What is it?" Quinn said. "Have you heard something?"

"It's Wally," Emily managed. She didn't know where to go from there, so she just plunged in. "He's dead."

A gasp from Quinn, as if the news had knocked the air out of her. "He can't be."

"I'm so sorry."

"You're sure?"

"I wanted you to hear about it before the police get there."

"Dead," Quinn whispered.

When she didn't say anything else, Emily said, "Quinn?" No response. "I'm so sorry." More silence. "Are you there? Are you okay?" Emily asked, even though she knew Quinn couldn't possibly be.

"I can't believe it." Quinn's voice was raspy. "It's just . . . How do you know?"

Before she spoke, Emily realized how strange this was going to sound. "He was in a storage unit I was working on."

"I don't understand," Quinn said.

"Honestly, neither do I. We were clearing out a storage unit for another client and . . . Listen, is there someone you can call to be with you? Do you want me to come over?"

"No! God, no. I need to think. This wasn't supposed to happen."

"I'm so sorry." Emily knew she was repeating herself, but what else was there to say?

"Just remember," Quinn said. "Whatever happens? I've got your back. We're in this together."

In *what* together? When Emily disconnected the call, she felt as if she were in free fall. She tried to grasp what Quinn was suggesting. She started the car. Immediately the windshield fogged. She cranked the air conditioner and waited for the glass to clear. Ran the wipers a few times. Then she started driving home.

Halfway there, she remembered she'd agreed to go to the

police station to give a statement. She made a U-turn and drove there instead. Outside the police station, she checked to see if she'd missed Frank returning her call. She hadn't. She texted her mother, Home in an hour, so she wouldn't worry.

The officer at the desk at the police station was much younger than the one who'd been there when she'd come in with Quinn. He asked her to sign in, then whisked her past the front counter. He led her around back and delivered her to a familiar uniformed officer waiting in the corridor. Sergeant Stanley.

"Mrs. Harlow?" Stanley rose up on his toes and hooked his thumbs into his belt. "I understand you're back? This time to give a witness statement?" All business, he escorted her to a small room with a table and four chairs. He pulled out a minia-ture recorder from a drawer and placed it on the table between them.

"Tuesday, August sixth, three twenty-three p.m. Sergeant Brian Stanley with Emily Harlow." He stopped and played back the recording. Satisfied, he pressed RECORD again. "In your own words, can you describe what happened this morning when you arrived at Inner Peace Storage at 1501 Washington Street in East Hartwell, Massachusetts?"

Emily reached across and shut off the recorder. "I thought this was supposed to be a written statement."

"No problem. If that's what you'd prefer." He reached into the desk, pulled out a form, and pushed it across the table to her. "I was going to have someone transcribe your statement and have you sign it. Easier that way. But if you prefer to write it out yourself . . ." He offered her a pen.

It would be easier just to tell him what happened. "Okay. You threw me. This isn't what I was expecting." She waited until he'd turned the recorder back on, then began. "I left my house this morning at about nine-thirty. It was raining." She described her arrival at the storage facility, watching the manager break open the unit, and the moment she'd noticed the rug rolled up under the workbench and realized what it was. She ended with, "We immediately called the police."

"Thank you," Stanley said, nodding. Emily rose to her feet, thinking she was done, but he motioned for her to sit back down. "Just a few more details that we're hoping to get straight. Don't want to have to ask you to come back."

Emily didn't like the sound of that. She waited, perched on the edge of the seat.

"Can you describe your whereabouts and actions going back to Sunday afternoon?"

Sunday afternoon? Why was he asking her that? "I thought this was about what happened today."

"That, and we're trying to tie up a few loose ends. We believe that you spent part of Sunday—late afternoon and evening—with the victim's wife. Is that correct?"

Emily nodded.

"Can you speak? For the tape."

"I did."

"And we know a witness reported that his car was involved in a car accident that same night in the Square. He hit your car. Would it surprise you that we have that on CCTV?" He didn't wait for her to respond. "You didn't report the incident to the police? Why was that?"

Emily's stomach rolled and she felt her face flush. "I had no idea that it was Walter Newell who hit me. I'd never met the man. I didn't report it because it was no big deal. It's an old car.

I don't even have collision insurance. Besides, at first I didn't realize my car had been hit."

"You hadn't met the man," Stanley said, deadpan, "and yet you'd just come from his house."

Shit. She avoided Stanley's gaze, instead looking down at the red light on the recorder. He made it sound damning, but it was purely circumstantial. In the silence that followed, Emily could hear the second hand on the clock behind her on the wall ticking. A door slammed down the hall.

Stanley went on. "By the next day, you knew who he was, didn't you? You knew he'd hit your car. You knew all of that when you came here with his wife to report him missing."

She started to deny that but stopped herself. She knew what Frank's advice would be if he'd answered his damn phone. She stood and announced, "I came here to give a statement about finding a body. I've done that. I'm leaving."

"Of course you can go." Stanley rocked back in his chair. "But we'll be keeping your car."

"You have a warrant?"

"We can get one, and hold your car until we do. Or you can give me the keys and we'll return it to you as soon as possible."

Emily tried to keep her expression neutral. What she wanted to do was tell him to stuff it. "How long will you need to keep it for?"

"That depends," he said, relaxing a notch, as if sensing his advantage. "Depends on what we find. But I can guarantee that you'll get it back faster if you leave it and let us examine it."

What choice did Emily have? Reluctantly, she removed her car key from her key ring and handed it over.

❧

Emily was still shaking when she called her mother and asked her to come pick her up at the police station. She hung up before Lila could ask why, all the while kicking herself for coming alone to give what was supposed to have been a *written* statement.

She took a seat in the lobby. A teenage boy sat in a chair, furiously thumbing away at his cell phone. A couple was huddled together near the exit, their backs to her. When the woman turned, Emily recognized Quinn Newell. She was clutching a tissue and her face was red and bloated. *She* knew better than to talk to the police without an attorney present. The man in a suit, to whom she'd been talking so intently, was Ryan Melanson, Frank's law partner.

"Mrs. Newell?" Sergeant Stanley held open the counter for Quinn and Ryan to pass through. "This way, please." Emily was worried about how Quinn's *I've got your back* would play out under Stanley's relentless questioning. When push came to shove, would Quinn throw Emily under the bus?

As Ryan escorted Quinn across the lobby, he spotted Emily. He came over to her, bent down, and rested his hand on her shoulder. "You missed a great game," he said quietly.

Emily recoiled from Ryan's touch, remembering the feel of his hand on her behind. And if it had been such a great game, then why had he left early? He backed off, hands raised in mute surrender, and said, "I'm only here because Frank asked me to help out."

Frank had asked him to help out? *As if.*

Please, Emily thought, *don't do us any more favors.* Without

Ryan's referral, Emily never would have met Quinn Newell and she wouldn't have gotten tangled up in this mess.

Ryan returned to Quinn, leaving behind a wake of after-shave. Quinn dabbed at her eyes and steadied herself. Attached once again to Ryan's arm, she followed Stanley past the front counter. She turned back to Emily for a moment and signaled a covert thumbs-up. Stanley's speculative gaze anchored for a few moments on Emily before he turned and followed Quinn and Ryan.

23

"SO YOU JUST answered their questions and left your car there?" Frank said after he got home that evening and Emily told him what had happened. "Really?" He took off his suit jacket and threw it on the back of a kitchen chair. Loosened his tie and whipped it off, then unbuttoned the neck of his shirt. Lila had greeted him and then disappeared to rest and take a shower, or so she'd said.

"What was I supposed to do?" Emily said. "He told me I had to—"

"He who?"

"Sergeant Stanley." Emily opened the oven and took out a lasagna she'd frozen more than a month ago. She removed the foil and put the pan back in to let it brown, then turned on the fan over the stove and opened the back door. It was too hot for lasagna, but it was what she had. "He's the same officer that Quinn and I talked to after the police found her husband's car."

"Stanley. Short guy with a lisp?"

"Shortish. No lisp. He told me if I didn't leave the car voluntarily he'd impound it while they waited for a court order."

"That is such pure and utter bullshit." Frank cracked his knuckles.

Emily choked up and her eyes filled with tears. "I tried to call you."

Frank slid his phone from his pocket. "Shit. Battery's dead. I was in court all day, or else I'd have noticed. I still don't get why they took your car."

"They have CCTV footage that shows Quinn's husband hitting my car while I was getting your coffee."

Frank sank down on a kitchen chair. "They *have* it on camera? Or he *told you* that they have it on camera? Did you actually see it?"

"No. But—"

"They were fishing."

"I didn't tell them about the hit-and-run. Someone called it in."

"Right. The serendipitous anonymous caller. Next they'll be selling you a bridge."

"Even if they don't have it on video, all they'd have to do is go to the coffee shop and talk to—"

"You have no idea what they're looking at or who they're talking to because you're the last person they'd tell. This is serious, Emmy. You'll get yourself in deep shit if you're not careful. Please." He pointed his finger at her. "Don't talk to the police again. Not alone. Understand?"

Emily always found that tone and the finger-pointing irritating, not to mention Frank's cocksure attitude. He was always right and she was always wrong. Though at this moment he probably was right. She swallowed her annoyance. "They're going to let me know when I can come back for the car."

"Just to get your car?" He got up, opened a bottom kitchen

cabinet, and pulled out a bottle of Maker's Mark. Got down a glass and poured an inch. "You watch. They're not done jerking you around. They're going to try to get more out of you." He knocked back the bourbon and grimaced. Smacked the glass down on the table and pointed the mouth of the bottle at Emily. "Please, please, the next time you talk to the police, take me with you." He poured another inch of bourbon into his glass and slammed the bottle down on the table. "And if I'm tied up in court, make them wait. So what if they end up impounding your car? Better that than impounding you."

Frank opened his mouth, about to continue his rant. Instead, he froze. Blinked, and shook his head. "What am I doing?" he said. "None of this is your fault. It makes me so angry when the police use their status to manipulate . . . to *con* unsuspecting people whose worst sin has been to try to be helpful. People who take what they're told at face value. And here I am"—he stood, his expression softening—"taking it out on you. I'm sorry," Frank said, and pulled Emily into his arms. "I'm really sorry."

Emily surrendered to the hug and a wave of self-pity. She closed her eyes. For the moment, at least, she felt sheltered and safe.

"I'm sorry you're having to deal with all this," Frank said. "And I shouldn't have lost my temper." His reassuring words were warm in her ear. "I love you so much, and I don't want you to get hurt."

Emily broke down in tears.

In bed that night, Emily tried not to let the panic that bubbled in her stomach overwhelm her. Frank was right. She never should have trusted the police. She never should have spoken with them alone. And the worst part was, she'd known better. Her only sin had been to find Walter Newell's body, and how the hell had he ended up in the Murphys' storage unit, anyway? There had to be some link between the Newells and the Murphys—a link other than Emily.

Emily turned on her phone and googled *Walter Newell.* The item that caught her eye was nearly three years old, a wedding announcement in the *Boston Globe* that had featured a shot of the couple standing side by side and grinning. In those days, Quinn had been channeling a Kristen Stewart vibe, with shoulder-length platinum-blond hair, ironed straight, a dark inverse-skunk stripe lining the center part. Her face was pale and her eyes were smudged with kohl.

Emily stared at the picture of the groom. She tried to overlay the features of this smiling hipster on either the face she'd glimpsed behind yellow aviator glasses at the coffee shop, or the port-wine-stained face of the dead man. Frustrated, she turned her attention to the announcement below the photo.

Amanda Quinn and Walter Halsey Newell were married May 11 at Four Seasons Hotel in Boston.

Amanda? The name lacked the panache of *Quinn.*

The bride is an associate at T. E. Kalmus Fine Art and Auctions. She was previously married to the late Michael Safstrom.

Huh? Not only had Quinn been married before, she'd been *widowed* before. And so much for that bullshit about Quinn being a desperate spinster, her *biological clock ticking* when she'd met Wally. Or that she'd been clueless about her husband's collections. She'd worked for an auction house.

Walter Newell, according to the announcement, was a graduate of Boston University and a real estate developer. Another line that caught Emily's eye: "The groom's father is a vice chairman of the Newell Group, the global investment banking firm."

Even Emily had heard of the Newell Group. They'd been involved in developing Boston's Seaport District.

Emily rechecked the search results for more information. She tried *Walter Newell* and various permutations of Quinn. *Amanda Quinn. Amanda Safstrom. Quinn Safstrom. Quinn Newell.* But all she came up with was some charitable giving in Quinn's name and a raft of real estate transactions in Walter's. They'd kept a low public profile.

That would soon change.

She turned on the television and tuned to Boston 35. A chef was basting chicken parts with barbecue sauce on a cooking show. It was another twenty minutes before the ten o'clock news. Emily dozed off as the chef grilled husk-wrapped corn on the cob. She opened her eyes when she heard the fanfare that preceded a news bulletin.

BREAKING STORY! streamed across the top of the screen, white letters against a band of red. Then, *BODY FOUND IN STORAGE UNIT.*

Voice-over, a woman newscaster: "A gruesome discovery today. East Hartwell police are investigating a man's body found in a self-storage unit. Stay tuned for an update on this late-breaking story."

Emily pushed the pillow behind her and sat up in bed, waiting out what felt like an endless stream of ads until finally the same introduction ran, this time over video of the entrance to Inner Peace Storage.

Frank came out of the bathroom, toothbrush in hand, and watched as, behind the newscaster, a police cruiser drove out of the storage facility.

"Isn't that your car?" Frank asked.

Emily cringed. Sure enough, there was her Honda, trailing behind the cruiser. At least the camera was angled so that viewers couldn't see the Clutter Kickers logo on her door.

"Good thing—" Their front door chimed and Frank broke off. He looked at his watch. "What the hell?"

Emily went to the window and looked out. She fully expected to see Quinn's red Miata or a police cruiser in front of the house. But the vehicle parked in front was a dark green pickup truck.

Frank looked out the window from behind her. "I'll go see who it is." He went into the bathroom and emerged moments later, wiping his face on a hand towel.

"Emily? Frank?" Lila's tremulous voice came from the other side of the bedroom door. "Do you want me to get that?"

"No, thank you, we do not want you to get that," Frank said, enunciating each word. He pulled open the bedroom door and brushed past Lila. "Stay up here, both of you." Delivered like they were a pair of dogs who'd mastered *sit* and *stay*.

Emily put on her robe and joined Lila in the upstairs hallway. She couldn't see past the bend in the staircase, but she heard the front door open. Then Frank's voice, barely audible. "What do you want?"

Emily couldn't make out the reply, just a man's gruff voice. She crept down to where she could see Frank's legs.

"We're done." Frank's voice. "Case closed. There's nothing left to discuss."

"You lied. You wouldn't want me to go public—"

"I didn't lie. I *don't* lie."

"Left out a few details, then—"

After a hushed back-and-forth, Frank said, "You have nothing to worry about. Just calm down. It's what you agreed to. You cashed the check and signed a nondisclosure."

The man spoke some more, but Emily caught only the tail end when his voice rose. "You can't seriously think—"

"Shhh. You'll wake my wife."

Her heart pounding, Emily backed up a few steps. She bumped into Lila. "Who's that?" Lila whispered.

"No idea," Emily whispered back.

Frank again. "You need to leave. Right now. We're done."

"We're not done," the man snarled.

A scuffling sound. Then a thud and a grunt. Emily would have raced down the stairs except Lila caught her arm. Emily was glad to have her mother there, a sanity check.

"Take your hands off me," Frank said, his voice cold and steady. "Believe me, you don't want to play this game." There was a long silence. Then Frank again. "Okay. You want to talk? In my office."

The front door slammed and the banister that Emily hadn't realized she was gripping vibrated. Then the sound of receding footsteps to the back of the house and Frank's office. Emily breathed a sigh of relief and turned around. Lila was right behind her at the top of the stairs, biting her knuckle.

"Who is that man?" Lila said. "Is Frank okay alone in there with him? Shouldn't we call the police?" It was just like her mother. Calm in a crisis, panicked in its aftermath.

"I have no idea who he is," Emily said. And, knowing how much Frank distrusted the police, she wasn't about to call them unless he'd specifically asked her to. She started down the stairs, pausing halfway to listen, with Lila right behind her. She could hear the rumble of voices from Frank's office. It sounded as if they were arguing.

Emily tiptoed to the front door and peered out through its glass panel. The front yard was dark. The pickup truck was still parked out there. She stepped aside and let Lila look out.

"We could at least get his license plate," Lila said.

"We?"

"Take a picture. Just in case he punches a hole in one of your walls or throws a chair at Frank."

It wasn't a bad idea. Emily ran upstairs for her phone. She came back down and slipped outside. Lila watched from behind the screen door.

Emily approached the truck. The pavement under her bare feet was warm. The truck was a fancy version of a classic Ford pickup with front and back seats in the cab. She risked using the flash and snapped a close-up of the plate on the back of the truck, then hurried up the front walk.

She was nearly to the screen door when she realized that Lila was no longer waiting there for her. Instead, Frank's back filled the doorframe. The porch light came on. Before Emily could dart into the shadows, Frank moved aside, the door opened, and the visitor hurtled out.

He came to an abrupt halt within inches of running into her. Jeans. A black shirt stretched over a muscular gut. Dark, close-cropped hair. He glanced at her, surprised at first. *You?* he mouthed. Then he barked a laugh, exhaling beer breath, turned back, and gave Frank his middle finger. When he wheeled around to face her again, Emily looked down, avoiding eye contact, anxious to get back inside the house.

That's when she noticed his shoes. He was wearing loafers. Loafers made of leather the color of butterscotch. And they were stained.

The man pushed past Emily. He got into his truck, slammed the door, and screeched off into the night. She stood there for a few moments as the smell of burnt rubber wafted over to her.

Coffee-stained loafers.

Minus the tinted glasses and the baseball cap, minus the beard and mustache (was it her imagination, or was the skin paler on his upper lip and chin, as if he'd recently shaved?), was this the man who'd run into her at Java Connection? The man whom a witness had reported hitting her car and then driving off, not in a green Ford pickup truck, but in Walter Newell's car, which the police found abandoned later that night?

She could still hear his snarky voice: *Stupid cow.*

"Emily?" Frank called to her from the open screen door. "What are you doing out there?"

"Are you all right, dear?" Lila asked, coming up behind Frank. "You look like you've seen a ghost."

That was exactly what she had seen. Emily came back into the house. "Frank, how do you know that man?"

"He's one of our clients. Why?"

Emily came inside. "I've seen him before. At the coffee shop when I went to get your coffee Sunday night. I think he's Walter Newell."

Frank's brow furrowed. "How could it be? Walter Newell is dead."

"Is he?"

"Didn't his wife identify his body?"

"I don't know. I haven't talked to her."

"It's not as if she was looking at skeletal remains. She'd know, wouldn't she?"

She certainly would. "Would they go on that?" Emily asked. "Just her say-so?"

"What are you getting at?"

"Maybe she wants people to think he's dead. I don't know, sometimes wealthy people need to disappear. Maybe it was an act, Quinn telling me how much she hated being married to him."

"Seriously?" Frank looked at her, slack-jawed. "She came right out and said that?"

Emily squirmed. Her conversations with clients were supposed to be confidential.

Frank waved his hand as if it didn't matter. "Okay, so suppose the dead man's not Walter Newell. Then who is he? How come no one's reported *him* missing? You can't just pick up a spare corpse at Whole Foods."

"What makes you so sure that someone else hasn't been reported missing?"

"Whoa. Time out." Frank reared back. "That guy who just left here? He's one of Ryan's clients."

"And Ryan's the one who recommended us to Quinn Newell."

Frank stared out through the screen to the street where the green truck had been parked. "You're sure that's the man from the coffee shop?"

Emily was about to explain about the shoes when her phone pinged with a text message.

Releasing your car tomorrow 10AM—E HARTWELL POLICE

24

WEDNESDAY

THE NEXT MORNING, Emily was awake long before Frank or Lila. She'd barely slept. One minute she had herself convinced that the man who'd come to their house was the man who'd run into her at the coffee shop. Those stained shoes, right? Plus *he'd* recognized *her*. But if he was, then the man who'd run into her at the coffee shop wasn't Walter Newell, because Walter Newell was dead. Unless he wasn't.

The next minute, the notion that the man who'd come calling on Frank was Walter Newell seemed patently ridiculous. The man had no beard. No mustache. And would someone who drove an Audi and owned a mansion in Mandarin Cliffs be driving around town in a green Ford pickup, even if it was pretty new? It all came down to who the dead man in the storage unit was.

As soon as she got up, Emily checked the news feeds. None were reporting the victim's identity.

At eight o'clock, moments after Frank, his usual nonverbal morning self, came downstairs in his bathrobe and poured himself a cup of coffee, Emily's cell phone chirped. The readout said NEWELL. Emily showed Frank and answered the call.

"I wasn't sure if it was okay to call you," Quinn said. "This has been such a nightmare."

"Ask her if she identified her husband's body," Frank whispered.

Emily shushed him and turned away. She couldn't very well lead with such an intrusive question, though it was what she wanted to know. "I thought you might need some space," Emily said. "I can't even imagine what you must be going through. What with the police and all."

"Yeah, well, the police treated me with kid gloves . . . up to a point. Then they started in on whether Wally and I had been getting along. Did we have any financial problems? Did he have anger management issues? Was he screwing around? Was *I* screwing around?"

"Fishing," Emily said. Sounded familiar.

"There were a few awkward moments. It was sort of a minefield. Because, well, I don't need to tell you, marriage is never uncomplicated, and with the police, honesty's not always the best policy." She sounded like Frank. "I was glad Ryan was there. He kept me from saying too much."

Maybe Ryan did have a few redeeming features.

"Have they been giving you a hard time, too?" Quinn asked.

Did cross-examining her on her whereabouts and impounding her car count? Quinn didn't need Emily's woes piled on top of her own. She said, "It must have been hard, identifying the body," cringing at how intrusive that sounded.

"It was hard," Quinn replied, without skipping a beat. "And horrifying. I could barely do it. Like, you know, I've only seen a dead person once before. My nana when I was seventeen. She didn't answer when I rang the bell at her apartment, so I let myself in. I found her tipped over in her chair, the newspaper still in her lap. She'd been doing the crossword puzzle." A long pause. "But of course this was nothing like that. Because he died . . ." There was silence on the line for a few moments. Then Quinn cleared her throat and continued, her voice strained. "Blunt-force trauma, they said. I don't even know what that means."

"But at least you got to see him," Emily pressed. She had to know if Quinn had identified the body. "How did he look?"

"He looked, I don't know, peaceful. You found him, so you know."

The rolled-up area rug had been lying in a puddle of water. All she could see were pale gray fingers. Then, later, the corpse mercilessly exposed under the spotlights. *Peaceful* would not have been the word Emily would have chosen.

Quinn added, "At least they let me have some time alone with him. I felt terrible leaving him in the morgue. It was so cold there, I felt like I needed to cover him up. Is that weird?" She gave a bitter laugh. "You know I wasn't happy being married to him, but I didn't want this."

"It must be hard," Emily said. Empty words, she knew.

"Emmy, we're still going to finish what we talked about, right? I don't want you to think I'm going to just let it go."

"I . . . uh . . ." Emily stammered, not sure what to say. Because she wanted as little as possible to do with Quinn Newell, even if she offered to pay ten times their usual rate. "Seems like now's not the best time for you to be making any major decisions. I'll return your deposit first thing."

"Not at all. Now we can do the whole house. It will be a piece of cake; I really don't care about any of it. Then I won't have to be reminded everywhere that I wasn't welcome. It wasn't just my stuff in the garage. Wally hogged the bed. Hogged the comforter. Filled the medicine cabinet with his stuff. We had to get his brand of coffee. His—"

"Quinn," Emily said, interrupting the flow of bile. She hoped Ryan had kept Quinn from venting like this to the police. "I'm not a psychologist, but I think you should wait. A few weeks, at least, and—"

"I don't want to wait. And I'm counting on the help you promised."

Petulant. Entitled. Needy. Impulsive. "Quinn, let's talk about it some more later, okay? After the funeral?"

Quinn groaned. "Oh God, the funeral service. I don't even know where to begin. I guess I have to wait until they release the body, and then what?"

"Talk to the people at the funeral home."

"What funeral home?"

Emily wasn't about to take the bait. She was done helping Quinn. "It's what they do. Help families."

A long pause. "You'll call me," Quinn said, "won't you?" When Emily didn't respond, Quinn pressed. "You've got the garage door opener. You can even come by when I'm not here. I want to get rid of everything. Just take it away."

"We'll see," Emily said. "Seriously, don't make any major decisions right now. Okay?" Without waiting for an answer, she disconnected the call, then stood there for a moment, looking at her phone.

"Well?" Frank's voice startled her. She'd forgotten he was in the room with her.

"You were right. She identified the body."

"What did I tell you? Walter Newell is dead. Satisfied?"

"Tell me again, who was the man who was here last night and what were you talking about?"

"He's . . ." Frank took a deep breath. "Emmy, I really can't. Attorney-client privilege and all that. But this much I can tell you." He looked up, as if the explanation were etched in the ceiling. "He's not my client. He's Ryan's. He's the son of a CEO we've worked with before. Deep pockets, or we'd never have touched his case. Drives around in that truck trying to look like Joe the Plumber. Bottom line? Guy's a jerk. Suing his neighbor, or at least I think that's what he's up to this time. All I know is, he agreed to the settlement and now he's balking at the nondisclosure and the contingency fee. As often as he sues people, you'd think he'd know the drill. Litigation costs."

"What's his name?"

"Come on. You know I can't tell you that."

Frank wasn't usually this circumspect about their clients. "If he's Ryan's client, how come he wasn't at Ryan's house, threatening him?"

Frank poured some more coffee into his cup, took a sip, and grimaced. "He wasn't threatening anyone."

"He was. I heard him."

Lila appeared in the doorway. "I heard him, too."

"Good morning, Lila," Frank said with a tight smile.

"We almost called the police," Lila said. She crossed the kitchen and poured herself a cup of coffee.

"I'm sorry if he upset you, but there was no need to be concerned. Asshole clients are a dime a dozen." Frank waved his cup in Lila's direction. "If I reported them, I'd be out of business.

The guy just needed to vent." He rubbed his chin. "And I need to shave." He put his coffee cup in the sink and left the room.

Lila watched him go. "I'm afraid I underestimated your husband." She got the milk from the refrigerator and poured an inch into her cup. "Either he's much tougher than I ever imagined, or he's a superb liar."

25

AT TEN, FRANK drove Emily to the police station to get her car. He stuck to the speed limit, slowing when the lights turned yellow. But his manner was anything but calm as he pounded the steering wheel and issued orders, getting louder and more emphatic the closer they got to the police station.

Just go in there and get your car.

Do not think for a moment that the police are just trying to get at the truth.

Do not trust them; they make things up.

They want information and they'll do whatever they need to do to get it.

And most of all (he said this three times), *Check with me before you say anything.*

He kept looking across at her, making sure that she was paying attention. How could she not? She folded her arms across her chest and waited for him to run out of steam. She didn't need him to remind her not to trust the police.

Sergeant Stanley was in the lobby waiting for them. "And who's this?" he said, eyeing Frank in his power suit.

"Frank Harlow," Frank said. He offered his hand to Stanley, who was at least a head shorter than him. "Attorney."

Stanley shook the hand and gazed up at Frank, appraising. "Harlow?"

Emily felt her face flush. "Frank is my husband." She glanced at Frank, realizing she'd already broken a rule, speaking without Frank's say-so, but he didn't seem to notice.

Stanley's gaze shifted to Emily. "Lawyered up?" A smirk tugged at the corner of his mouth. "Interesting."

"I'm just here to pick up my car," Emily said. "My husband drove me."

"Of course. Right this way, please." Stanley wheeled around and led them into the back, down the hall and downstairs. Walter Newell's Audi was still at the far end of the basement. Its front fender, bumper, and right headlight had been removed. Emily's car was parked nearby with portable lights and a rolling work-bench set up alongside.

"The keys?" Frank said.

Stanley faced Emily. "Don't you want to know what we found when we examined your car?"

"I—" Emily began. She looked at Frank.

"She just wants her car," Frank said.

Stanley ignored him. He crouched beside the back of her car. "We can tell that your car had some recent body work." He pointed to the back where Lila had spotted the crude repair. "Very recent. And traces of paint we found on the front bumper of Walter Newell's Audi match your car's."

"You told me he hit me, " Emily said. "You said you had it on surveillance."

"Why were you in the Square?" Stanley asked.

Frank nodded for her to answer. "I was getting coffee. I guess he was getting coffee, too."

"There are also surveillance cameras at the storage facility. We've examined their camera footage from the night your friend's husband disappeared."

"She's my client. Not my friend," Emily said before she could stop herself.

"Would it surprise you that the surveillance video shows you unlocking the unit on Sunday? Going inside?"

"I told you—" Emily began. Frank shushed her

"Right," Stanley said. "Then you left. But hours later, after midnight, you're back."

Emily was speechless. Frank scowled and shook his head. "Enough," he said under his breath. "She's just here for the car."

"No problem." Stanley went over to a red metal lockbox hanging on the wall. He punched in some numbers and opened it, then fished out a key and closed the box. "Here." He tossed Emily the key, but she missed it and it dropped on the floor. Frank picked it up.

Stanley pressed a button on the wall. With a loud clank, an overhead door rose on the adjacent wall. When it had risen completely, Stanley came over to Emily and stood a foot away. He lowered his voice. "You can leave right now. No one's stopping you. Or you can come upstairs and look at the surveillance footage. See what *you* make of it."

Emily took a step back. "I didn't go back to the storage unit Sunday night. I went home. I went to sleep. There's no reason why I'd come back."

"The surveillance footage says otherwise."

Frank hooked Emily's arm and tugged her toward the car.

"What doesn't your husband want you to see?" Stanley said.

"Don't react," Frank said under his breath. "Don't—"

"Mrs. Harlow," Stanley said, cutting Frank off. "Why not look at the tape? You don't have to say a word. Or maybe you'll be able to help us out by identifying the person."

Under her breath, she said to Frank, "What harm can it do, just to look?"

"This is not a good idea," Frank whispered back.

"I need to see what they have. I won't say anything."

"Then I'm coming with you."

"Sorry," Stanley said. "This offer is just for your wife. She comes alone or it's off the table."

"This is extortion," Frank said, a vein pulsing in his forehead. "See what they've done? They try to manipulate the situation so we're on opposite sides. Don't go. I'm giving you my best advice."

Only she wasn't one of his clients, and it was flat-out impossible that she was the person the CCTV camera had captured. "I need to see what they have."

"I'm telling you, it's a mistake." Frank squeezed her arm. "You'll say something. You'll react. You won't be able to help yourself, and then they'll twist it. This is the typical kind of bullshit they pull. For all you know, there are no pictures. It's nothing but a ploy to get you alone."

"We have pictures," Stanley said. "Mr. Harlow, your wife's a grown-up. She can see what's on the tape and judge for herself. Though I have to wonder why you're so adamant that she shouldn't." He gave a little salute, tugged up his belt, and strutted off.

Frank rolled his eyes at Emily as if to say, *Told you so.* He dropped her arm and opened the door of her car.

Emily glanced back. Stanley stood waiting, silhouetted in the stairwell doorway.

"Get in!" Frank said, gesturing for Emily to get in the car.

How long had they been married, and still he hadn't learned that ordering her around in that tone of voice was counterproductive? Why not look at the surveillance video? She could keep her mouth shut. Emily bumped the car door shut with her hip.

As she walked toward the stairwell, Frank called after her, "Emily, don't. This is not a good idea."

She turned back. "I get that. And it's also not a game. I appreciate that you're trying to protect me, but I need to see what they have."

"Okay, okay. Go." Frank shook his head. "But *don't say anything.* Understood?"

The advice was for her own good, Emily told herself. But a smart detective, and she had no doubt that Stanley was good at his job, observed as well as listened. She'd have to watch what she did as well as what she said. When she reached Stanley, she forced a polite smile and then followed him up the stairs.

26

SERGEANT STANLEY LED Emily to an office. It was a bare, functional space containing a desk and a pair of file cabinets, with a window overlooking the parking lot. He waited for Emily to sit across the desk from him. Then he pulled out a folder, set it on the table, and opened it. Inside was a stack of photos. The one on top was a grainy black-and-white shot. It showed an alleyway lined with storage units. Painted in white on the driveway of the closest unit was the number 218.

Stanley tapped the time stamp at the bottom of the frame. The picture had been taken at 1:16 a.m., hours after Emily had conked out after much too much wine and a soothing cup of hot chocolate. "See that?" Stanley said. He indicated a dark shadow with two pinpoints of light that, on closer inspection, looked like parking lights of a car facing the camera.

Stanley showed her the next picture. The time stamp was a minute later, 1:17 a.m. In this photo a car was sideways to the camera, backed up to the door of the unit next to 218. The car's hatch was raised. "That's your car, isn't it?"

Emily's stomach turned over. The car was light-colored, prob-ably white. Clear as day, the Clutter Kickers logo was stenciled on the door. She looked at Stanley. He didn't say anything, but his eyebrows rose in a question. When she didn't say anything, either, he slapped another picture on the desk.

"Here you are again." This photo showed a shadowy figure hunkered down on the far side of the car from the video camera, presumably opening the padlock.

Emily bit her lip.

"But you were home, right? So maybe you were sleepwalking." Stanley put down another picture. "Because here's you again, crouched inside your car and pushing something out the back."

It was a compelling narrative, but the picture didn't actually support it. Nothing was clear but the side of the car.

"You crawl out the back yourself," Stanley went on. "Disappear into the unit. Ten minutes later, here you are locking up." Deliberately he placed another picture down on the desk. This one showed the car's hatchback shut, and a shadowy someone hunched over the lock again on the far side of the car. But this time, even though the person was facing away from the surveillance camera, Emily could see that her top and pants looked like Emily's work uniform. A long ponytail hung out the back opening of a baseball cap. "That is you, isn't it?" Stanley asked.

Emily caught one detail that proved, to her at least, that it wasn't her. She pointed to the person's shoes, which were clearly not open-backed Crocs. "That day I'd hurt my foot. I would have been wearing these." She stuck out her foot for Stanley to see her Crocs.

"You're saying that's not you? Not driving your car?" Stanley said. "License plate QVC838?"

Of course Stanley would know her plate number. He'd had

her car right there in the police garage for the last twenty-four hours. Frank's warning was spot-on. *They want information and they'll do whatever they need to do to get it.*

"And perhaps you can explain something we found in your car," Stanley added. "Carpet fibers. I don't need to remind you that Walter Newell was rolled inside a rug."

Fibers from *that* rug? It wasn't remotely possible. Emily put her elbows on the table and leaned forward, head in her hands. *They make things up.*

"And by the way," Stanley said, "about the person who called in the hit-and-run? The witness? We traced the call. It came from Walter Newell's cell phone."

Walter Newell called in his own hit-and-run? Emily couldn't imagine why he'd have done that. Not unless he wanted to make sure that the police knew about it.

"We know he registered at the auction in Hyannis at about two in the afternoon," Stanley went on. "We know he didn't buy anything. We know the call reporting the accident came in from his phone eight hours later. I can play it for you. We keep all 911 calls. Maybe you'll recognize the voice."

He didn't wait for an answer. He picked up the phone on his desk and punched a few buttons. Waited and punched two more. Listened. Then he turned on the speakerphone and Emily heard a beep.

First, in a robotic voice: "Call received August four, twenty-one fifty-five." Then a woman's voice: "This is 911." The dispatcher sounded like an older woman. Tired. Alto. "Please state your emergency."

"Hello?" This voice was also a woman's. Low and raspy.

"Please state your emergency," the dispatcher repeated.

"I just witnessed a hit-and-run in East Hartwell Square." The voice sounded muffled. "Car pulled out of a parking space. Hit the car in front of it. Didn't bother to stop."

"What is your name?"

"He's gone now. The car was a light-colored Audi. He hit a Honda hatchback with printing on the door."

"Your name?" When the caller didn't answer, the dispatcher asked, "Is anyone injured?"

"No. The other car was parked." The caller gave the precise location in front of the coffee shop and the license plate of the Audi.

As the recording continued, Emily closed her eyes, trying to place the caller's voice. The person who'd most likely have had access to Walter Newell's phone was Quinn. But how could Quinn have known about the accident when Emily had left her at her home minutes earlier?

After the recording ended, Stanley hung up. "The caller says she saw the accident. But here's the thing about it. No one in the coffee shop remembers serving you."

Didn't remember? That seemed highly unlikely. Her nasty run-in had been witnessed by the barista. And what about that teenager who'd turned the sign in the door to CLOSED and started mopping up?

"Did you pay with a credit card?"

Emily said nothing.

"Cash, then? Did you get a receipt?"

She hadn't, because Ana—Emily remembered the barista's name—had given her Frank's coffee on the house.

Emily broke her silence. "They should remember me. I left a ten-dollar tip."

"Ten dollars? That was generous of you. I wonder, was that so they'd be *sure* to remember you?"

Don't say anything. Frank had been so right.

"Shall I tell you how Walter Newell died?" Stanley didn't wait for an answer. "Blunt-force trauma to the front of the legs. Trauma to the back of the head. Finally, his chest was crushed."

Emily closed her eyes.

"Bottom line?" Stanley went on. "It looks like he got hit by a car. The initial impact was too low"—Stanley reached down and touched the top of his shins—"to have been an SUV or a truck. Something like a Honda Civic, though, that'd be about right. Mr. Newell was knocked to the ground, then the vehicle ran over him. Twice. An accident? What do you think?"

Emily shuddered. She was trying not to think.

"After that—and now frankly I'm guessing based on the fact that his car was found parked at the wharf and his body was wrapped in a water-soaked rug—the killer rolled his body down the ramp and into the water. The shore on either side of the ramp is overgrown this time of year. Even at low tide he'd be well hidden. That staining on his face? You must have noticed it. It was on his chest as well. Tells us he was left lying facedown after he died. Blood pools at the lowest point.

"So, what happened?" Stanley continued. "After he dented your car, did you follow him to the wharf and confront him? Or maybe it was the other way around. You dented his car when you were parking and then *he* followed *you*. One way or another, you both end up at the wharf. It's late. Quiet. Just the two of you. You argue. Things get out of hand. Maybe he threatens you. You get in your car. Start the engine." Stanley stood and leaned toward her, his palms on the desk. "He's big. He's angry. He's standing in front of you, daring you to . . ."

Emily bit her lip, resisting the urge to put her hands over her ears. None of that had happened. But whatever she said, her words would end up getting twisted. *Ask my husband. I was at home.* Stanley would come back with a snort. *Of course he would say that—he's your husband. He'll say whatever you need him to say.*

"You'd have needed help," Stanley went on. "A dead body's a heavy thing, even heavier when it's wrapped up in a wet rug. Gravity works in your favor getting it into the water. But getting it out?" He lowered his voice. "That's a two-person job." Stanley sat down. "So who helped you?" He stared at Emily for a few moments, rubbing his chin like he was trying to figure it out. "Let's leave that for a minute. You could have done the rest by yourself. Driven to the storage unit. Rolled the body out of the car. Pushed it under that table. And before you left, changed the lock, buying at least another day before the body could be examined. Guaranteeing that there'd be even more uncertainty when we tried to estimate Mr. Newell's time of death."

Emily couldn't hold back. "I don't care what you think those surveillance images show, that is not me."

Stanley collected the photographs and struck the stack on the table to straighten them, then slapped them back in the folder. "Then you have nothing to worry about. Our officers won't find the original padlock to that storage unit in your house, will they? Because that's where they are right now, executing a search warrant."

Emily left Sergeant Stanley's office, her stomach in a knot. Frank was waiting for her in the lobby. He jumped to his feet and followed her out the door. She didn't break down until she got out to the parking lot, where Frank had parked her car alongside his.

Emily was expecting a big *Told-you-so.* Instead Frank opened his arms. Emily collapsed against him and sobbed, surrendering for a few moments as anger and frustration filled her. But this was no time to fall apart. That creep Stanley was probably watching out the window while his goons were searching her house.

She pulled away from Frank, wiping her eyes with the heel of her hand. "We need to get home. The police are probably already there, searching our house."

"Shit," Frank said. "What are they looking for?"

Emily glanced back at the police station and lowered her voice to a whisper. "The padlock to the Murphys' storage unit."

Frank gave her a long look. "Are they going to find it?"

"Frank!"

"Just asking. You're sure they won't?"

Emily didn't answer. She wasn't sure of anything after seeing the picture of a car that looked like hers pulled up to the storage unit. She opened her car's back door. The police had left the backseat folded forward. She touched the dark carpeting that lined the hatchback's empty cargo bay. It was damp, and when she smelled her fingertips, she gagged on the whiff of sulfur, like decaying plant matter.

"What?" Frank said.

"Stanley said they found carpet fibers back here. Walter Newell was rolled up in a rug."

Frank gave her a pitying look. "Emmy, they'd find carpet fibers in the back of *my* car. They'd find them in your mom's car. It's like saying they found hair in your bathroom. They say it to freak you out."

Emily pushed the seat upright. There was her gear bag on the floor where she'd left it. Surely the police had searched it. She opened the bag. Everything seemed to be in order—her face masks and cleaning agents, rubber gloves, all present and accounted for. The only thing that wasn't there that should have been was the key to the old padlock on Mrs. Murphy's storage unit. It wasn't at the bottom of the bag or inside any of the side pockets. The police had probably taken it.

"What did he tell you?" Frank asked.

Emily closed the bag and put it back in the car. "He said they think that the body was in the river. They have surveillance photos they say show me driving his body to the storage unit in the middle of the night, leaving it there, and changing the lock. And they say I'm not strong enough to have done it on my own." She looked at Frank. "I had to have had help."

"Huh." Frank was quiet for a few moments. "Did he actually show you the pictures? Because they talk a good game—"

"Frank, he showed me. It looks like my car." She slammed the car door. "But it's not me."

"Surveillance pictures are notoriously lousy. Low-resolution. Plus it was night. How far away was the camera?"

The security camera had been mounted just one unit away. "Maybe twenty feet. Though you're right, the camera angle is lousy."

"There. You see? Trust me on this, nine times out of ten, CCTV footage doesn't stand up in court."

"In court? Please tell me it won't come to that. Because he made it sound as if they think I killed Walter Newell. That after he hit my car, I followed him to the wharf, confronted him, and ended up running him down. They think—"

"Whoa." Frank held up his hand. "They think you ran him down and now they're letting you drive off in the murder weapon? How likely is that?"

Emily paused. It was true that didn't seem too likely. "But what about the carpet fibers?"

"Carpet fibers? *Pfff.* They'd have to run forensics tests before they'd be sure that the fibers match. That can take weeks. If they had enough to charge you, they'd have arrested you."

Emily let Frank's words wash over her. His confidence was bracing even if his words weren't all that reassuring.

"I'll meet you at home," Frank said, getting into his car.

Emily nodded and got into her car, too. Her hand shook as she started the engine. She lowered the window and touched the steering wheel. A trace of white powder came off on her fingers. The interior would have been dusted for prints.

Frank leaned out his car window, looking at her closely. "Sure you're okay driving?"

"Just keep me in your rearview."

"No worries. I've got your back."

Emily repressed a shudder. She'd heard something like that before. Recently. From Quinn Newell.

27

EMILY DROVE, FOLLOWING Frank through town and back to the house. The more she thought about the evidence the police had gathered—surveillance pictures that showed someone driving a car like hers and delivering something to the storage unit in the dead of night, carpet fibers in her car—the angrier she got. The person in the grainy CCTV footage was barely visible, and the car might have been hers, or it might have been any light-colored compact car with their logo painted on the door. But the person, indistinct as she was, did seem to be wearing an outfit like Emily's work uniform and she had a long ponytail. On any other night, the shoes would have been right.

Emily shivered. This was not a case of mistaken identity. Whoever it was had been *trying* to look like Emily. The person had also been fully aware of the location of the surveillance camera. What Emily couldn't understand was why the barista, who'd been so kind to her at the coffee shop, refused to confirm that she'd even been in there. That, at least, she could discover for herself later, after the police had finished executing their search warrant.

Emily turned onto her block. She gripped the steering wheel

even tighter when she saw that a police van was backed into their driveway and a cruiser was parked in front. The bulkhead doors to the basement were open, as was the front door. One of their neighbors—a retired postal worker who'd been living across the street for decades before they moved in—stood behind his screen door, looking out. Emily parked in front of his house and got out, giving him an awkward wave.

Lila, wearing a broad-brimmed straw hat and sunglasses, a gold tunic and white leggings, sat in a folding chair on the front lawn watching the house like she was watching a movie. When she saw Emily, she jumped up and waved some sheets of paper at her. Emily reached out for them. Across the top page, it read: *SEARCH WARRANT.*

Frank, who'd parked his car farther down the street, joined them.

"I'm sorry," Lila said, addressing her apology to Frank. "I didn't know how to stop them."

"You couldn't have stopped them," Frank said. "And if you'd tried, you'd have gotten yourself arrested."

"Why are they here?" Lila asked. "They can't possibly think that Emily had anything to do with that man who—" She broke off as a police officer emerged from the front door, wearing bright blue rubber gloves and carrying what looked like a pile of clothing. He laid the items down on a plastic tarp behind the police van. Emily could see several of her work uniforms, including her sneakers and cap.

"Can they just take whatever they want?" Lila whispered. "Coming in here like a battalion of goddamned storm troopers? You're an attorney. Can't you do something? Isn't there something in the Constitution about illegal search and seizure?"

"Lila," Frank said, "I know you're trying to help, but please, this is what legal looks like. There's nothing for it but to let them do their job. They can only take what's specified in the warrant." He eased the stapled sheets of paper from Emily's grasp, looked them over, then handed them back.

Emily read the warrant herself. It listed the places the police were allowed to go. The house. The garage. The yard. Vehicles on the property. All in search of *any property that is or has been used as a means of committing a criminal offense.* What did that even rule out?

Below that, written in by hand, was a list of items. It began, *PADLOCK.* After that, *WOMEN'S CLOTHING PER PHOTO.* Stapled to the search warrant was a copy of one of the surveillance stills—the woman in a baseball cap and a Clutter Kickers uniform. Emily wanted to wave the photograph in the face of the lead officer and shout, *"See? She's wearing the wrong shoes!"*

A uniformed officer emerged from the front door of the house. He stopped at the back of the police van to write on a clipboard. Frank went over to him and Emily followed, hanging back. The officer kept on writing, a lefty, his hand curled over his letters.

"Officer," Frank said.

"Sir?" the officer said without looking up.

"This is my house. Are you almost done?"

"We'll let you know," the officer said.

Another officer emerged from the basement carrying a medium-sized cardboard box. It looked heavy, from the way he was holding it against his chest. He set the box beside the tarp and exchanged a few words with the officer with the clipboard. The clipboard cop crouched by the box, opened the flaps, and sifted through its contents. He started to write.

Emily drew closer. The plastic label stuck to the side of the box read LOCKS. Inside were old padlocks and hasps, keys and keyhole escutcheons. One padlock was emblazoned with a Celtic cross. Even from a distance, Emily could see these were old, more collectible than functional.

"Those are mine," Frank said.

Of course they were. But the padlock the police were looking for—the one that had hung outside Mr. Murphy's storage unit, the one with a flaking 217 painted on it in red nail polish—would have stood out like an ugly duckling in this pack of swans.

"I need you to initial this receipt," the officer said, walking past Frank and handing Emily the clipboard.

"Frank?" Emily wanted to check with him before she signed. She was surprised when Frank gave her a distracted nod. He was staring at the box of padlocks, his fists clenched. That's when Emily realized: this was the first moment her misadventure had touched *his things*.

28

AFTER THE POLICE left, Frank went directly to the basement, closing the bulkhead door behind him. Emily pulled her car into the driveway and picked up her gear bag. She hoped that, with a more careful search of its interior, she'd find the padlock key. But even after she'd emptied everything out onto the passenger seat, she couldn't find it. What she did find at the bottom of the bag was her stun gun. Lila had taken one look at it and proclaimed it dead. Was it? Emily took it out, held it stiff-armed, and pressed the trigger.

No bug-zapper snap. All she got was a tiny spark and a dead-sounding clicking, a miniature version of the sound her car made trying to start on a dead battery. Emily had no idea where she'd stashed the charger. She returned the stun gun and the rest of the contents to her gear bag and put it on the backseat of her car. Then she entered the house.

The police had turned the place upside down and left the air smelling of testosterone and sweat and something almost medic-inal, like hand sanitizer. Lila was in the living room, restoring order: plumping sofa cushions and straightening piles of mail, lining up photos and books on their shelves.

Emily went through the first floor and opened the windows as wide as they'd go. Then she went up to her bedroom. She stood in the doorway and took in the mess. Bedding was pulled back. Bureau drawers and the clothes hamper were open, the contents spilled onto the floor, higgledy-piggledy.

Her closet door was open and the clothes she'd carefully folded and hung in her newly installed closet system were a jumbled mess. The clothing she'd bagged to give away had been dumped on the floor.

That smell was up here, too. Emily opened the windows, then scooped up all of her socks and underwear and dumped them into a laundry basket. She started to strip the bed, attacking the top sheet, then the bottom sheet. Hurling them into the laundry basket. If there'd been room, she'd have added everything else the police had laid hands on. In the closet. In the room. In the house.

"Emmy, dear?" Her mother stood in the bedroom doorway.

"What?" Emily grabbed a pillow.

"Can I help?"

"No." Emily yanked the pillow from its case. "Thanks."

"Okay," Lila said, but she came into the bedroom anyway, picked up one of the other pillows and shook it out of its case. "Spit, spot. We'll have this room shipshape in short order." She went to the closet and grabbed an armload of clothes from the floor. Dumped them on the bare mattress and started to fold.

"Stop," Emily snapped. Lila dropped the pants she'd been folding and froze. "Sorry," Emily said. "It's just that I was giving those away."

"So what can I do?" Lila asked, hands on her hips.

"Nothing."

Lila surveyed the disarray in the room with a jaundiced eye.

"It all feels contaminated." Emily's throat closed. She tried to swallow. "I have to do laundry."

Her mother came over and put her arms around her. "It's all right," Lila said, though Emily knew it was anything but. "Sometimes we all need to do laundry. Here." She gave Emily a tissue.

Emily sat on the bed and Lila sat next to her. "I see they gave you back your car," Lila said.

"My car," Emily said. "Yes, they did. But they think I used it to kill that man in the storage unit and move his body."

Lila's jaw dropped. "Why on earth would they think that?"

In a rush, Emily told her about the CCTV stills taken in the dead of night. When she finished, Lila got up and stepped to the window. She stood there, staring out for a few moments. Then she turned back to Emily. "Darling, can I tell you the one thing that's bothering me most about all this? From the moment you opened up that storage unit the first time and were astute enough to realize that something was off, there's been a chain of bad events, one after the other. Your car gets hit. Your client's husband goes missing. His dead body turns up in that infernal storage unit. I know you feel as if you did something to trigger the chain, but you didn't." She put her hand under Emily's chin. "Right? Keep telling yourself that. So the question is, what did?"

"And the answer?"

"The answer is . . ." Lila paused and thought. "I don't know what the answer is, but I have an idea where to look. For starters, I'd go back to that storage unit. It began there, didn't it? The police are allowing us to go back in, and I promised Ruth that I'd meet her there in the morning. Becca's meeting us there, too. If nothing else, getting out of here will do you a heap of good. God knows you need to, or before you know it you'll be power-washing the driveway."

Emily gave a weak laugh. As always, Lila's logic was impeccable.

"Tomorrow?" Emily said. "I need to take care of something first. Then I'll meet you guys at the storage unit. I'll bring coffee and donuts."

"Donuts?" Her mother made a sour face.

"Trust me. You'll like these donuts. I wonder if I should bring the camera I use for making the videos."

"Bring it. Though I don't think Ruth is going to feel sentimental about disposing of stolen property."

It struck Emily that a few days ago her biggest concern had been figuring out how to deal with Mr. Murphy's potentially stolen property without getting arrested. Now that was the least of her worries.

29

THURSDAY

THE NEXT MORNING, Emily checked up and down the street before leaving the house. She knew she was being paranoid, but if the police were seriously considering her a suspect in Walter Newell's murder, they'd be tracking her movements. But there were no cars she didn't recognize parked on the street. Nevertheless, she took a circuitous route to Java Connection and scanned the main street after she parked, hesitating before she got out. There was a line of cars at the shop's drive-through. From the sidewalk you could smell coffee and the lingering aroma of hot fat from frying donuts. The day hadn't heated up yet, and the door to the café was propped open.

Emily paused by the spot where she'd parked in front of Walter Newell's car on Sunday night. A silver SUV was parked there now, and rain had long ago washed away the coffee spilled in the gutter. She looked around for the CCTV camera that Sergeant Stanley claimed had captured the hit-and-run. The closest one was at least a hundred yards away at the corner, mounted on a pole over the stoplight. If Frank was right, that camera was much too far away to get a clear picture of anything that had been going on where she'd been parked. Plus it was aimed down toward the intersection.

She entered the coffee shop. The air was filled with thumping percussion and jazzy guitar riffs along with the whir of beans grinding and the sucking sound of an espresso machine, though most of the customers sitting at the tables seemed to be drinking their coffee iced as they stared mesmerized at cell-phone and laptop screens. Three registers were open, fed by a single line of customers.

Emily looked for the barista who'd come to her rescue the other night with paper towels and coffee on the house. Not at any of the registers. Or clearing tables. Then Emily spotted her behind the counter twisting a coffee scoop onto an espresso machine. Today she had her hair pulled back in a ponytail, but she wore the same gold hoop earrings and macaroni bracelet.

Emily got in line and, when it was her turn, ordered three iced lattes and a dozen cider donut holes. Her mouth watered as she watched the clerk dust the donut holes with cinnamon-sugar and scoop them into a bag. She paid, and then waited off to the side. Minutes later, Ana put three tall lidded cups into a cardboard carrier and set them on the counter. "Emily," she called out.

"Ana?" Emily said, approaching the counter. When Ana looked at her, Emily waved and mouthed, *Can we talk?* Ana's eyes flickered with recognition and quickly morphed into a blank stare, like a wall had gone up.

Emily took the coffees. Louder, she said, "Excuse me, Ana?"

Ana turned her back to Emily, scooped beans into the grinder, and switched it on.

Emily raised her voice. "Ana? Remember me? I was in Sunday night right before closing? A man ran into me and spilled his coffee?"

The bean grinder shut off and Ana turned to face Emily, avoiding eye contact. "Sorry. I no remember," she mumbled, barely audible.

"You were here," Emily said. "I'm sure it was you." The clerk at the nearest register stared at Emily. Emily smiled. She lowered her voice and pointed to Ana's macaroni bracelet. "You were wearing that bracelet. I thought it was so sweet."

Ana put her hand behind her back.

"You have a daughter?" Emily asked.

"Sobrina." Ana whispered the word. *Niece.*

"You recognize me. I know you do. I wouldn't be here bothering you, really I wouldn't, if it weren't important." When Ana didn't respond, Emily pressed. "Do you remember the man that ran into me a few nights ago, just before closing? The police came in and asked about him?"

Ana took a step back, bumping into the counter behind her. Her eyes widened. Under her breath, she said, "Please. Go. Away."

Emily said, "I just want to know what you remember about the man. I was so upset and my memory's all confused. It turns out that it matters. A lot. Maybe the police—"

Ana squeezed her eyes shut. That's when Emily realized Ana wasn't afraid of Emily. She was terrified of the police.

"No police. I promise," Emily said. "Just talk to me. No one will know. Please. I'm begging you."

Ana opened her eyes and took a deep breath. She went over to one of the other clerks and whispered to her. Then she returned to Emily and motioned her through a back door.

Emily followed her into a storage room stacked with supplies, past a coatrack hung with purses and messenger bags, through another back door, and into the shadowy alley behind the store. Ana stopped beside a dumpster, the ground around it littered with cigarette butts and the air reeking of ripe garbage.

Ana folded her arms across her chest and glared at Emily. "Okay? So?"

"Did you talk to the police?"

Ana pressed her lips together. Emily took that for a no.

"But they were here, weren't they? And they asked about me and that man?"

"I don't talk to police. Never. I have family. You understand? If they send me back, what will they do?"

"I promise I won't tell the police I talked to you. But I need to know what you saw. I was so upset at the time and not thinking clearly. And the man was so nasty. When he drove off, he hit my car. And then"—Emily paused until Ana met her gaze—"he was killed."

Ana's eyes widened and her arms dropped to her sides. "Killed?"

It was a small opening, and Emily rushed into it. "Maybe you heard about it in the news? He was found in a storage unit near the town wharf? But you saw him. He must have gotten here right before I did."

Ana gave her head a tiny shake.

"No?" Emily said.

"No right before. He waited."

"You mean he'd been here awhile?"

"No drinking. No many other customers, so I noticed. He's making me uncomfortable, him, just sitting there."

That explained why the coffee that splashed all over Emily hadn't been hot. "Watching you?"

"No watching me. Watching out the window."

Emily shivered, folding her arms across her chest. "Like he was waiting for someone?"

Ana nodded.

"How long?"

"Twenty minutes. Maybe more, even."

Emily didn't like where this was going, but there was no turning back. "But he was at the counter when I came in."

"I'm cleaning up. Ready to close the accounts. He come back up to me and ask, how much for coffee beans. Then, what kind do we have. I show him the shelf. Next thing, he's shouting at you."

"And you helped me. That was so kind of you. You told me that he wasn't a regular customer."

"No." A whisper. "I never seen him before."

"Thank you. Thank you so much," Emily said.

So the man who'd spilled his coffee all over Emily hadn't simply run into her. He'd been waiting for Emily to get there. Which meant he'd been tipped off that she'd be stopping there on the way home—tipped off in time to get there twenty minutes before she did.

"So who was he?" Emily murmured the words to herself. Trying to control the tremor of emotion in her voice, she asked Ana, "You said you closed the accounts that night. Could you look up whether he paid with a credit card?"

Anna pursed her lips and shook her head. "I'm not supposed to—"

"But you could. Right?" Emily paused.

Ana flinched.

"All I need is a name," Emily said. "Then I won't have to

ask the police to look into it." The minute the words were out of her mouth, Emily regretted saying them. Ana looked stricken. "I didn't mean that. Desperate, I guess. I'd *never* sic the police on you. Don't worry. I promise. Just think about it. Okay? And when you feel comfortable, *if* you feel comfortable looking up who it was, call me." She circled her cell-phone number on one of her business cards and offered the card to Ana.

Ana hesitated. Then she took it.

30

AS EMILY DROVE from the coffee shop to Inner Peace Storage, her face went hot with shame. There was no excuse for bullying Ana the way she had. On the other hand, she felt some satisfaction that at last she'd discovered something: the man in the coffee shop had been waiting for her to get there. She hadn't been a victim of chance—wrong place, wrong time. She'd been set up, and set up by someone who knew she'd be stopping at the coffee shop on the way home. That changed everything.

Walter Newell could have been, as Frank suggested, upstairs listening as Emily and Quinn rhapsodized about killing their husbands. Heard Emily take Frank's call and say she'd be stopping for coffee on the way home. Or Quinn could have alerted him. Though why would she have done that?

The only other person who knew Emily would be stopping at the coffee shop was Frank. All he had to do was ask and he knew she'd stop on the way home and pick him up a coffee. He'd even know when she'd be likely to get there, since the coffee shop closed at ten. It was Frank—and putting this together felt like peering into an abyss—who'd insisted that the guy who came to their house wearing coffee-stained loafers was Ryan's client, even though the man was clearly pissed off at Frank.

She desperately hoped that her soft sell worked, and Ana was taking pity on her and looking up whether Mr. Congeniality had paid with a credit card. Walter Newell's or someone else's? She needed a name to go with those shoes.

When Emily got to the Murphys' storage unit, it was open and Lila's car was parked in front. Emily sat in her car for a few moments, willing her fingers to loosen their grip on the wheel. She checked her face in the rearview mirror. Then got out of the car.

The hum Emily heard when she entered the unit turned out to be the ventilation system. The thermostat was now functioning and reading seventy-two degrees. Cool air was pouring in from the ceiling vent.

At a glance, Emily could see about a quarter of the shelves had already been cleared. Books had been transferred to stacks on the floor. Mrs. Murphy sat in a folding chair at the worktable, looking for all the world like she was playing solitaire with due-date cards and library pockets. Lila stood on a cinder block. As Emily watched, Lila eased a thick volume from the topmost shelf. Ran her hand over the front cover and gently opened the book. "Morris, William," she called out. "*The Wood Beyond the World.*"

After a pause, Mrs. Murphy said, "Got it!" She held up a due-date card. "Francis Lewis Memorial Library."

Becca, who was sitting cross-legged in a cleared space on the floor with her computer on her lap, repeated the title and the library as she typed.

"Ex-lib," Lila said. That was shorthand for ex–library book. *Tap tap tap*, Becca typed. Lila sniffed at the book, riffled the pages, and frowned. "Good condition." Becca typed some more.

In antiquarian book-speak, *good* didn't mean good. It was like getting an exam grade of C.

"Let's stack it," Lila said. "It's in rough condition, but they'll be happy to have it back where it belongs." Lila walked over and picked up the card from Mrs. Murphy, tucked it into the book, and set the book on top of one of the piles on the floor.

"Hey, guys," Emily said. "How's it going?" She sidestepped around the stacks in the unit to give Lila, Becca, and Mrs. Murphy each a coffee. "I have sugar and milk if you want, and delicious cider donut holes." She handed one to Lila, who sniffed it suspiciously. Took a nibble. A bite. Then popped the whole thing into her mouth.

"We're turning back history," Becca said. "It's very satisfying."

"Can I help?" Emily asked.

"You can help by not helping," Lila said, snagging another donut hole. "Please. It's tight quarters in here. Standing room only. And we have a system."

"Really, we've got it under control," Becca said. She looked around. "Actually, you could help me move those boxes out of here. The books in them are so far gone, I can't even tell where they're from. Be careful. They're full of mold."

So don't inhale. Emily helped Becca push one of the boxes of books out of the unit and came back for the second one.

"Hang on," Becca said. Emily examined the unit, shelf to shelf, while Becca tossed several more books into the box and checked for others. They'd made good progress. About a quarter of the books had been sorted. After that they'd have to do the document tubes—at least it looked as if those were clearly labeled and properly sealed in the first place. And after that, the boxes of assorted building hardware. Was it Emily's imagination, or did there seem to be fewer of those?

"Here you go." Becca closed the flaps on the box of discarded books and gave it a shove in Emily's direction. "Oh, I need to send you the combination to the new padlock." She sat back down on the ground and picked up her laptop.

"Thanks," Emily said. But her attention was focused on Mr. Murphy's dozen or so remaining boxes. Stuck to each of them were green plastic labels, punched with white capital letters. HINGES. KNOBS. BRACKETS. They reminded her of something. Something incongruous that she'd barely noticed at the time.

But before Emily could follow the thought, her cell phone pinged. She'd missed a call and had a voice message waiting. Caller ID read ANA PEREZ. The barista at the Java Connection.

"Catch you later, guys," Emily said.

Becca waved. Lila, standing on the cinder block, was already pulling down another book. Mrs. Murphy was straightening an array of library pockets. Emily pushed the last box of discarded books across the floor and out to the curb. Then she got in her car and listened to the message.

In a lightly accented voice, "That man. He charged his coffee." There was a brief pause filled with the background chatter of conversation at the coffee shop. Emily waited for the name she expected, *Walter Newell*.

Instead, Ana said, "Rafe Bartok." She spelled the name, and then hung up.

WHO IN THE hell was Rafe Bartok? The name sounded like a Las Vegas lion tamer's nom de guerre or a losing contestant from *The Bachelorette*. And why had this stranger been waiting for Emily to enter the coffee shop? And had the same man shown up at her house threatening Frank two days later, clean-shaven but still wearing coffee-stained loafers?

Emily typed the name into the Google app on her cell phone. Then she narrowed the search to images. The first photos that came up were of a man in his forties. Thick dark hair. Intense eyes. Emily's heart skipped a beat. He looked like the man who'd driven the green pickup truck to their house.

She tapped one of the images and up came a record from IMDb. Turned out Mr. Bartok was an actor. He'd been at it for decades, struggling, it would seem from the list of parts he'd played. Coroner's Assistant on *CSI*. Delivery Guy in *Gone Baby Gone*. Most recently, Desk Sergeant on an episode of *Boston's Finest*. The high point of his career had been ten years back when he'd played a serial killer for three episodes on *Bones*. Low points included multiple credits, back in the 1990s and then again more recently, when his role in a movie had been behind the camera as "grip."

Emily also found a photograph that was a whole lot less flattering than his headshot: a mug shot from a news story dated May 2017. Jaw set. Expression sullen. Hair tousled. Eyes watery. The text said Bartok, forty-five, a "local actor," had been arrested for OUI outside a restaurant in East Hampton: "An employee called the police at about 9:45 on Tuesday to alert them to a possibly intoxicated driver who was attempting to leave the parking lot with his truck's emergency brake engaged." Sounded like a down-on-his-luck guy who'd be willing to take a sketchy gig if the price was right, though Frank had described him as "the son of a CEO."

Emily hurried home and ran upstairs to her office. She logged on to her computer and found one of Bartok's more recent headshots. She pasted it into Photoshop. Next, she captured a photograph of Walter Newell from the wedding announcement she'd found earlier and pasted it into Photoshop, too.

Side by side, you'd never have mistaken Rafe Bartok for Walter Newell. Bartok had a blocky face with deep-set eyes. Newell was more of a pretty boy with a devilish heart-shaped face, his hairline a widow's peak. Newell's face spoke of a Gaelic ancestry; Bartok's sturdy Balkan. On the other hand, they had the same general build, dark hair, and dark features. Tweak the hair, add a few accessories . . . Emily set to work doctoring the photographs. She Photoshopped a beard and mustache onto Bartok's face. Then gave both men yellow-tinted aviator glasses and baseball caps. Emily gazed with some satisfaction at the doppelgängers she'd created. She realized it was a whole lot easier to make two people look alike on a computer screen than in person, but she'd demonstrated, to herself at least, that it wouldn't have taken much for Rafe Bartok to pass himself off to strangers as Walter Newell. He was, after all, a character actor.

She was so immersed in Photoshop that she was startled when she heard Frank's voice. "I'm back."

She whipped around. Frank stood in the doorway, dressed in a dark suit—his court clothes. "I didn't hear you come in." She checked the time on her screen. One. "What are you doing back?" She snapped her laptop shut.

"Court's recessed."

"Didn't the plaintiff settle?"

Frank waved off the question. "What are you up to?"

"Just messing around."

"Can I see?" Frank didn't wait for an answer. He reached past her and opened her laptop. The screen bloomed with the images of the two Photoshopped faces, side by side. Frank drew closer and squinted at the screen. "Who's that?" Emily felt a surge of triumph. Evidently he thought the two images were the same person.

"It's supposed to be Walter Newell," she said.

"That's the guy who ran into you at the coffee shop?"

Not *That's the dead guy in the storage unit.* Or *That's Quinn Newell's husband.* Instead Frank was reminding her that the man in the coffee shop had been Walter Newell, though she was now convinced that he wasn't.

Emily pretended to ponder the faces. "Doesn't he look like your visitor from the other night? The man with the pickup truck who—"

"Ryan's client," Frank said quickly. Too quickly. "Now that you mention it . . ." He tilted the screen and stared into it. "Nah. This guy looks nothing like him." He stood. "But where are you going with this? Because you told me you only got a brief glimpse of Walter Newell before his coffee spilled all over you. On top of that, you were a bit . . . more than a bit compromised. I could tell the minute you got home. You were plastered. *He* ran into you? I'm surprised"—Frank's tone softened, like this was just between the two of them—"the police haven't charged *you* with hit-and-run and driving under the influence."

Emily recognized one of Frank's tried-and-true techniques: *If a witness gives you a hard time, make him look like a jerk.* Still, his comment struck a nerve. She had behaved like a rank amateur, drinking with Quinn Newell. Oversharing. Toasting dead husbands. She'd still been under the influence when she arrived at the Java Connection. And if it had been only that man's facial appearance, she'd readily admit that she hadn't gotten a good enough look at him to say whether or not he was the same man who'd arrived in the green truck. But she had not, she reminded herself, Photoshopped a pair of coffee-stained loafers onto the guy's feet.

Emily knew she should let it drop, but she couldn't help herself. "According to the police, Cape traffic was so bad on Sunday that Walter Newell couldn't have gotten back in time to run into me if he left when he told Quinn he was leaving. So maybe he wasn't the man at the coffee shop. Who knows, maybe Walter Newell was already dead."

Frank put up his hands. "Whoa, whoa, whoa." He blinked, like he was trying to put the pieces together. "*If* he left when he said he did? That's a big *if.*" Frank gave an exasperated sigh. "Isn't it possible that he was lying to his wife? Emmy, think about it. What do you actually know about Walter Newell?"

32

FRANK LEFT EMILY alone in her office. The two faces on her computer screen felt like Halloween masks as they stared at her from
behind matching aviator glasses. Frank was right. Again. What
did she know about Walter Newell? He'd come from a wealthy
family. He'd been in real estate. Owned a ridiculous number
of suits and shoes. Collected retro advertising signs and magazine cover art. According to Quinn, he was a control freak. And
something that Quinn had neglected to mention: he was her
second dead husband.

Full stop. That felt like lightning striking the same spot twice.
Again Emily pulled up Quinn and Walter's wedding announcement that had run in the *Boston Globe.* It named her previous
husband, "the late Michael Safstrom."

Michaels were a dime a dozen, but Safstroms, not so much.
Emily googled his name and got hundreds of hits. As she
scrolled through them, articles that Michael Safstrom had
written for *Collectors' Quarterly* caught her eye. "Collecting Original Cover Art." "The Disappearing Art of Porcelain Advertising Signs."

Safstrom's article on signs began, "Perhaps the most easily recognizable advertising medium of the late 19th century was the porcelain sign." It went on, extolling the virtues of porcelain signs, their durability and weather resistance, their bold colors and eye-catching graphics. As collectibles, they were much-sought-after because they were rare—many had been melted down for their base metal at the onset of World War II. The article was illustrated with pictures of signs marked "from the author's collection." LE PNEU MICHELIN—the familiar Michelin man riding a bicycle. ZENITH RADIO—a bright red sign emblazoned with zigzag lightning. A flying red Pegasus for MOBILGAS.

The article on collecting cover art was peppered with names even Emily recognized. Norman Rockwell. Maxfield Parrish. N. C. Wyeth. It discussed the ins and outs of evaluating an illustration. How to spot a forgery or giclée print reproduction, the digital technology Lila had mentioned to Emily.

Safstrom's columns on collecting had been published regularly, every few months, from 2005 until 2011. A news article in the *Nassau Times* dated March 2012 explained why they'd stopped: "Hermès Cruise Ship Passenger Remains Missing." Forty-three-year-old Michael Safstrom had been on his honeymoon cruise when he went overboard from the eighth deck of the ship on its way to Bermuda. His wife, Amanda Quinn Safstrom, had reported him missing two days later when the ship reached Nassau.

Emily found his obituary, which ran in the *Boston Globe* four months later. It included the announcement of a memorial service at a church in Gloucester. There was nothing about burial. She wondered if his body had been recovered.

Emily pushed away from her computer, thinking. Four years after Michael Safstrom's death, his widow, Amanda/Quinn, married Walter Newell, a man she claimed was so jealous and controlling that he wouldn't let his wife bring so much as a photo album or a stuffed toy from her past into their home. And yet all over the house he'd displayed porcelain signs and magazine illustrations that looked suspiciously similar to what her first husband collected.

Similar to or identical?

For a start, Emily needed to take a closer look at those advertising signs, because how likely was it that a hyper-jealous, controlling husband would have allowed himself to be surrounded by items that had been coveted by his wife's ex?

Getting into the Newells' house wouldn't be a problem. Quinn had given Emily the garage door opener and invited her to feel free to use it *whenever.* But Emily wasn't about to spend another minute with Quinn Newell if she could help it. It would be much better if Emily got in and out of the house when Quinn wasn't there. But when was that? Quinn didn't have a job that took her out of the house. But she did exercise. Regularly. Emily remembered the morning vinyasa yoga classes circled on the fitness center calendar hanging in Quinn's kitchen.

It took a minute for Emily to find the schedule of the local fitness center on its website. A yoga class was scheduled for tomorrow morning at eleven. It was worth a try.

FRIDAY

BEFORE EMILY WENT to bed, she had posted her stop-motion closet-sorting video to Instagram and Facebook along with a link to her website. When she checked the next morning, it had "reached" more than five hundred people and been shared by ten. It was nothing like the way her sock-sorting video had gone viral, but when she checked her email she was gratified to see a few queries from potential new clients. She forwarded them to Becca.

Lila was in the kitchen eating a bowl of cereal with sliced banana and reading the paper when Emily came down. Lila had on a dark blazer and skirt, her red hair de-spiked. A black coat was draped across the back of her chair, though Emily couldn't imagine Lila needing it.

"Good morning, dear. There's a pot of coffee," Lila said. "Frank said to tell you he had to leave early."

"Good morning," Emily said, eyeing her mother. That outfit she had on looked all too familiar. "You look—"

"I know. Boring."

"Stand up so I can see."

Lila stood. Twirled. Then held a pose with her head to one side, chin up, as she tugged on the cuffs of the blazer. The sleeves were a tad too short. Despite that, Lila looked surprisingly chic, given that Emily's skirt was also too short and that boxy blazer was at least ten years old. Emily's silk scarf, which Lila had artfully draped around her neck, did wonders pulling the look together.

"I didn't think you'd mind," Lila said. "You *were* getting rid of them, weren't you? I needed something that looked professional and conservative. And, yes, boring. What do you think?"

"I think you nailed it on all counts." Emily poured herself a cup of coffee and added an inch of milk.

"We're launching our first trial balloon," Lila said. "I'm going to South Hadley with Ruth and Becca to return some books and lithographs to their District Collection. Folio prints from Gould's hummingbirds. Not as valuable as any of Audubon's birds, thank goodness. Any library would have noticed the instant an Audubon bird print disappeared. That's how her husband was able to fly under the radar, lo these many years. He didn't overreach."

"It's a long way to South Hadley."

"Not too bad. Under two hours. We'll be back early afternoon." Lila sat down.

"Unless you get arrested."

"And if that happens"—Lila spooned some cereal with a slice of banana, ate it, and shook the empty spoon in Emily's direction—"I'll be counting on you to bail us out."

"You don't seem overly concerned." Emily sipped her coffee.

"I'm not, particularly. I've known their director for years. We went to Simmons together. That's why I thought it would be a safe place to start. If I'm right, they have no idea what they're missing. Once they find out? It's a tricky thing, letting your board know about items that disappeared years ago, under your watch, without your noticing. You can't inventory the contents of every book. I'm hoping that a discreet return will be in everyone's best interest. And who knows what else of theirs we'll find when we've finished going through that storage unit? The important thing is to restore the losses. Especially since the thief has already gone to meet his maker.

"By the way, I thought you'd appreciate this." Lila twisted around and lifted the black coat that was on the back of her chair. "Ruth found it in her husband's closet." She opened the coat. "Here's how he got away with it." A patchwork of pockets had been sewn inside. "And look at this." She showed Emily a hook in the lining. Hanging from it was a thin black-felt pocket. From it, Lila drew out an X-Acto knife with a plastic sheath.

Emily took the coat from Lila and shook it out in front of her. She draped it over her own shoulders, then threaded her arms through the sleeves. She buttoned two top buttons. The coat fit snug across her shoulders but loose, almost tent-like, in the middle. Plenty of room for whatever you wanted to slip into those deep pockets. Plus the coat was a lot heavier than you'd have expected. Feeling around the lining, she realized why. Like a curtain, its hem had weights sewn into it. "Do you think Mrs. Murphy knew what he was up to?" Emily asked.

"I suppose it's possible." Lila gave a heavy sigh and sank back into her chair. "But if she did, then why would she bring us his coat?" Lila carried her empty cereal bowl and coffee cup to the sink, rinsed them out, and put them in the dishwasher. "Unless . . ." She turned around and leaned against the counter, resting her chin on her hand, considering. Then gave her head a shake. "She really knows next to nothing about books and prints. More likely she was the naïve magician's assistant. Enthusiastic old biddy, chatting up librarians. Lowering their guard. Not realizing that he brought her along to divert attention while he made things disappear." Lila glanced at her watch. "I hope I'm right. Time to face the music." Lila picked up her purse, fished out her car keys, and left the house.

Alone in the kitchen, Emily unbuttoned the coat and started to take it off. That's when she realized something else odd about it. The buttons were on the left side, buttonholes on the right.

Emily ran to the door, hoping to catch Lila, but her car was gone. She considered calling, but she knew her mother never answered her phone when she was driving. Instead she sent a text that she hoped Lila would understand:

It's a woman's coat. Let Becca know.

33

EMILY PULLED INTO the parking lot across from East Hartwell's fitness center thirty minutes before Quinn's eleven o'clock yoga
class was scheduled to start. Quinn's Miata wasn't there yet.
Emily parked and waited, watching as the lot filled and women
in leggings and carrying yoga mats got out of their cars and
made their way across the street. At eleven, Emily was about
to give up when Quinn's Miata pulled in. As Quinn raced
from her car to the fitness center, Emily headed for Quinn's
house.

Mandarin Cliffs felt deserted. Few cars were parked in front
of the houses. No children played in what would have made an
excellent street hockey or basketball court. Signs sprouted in
front yards proclaiming the security systems that protected the
homes.

Emily made a U-turn in the mouth of the cul-de-sac and
parked facing out, leaving the car door unlocked in case she
needed to make a quick exit. She'd get in and out, staying just
long enough to ascertain whether Husband #1's treasures were
on Husband #2's walls.

With her gear bag over her shoulder, she rang the bell, making sure no one was home. Then she crossed the lawn to the garage, took out the controller that Quinn had given her, and pressed the button. One of the garage's two double doors rose and folded back, revealing the empty bays where Quinn and her husband's cars were usually parked.

Emily entered the garage. It smelled of car wax and leather, plus the residual musky smell of whatever dealers used to permanently perfume the interior of luxury cars. Off to the side, in the pair of bays behind the still-closed garage door, sat the pile of possessions that Quinn had said she was ready to deep-six.

Emily heard a plaintive cat's meow coming from the kitchen. She closed the garage door and let herself into the house. The calico cat greeted her, rubbing its head against her leg. Emily resisted the urge to pick up the cat and give it a nuzzle. She didn't have much time before Quinn could be back.

An open package of English muffins sat on the counter. In a shallow cobalt-blue glass bowl lay a loaded key ring that had probably been Wally's. Beside the bowl was a brochure from Dunmeyer and Wellington Funeral Home, touting "Professional Services with Personal Care."

Emily unfolded the printouts she'd made of the photos that illustrated Quinn's first husband's articles on collecting. The moment she entered the front hall she found a match, the metal sign at the bottom of the stairs that advertised Sunlight soap. When she'd been there last, the content hadn't registered—only the hole in the wall that it covered. Halfway up the stairs she found another match, a sign for Omega watches. The striking image was of a gold pocket watch viewed from the side, with the word OMEGA in stylized black letters on a bright red background. Peeling enamel revealed the sign's rusted metal base.

Emily photographed both signs. Then she made her way to

Walter Newell's study. There, hanging on the walls, she found many of the magazine covers reproduced in another of Michael Safstrom's articles. Not magazine *covers*, Emily confirmed when she slipped behind the desk and examined them close up. They looked to be artist-signed, original art. The *MAD* magazine cover alone had to be worth a small fortune.

Emily took another picture and lowered her cell phone. She felt satisfied that she had what she'd come for, evidence that the objects that took pride of place in Walter Newell's house had been collected by his wife's previous dead husband. Which meant that Walter wasn't the crazy jealous husband Quinn made him out to be. Maybe he was just rich and inconvenient.

Emily hurried through the kitchen and into the garage. But before she could close the door behind her, the cat darted past and was instantly lost in the shadows.

Emily cursed her own carelessness. If she didn't get the cat back in the house, Quinn would know someone had been here. "Here, kitty kitty kitty." She didn't even know the damned cat's name. She dropped her gear bag and fished out her cell phone. She turned on its flashlight and shone the beam from one end of the garage to the other. "Come on, you stupid cat." Emily made kissing sounds and held the kitchen door open, but the cat was having none of it.

Emily went back into the kitchen, poured a saucer of milk, and brought it out to the garage. She clicked her tongue and rattled the saucer on the concrete floor. Crouched. Listened. At last, a faint rustling sound seemed to come from the pile of belongings that Quinn had claimed her husband kept her from bringing into the house.

Emily shone the light, trying to penetrate the pile. The glassy eyes of a Care Bear gleamed back at her. It sat in a box of stuffed toys on the floor between the bureaus. Emily realized that box had been moved since she was last there. She thumbed back through the pictures she'd taken on her first visit. The stuffed animals had been on top of a bureau. And the dark stain which was now visible across the papasan chair's gold seat cushion had been hidden beneath a burlap-backed area rug.

Her heart racing, Emily stepped closer to the pile and examined it from end to end, top to bottom, in the flashlight beam. The rolled-up rug had vanished.

She switched to the camera and zoomed in. Took a shot of the empty chair seat, and then another. That's when she heard it. A lapping sound. The cat was drinking from the saucer. Emily slipped her phone into her pocket, snuck over, scooped up the cat, and unceremoniously dumped it back in the kitchen. Raced the saucer to the sink, rinsed and dried it, put it in the cabinet, and then hurried back out to the garage, taking care not to let the cat slip past her this time.

She found where she'd dropped her gear bag, picked it up, and got out the garage opener. But before she could activate the mechanism, it clanked and whirred and the door started to rise. Just audible, beyond the sound of the door opening, was a car engine revving. A band of sunlight appeared at ground level. When the door was inches off the ground, a red car bumper came into view. Then a black grille with a license plate affixed to it, flanked by squinty-eyed headlights. Quinn's Miata.

Emily drew back as the garage door rose. She could see the silhouettes of a driver and a passenger in the car. She considered sauntering out to greet Quinn and her companion as if everything were hunky-dory. After all, Quinn had told her to come back anytime. But Emily was a lousy actress and a worse liar.

Counting on it taking a few moments for Quinn's eyes to adjust to the relative darkness in the garage, Emily hid behind one of the bureaus as the Miata slipped in and stopped. The engine shut down and the garage door descended. A car door creaked opened and slammed shut. Through a sliver of space between the bureaus, Emily could see the driver had gotten out. Yoga pants. Light-colored sneakers. Quinn. Emily ducked lower and prayed that Quinn wouldn't sense her presence.

The passenger door opened, and, moments later, there was a click as it was pressed shut. The *squeak-squeak* of soft soles on the concrete floor. Emily heard what sounded like a man clearing his throat.

Emily crouched, clutching her gear bag to her chest, her legs trembling as she tried not to make a sound, not daring to raise her head.

The door to the kitchen opened. "Emily?" Quinn called into the house. Emily's hand flew to her mouth; she panicked for a moment before she realized Quinn must have spotted Emily's car parked outside.

"Emmy?" Quinn called out again. *Don't call me Emmy!* Emily wanted to scream. "According to this," Quinn said to her companion, "she's here somewhere."

According to this? A chill went down Emily's back. More soft footsteps. The door to the kitchen closed. Seconds later Emily heard the sound of crickets. Her phone. In the empty garage, its chirp was like a clap of thunder.

34

EMILY SLID THE phone from her pocket and, her hand shaking, held it at arm's length. It felt radioactive with its screen lit up: QUINN NEWELL. When the screen went blank, she powered it off completely.

How could Quinn be tracking her location? When Frank installed the friend-finder app on Emily's phone, he'd explained to her just how safe it was. Only people she'd specifically granted permission could track her, and only when her phone was turned on. He'd linked her to himself and Becca and Lila. So who'd added Quinn?

Emily had to get out of here *now*. It wouldn't take long for Quinn to realize that Emily wasn't still in the house. But activating the garage door opener would be like triggering a burglar alarm. There had to be another way out.

That's when she noticed the standard door sandwiched between the two overhead doors. She picked up her gear bag and made her way over to it. She tried to turn the knob but it was locked. Panicked for a moment, she felt for a lock in the handle. Bingo. She twisted it, opened the door, and slipped out.

Squinting into the sun, she raced to her car. She stumbled as she took a quick look back. No one called out to her. No one came after her. She could only hope that Quinn or her friend didn't look out a window. She jumped into her car, threw her bag and cell onto the passenger seat, jammed her key into the ignition, and turned it. The engine roared to life. Her tires squealed as she accelerated out of there.

Emily checked her rearview mirror, expecting the Miata to pull up behind her at any moment. She kept going until she was well out of Mandarin Cliffs. As she drove, she reached for her cell, swerving to avoid oncoming traffic. How in the hell did you turn off the damned locator beacon? She stopped on a side street and pulled over. She switched the phone on and fiddled with the settings until she found LOCATION SHARING and set it to OFF for every one of her apps. She hoped that would do it.

Then she drove on, checking her rearview mirror and looping through backstreets. The farther behind that she left the dot that marked her last tracked location, the calmer Emily grew.

She tried to sort her thoughts. Frank could have tinkered with her friend-finder app. She left the phone lying around the house all the time and he knew her passcode. But why would he have added Quinn? It seemed more likely that Quinn had added herself. She could have done it the other night when Emily was sloppy drunk. They'd been together in Quinn's kitchen when Frank texted, asking Emily to stop for a coffee. She couldn't remember the details of what had happened next, but it seemed likely that she'd left her phone on Quinn's kitchen counter when she'd gone to the bathroom before leaving. Quinn could easily have picked it up and made the change.

All roads seemed to lead back to Quinn Newell. Quinn hadn't

needed Emily's help decluttering her garage; she'd needed someone to declutter her life and take the blame for her husband's
murder.

As Sergeant Stanley liked to point out, moving Walter Newell's
body, especially once it was rolled up in a wet area rug, would
have been a two-person job. Had Ryan helped Quinn, with an
eye toward becoming her third husband? Or maybe Quinn's
helper had been her first husband, Michael Safstrom, whose
body had never been recovered. Or maybe it was Rafe Bartok,
the actor in coffee-stained loafers, who Frank had said was one
of Ryan's clients? She swallowed hard. Or could it have been
Frank?

Emily felt her thoughts spiraling out of control, conjectures
caroming off one another. If Becca were here, she'd have been
calm, thinking clearly, and asking the right questions. Her
mother would have had a rational take on it, too. But best-case,
Becca and Lila were right now finessing a delicate meeting with
a head librarian, leaving behind books and prints that Mr.
Murphy, with more than a little help from his wife, had "borrowed" from South Hadley's District Collection.

She slowed as she passed the police station. She wondered
if she should tell Sergeant Stanley about the rug that was no
longer in Quinn Newell's garage. Such a flimsy piece of non-
evidence—from the back, one piece of carpet looked pretty
much like any other. Still, a rolled-up rug had disappeared from
the Newells' garage, and one like it had appeared in the Murphys'
storage unit.

So how did Wally's body get from the wharf to the storage
unit? Was there any way that Quinn could have managed it
alone? Emily wondered if she had time to drive to the wharf

and look around before meeting Becca and Lila at the storage unit . . .

As if on cue, her phone pinged with a text from Becca.

Heading back
See you at Inner Peace in about an hour

The commuter lot at the wharf was full when Emily got there. She continued to the boat basin and pulled over in a no-parking zone near the boat ramp. A couple was hauling a kayak out of the water. Both of them had binoculars hanging from around their necks. The man suddenly lowered his end of the kayak and pointed out over the water. A huge bird, dark with a white head, swooped down and landed on a branch at the near shore.

Emily sat forward in her seat and loosened her shirt, which had stuck to her sweat-soaked back. Suddenly chilled, she turned down the air conditioner and took a few deep breaths, trying to slow her heartbeat.

She'd almost succeeded when her phone chirped. The read-out said QUINN NEWELL. Again. Emily dropped the phone. It bounced from her lap onto the car floor. Chirped again. A third time. A fourth time. In the blessed silence that followed, Emily could hear her own labored breathing and the car's wheeze. When the voice-mail message chimed, she felt around on the floor for the phone and picked it up. She stared for a few moments at the red dot that said she had two new messages before playing them.

Quinn's voice: "I just got home. I thought you might be here but it looks like I missed you. Call me as soon as you can." That was the call that had come when Emily was still in the garage.

The second message: "Me again. Did you get my message? There's something I need to show you. Can you come back right away?"

Emily had no intention of returning to Quinn's house, now or ever. She pocketed her phone, got out of the car, and walked to the water's edge. Four days ago she'd pulled an auction bidder card from the weeds right here. Quinn had taken one look at the card and broken down in tears. Looking back, it seemed bizarre that Wally had last been seen at an auction and that bidder card had washed up right under Emily's nose. *Almost as if* . . . she'd been meant to find it.

Auctions. They seemed to keep coming up. Wally had been attending one the day he was killed. According to Quinn's first wedding announcement, she'd worked in an auction gallery. And hadn't there been auction catalogues on Mr. Murphy's desk?

Emily scrolled back through the pictures she'd taken the first time she and Becca had visited the Murphys' house. There was Murph's boat. His carved birds. And before that, his desk. Emily zoomed in. On top was a catalogue from Kalmus Fine Art.

Kalmus. That was the auction house where Quinn had once worked. Maybe Quinn knew the Murphys. Maybe she'd helped them sell ill-gotten maps and books. And maybe it was Quinn who'd been spotted by the observant security guard, making trips to the storage unit where they kept their treasures. That would make it a whole lot less surprising that Wally's body had ended up in the Murphys' storage unit, and it explained why Mrs. Murphy wasn't about to reveal that she knew the dead man's wife.

Emily looked past the parking lot and out across the water. The tide was low and the wind off the river was coming in gusts. Had this been yet another stage set? It was supposed to look as if Emily had followed Walter Newell here after he'd bumped into her at the Java Connection. She'd confronted him here. Run him down. Rolled him up in a rug she'd conveniently had with her. Stashed his body in the water for a while, then driven it across the river to Inner Peace Storage. With evidence the police had collected—paint from her car on Wally's front fender and CCTV footage of her car at the storage facility in the middle of the night—they had to be a whisker away from charging her with murder or, at the very least, manslaughter.

And yet, they hadn't.

The kayaking couple had dragged their boat to their SUV. It took both of them to wrestle it up onto the roof. It occurred to Emily how much easier it was to maneuver that kayak in the water than it was on dry land. Which made her wonder if it wouldn't have been a whole lot easier to tow Walter Newell's body across the water to the storage facility. The distance—it couldn't be more than two hundred feet from shore to shore—and the current would make the trip a quick one. Then, assuming there was access to the water from the storage facility and an opening in the chain-link fencing that surrounded it, all you'd have to do was dock the boat and drag the body to the storage unit. It would have taken two people to pull it off, but in the dark of night, it was a route that afforded plenty of privacy.

35

EMILY GOT BACK in her car to find another text from Becca. She and Lila and Mrs. Murphy were at a rest stop and would meet her at the storage unit in a half hour. That gave Emily time to poke around the riverbank behind the storage facility. When she got there, unit 217 was secured by the new combination lock. She could smell the river as she walked around the row of storage units numbered in the one hundreds and down a grassy embankment. Beyond a perimeter of chain-link fencing was a sheer ten-foot drop to the water. Across the water and upstream was the town wharf where she'd just been. Somehow it seemed farther away from this side.

Emily walked the fence from end to end, wading through knee-high grass and slogging through the occasional muddy patch. More than once, one of her Crocs was nearly sucked off her foot.

So much for her conjecture that Walter Newell's body could have been towed across the water from the wharf to the storage unit. There was no obvious place for a boat or even a kayak to dock at the water's edge, the chain link was unbroken, and lugging a body up the steep embankment would have been arduous, even for two people working together. Anyone who'd attempted it would have left a significant trail, and she'd found none.

Emily returned to the Murphys' storage unit. It took a moment to once again spot the CCTV camera mounted at the roof of the adjacent unit. It would be easy to back up a car to the door, dump a body even in broad daylight, without giving the security camera a clear view.

The toot of a car horn announced Becca's arrival. Lila pulled in behind her with Mrs. Murphy.

"Hey, how'd it go?" Emily asked as Becca got out of her car.

Becca didn't answer. She unlocked the unit as Lila and Mrs. Murphy exited, too. Lila's face was solemn, her arms folded. Judging from Mrs. Murphy's red face and the way she clutched a tissue, things had not gone well.

Lila said, "Turned out they knew exactly what they were missing."

Becca stood, the padlock in her hand. "And they had a pretty good idea who'd taken them."

"They had our picture," Mrs. Murphy said, "like a pair of common criminals on a WANTED poster, pinned to a bulletin board in their work area." She dabbed at her eyes.

"They were happy to get back *some* of what they lost," Becca said. "But they gave us a list of more items that went missing at around the same time as the Goulds." She threw open the door to the storage unit, then came over to Emily and handed her a printout. Under her breath, she said, "Mr. Murphy dropped an X-Acto blade the last time he was in there. That's why they started looking for losses. A little over a year ago they alerted other libraries to what the pair was up to and had an attorney contact Mr. Murphy."

A little over a year ago. That was when Charles Murphy died. Emily wondered if that was what had pushed him over the edge.

Emily scanned the list of missing items. More bird prints. Maps. And three carved birds. Emily groaned, remembering the entire shelf of carved wooden birds in Mr. Murphy's study. Which meant his stolen cache wasn't confined to the storage unit.

"Believe me when I tell you," Mrs. Murphy said, "I had no idea what he was up to." Her eyes filled with tears. "I know I should have realized. I mean, he kept wanting to go back. He wasn't a bad man. Really he wasn't. He was just"—she blew her nose—"weak."

Emily could tell from Lila's expression that she wasn't buying it.

Emily approached the open storage unit. Cool air oozed out. Emily went inside and motioned for Becca to follow. She tried to avoid looking under the worktable where the body had been stashed.

"I said we'd help her inventory the rest of what's in here," Becca said quietly. "Lila's putting together a list of institutions and people for her to contact. But after that—" Becca sliced the air with the side of her hand.

Emily got it. They'd be cutting their losses and hoping to keep their reputation intact. She remembered what Frank had told her: knowing about stolen goods wasn't a crime, but helping to dispose of them could be a felony. But the line between the two wasn't all that bright, and Emily didn't trust Mrs. Murphy to accurately explain to the police what kind of "help" she and Becca had provided.

"And here we've been making such good progress," Becca said with a wry grimace as her gaze traveled across the books and tubes they'd stacked in a dozen or so piles.

"Amazing progress," Emily said, "given the circumstances."

Only a few dozen neatly labeled cardboard boxes remained on the shelves—Mr. Murphy's beloved *thingamabobs*. Doorknobs. Hinges. Every box clearly labeled. He'd been such an orderly collector. His method, or maybe it was madness, would spark joy in the heart of any professional organizer.

But, looking at those boxes now, Emily felt unsettled. She'd recently seen a box of padlocks carefully labeled, just like Mr. Murphy's. It had been disinterred by the police from her own basement, and the sight of it had left Frank visibly shaken.

Frank, who claimed labels were for sissies. Frank, who poked fun at what he called Becca and Emily's *labeling schtick*. He liked to compare boxing and labeling clutter to rearranging the deck chairs on the *Titanic*. In his basement and attic and garage, according to Frank, he had no need to impose the kind of orderliness that Mr. Murphy had apparently craved. He knew just where everything was.

So why had that box of padlocks the police pulled out of her basement been tagged with labeling tape? The obvious answer: It wasn't Frank's. It was Mr. Murphy's. Emily remembered how Frank had lit up when Emily had described the contents of the storage unit. How the shelves were chockablock with all kinds of objects collected by a man who'd surely have been Frank's kindred spirit. Emily had told Frank that she had a key to the storage unit, maybe even showed him where it was, and—

"What are you thinking?" Becca asked.

"Nothing," Emily said. When Becca looked skeptical, she added, "It's just this whole situation is such a mess."

"Your mother was amazing. I think we'd all be in jail if she hadn't been with us."

"Emily? Becca?" Lila called from outside. "You all okay if I drive Ruth home now?"

Becca looked relieved.

"Sure," Emily called back.

"You want me to come back?" Lila asked.

Becca gave a tight headshake.

"No need," Emily called. "I'll see you at home."

Becca held Emily's gaze until Lila and Mrs. Murphy had driven off. "She knew," Becca said. She looked vexed, her mouth set in a taut line. "The library had pictures of the pair of them consulting a little notebook that she kept in her purse. Like a shopping list."

"I was afraid that it would turn out to be something like that. After I saw the coat."

Becca said, "All those pockets, and it's not a man's coat."

"Not a man's coat." Emily repeated the words, but she was thinking about Frank. Had he taken the key and snuck into the storage unit after he was sure Emily was sound asleep? Had he helped himself? Had that been before or after Walter Newell's body was delivered to the storage unit and whoever delivered it changed the lock? Or had Frank helped Quinn move the body and helped himself to a box of hardware as a reward for services rendered? "I can't believe it," she said, belatedly realizing she'd spoken the thought.

"I can't believe it, either," Becca said. "I knew that we'd have clients who'd make up excuses for what they hoarded. Who'd delude themselves, thinking that it's healthy to become emotionally attached to inanimate objects. Who'd be pathologically disorganized in all aspects of their lives. But I wasn't prepared for clients who'd outright lie and get us to help them break the law."

"So much for trust and integrity," Emily said.

"So much for my so-called intuition about people." Becca shook her head and gave a wry smile.

"People can really fool you," Emily said.

Becca did a double take. "You're not talking about the Murphys now, are you?" Emily felt her face flush. "Quinn Newell?" Becca said.

Emily faked a surprised look. After all, it was true, at first Quinn Newell had fooled her. "Quinn Newell told me her husband collected the advertising signs and magazine art that's in their house. But that collection belonged to her *first* husband, and he disappeared from a cruise ship off the coast of Bermuda while they were on their honeymoon six or seven years ago."

Becca's eyes widened. "Disappeared?"

"Jumped. Fell. Or was pushed. Or maybe he just vanished into the night. I can't tell if his body was ever recovered. Curious, isn't it, that Quinn never mentioned that she'd been married before?"

Becca tilted her head, thinking. "There could be a lot of reasons for that."

"The rug we found Walter Newell wrapped up in? I think it came from their garage." Emily swiped through the photos on her phone and showed Becca the picture that she'd taken of the rolled-up rug the first time she'd been in the Newells' garage.

Becca looked at the picture and winced. Her gaze traveled to the workbench under which they'd found Walter Newell's body.

"Thing is, I was just in their garage," Emily went on, "and that rug's not there now."

"You were there?"

"Should I tell the police?" Emily said, watching Becca for a reaction. When Becca didn't respond, Emily added, "I need a good reason not to."

"How about because we're up to our armpits in stolen goods, our clients are lying to us, and the security in this place isn't bringing us any closer to inner peace?" Becca enlarged the photo on Emily's phone. "And because sometimes a rug is just a rug."

Emily looked across at the boxes that remained on the shelves. "We haven't done anything with the boxes of hardware that Mr. Murphy collected, have we? Because it seems to me there's not as many of them as there were when we first got in here."

Becca stood stock-still and looked around. Emily swiped through the shots she'd taken of the storage unit. She showed Becca a picture. There was no question about it: boxes were missing.

"This is freaking me out," Becca said. "Who would have taken those boxes? The person who changed the lock? Walter Newell's killer?"

Emily didn't dare look at Becca, who'd immediately have sussed out the evasion.

Becca added, "Too bad there's no surveillance cameras *inside* these storage units."

At least Emily could fix that. She marched out to her car and returned with the spare camera she carried in the gear bag. She took a series of pictures of the interior of the storage unit—the floor stacked with books and tubes; empty shelves; boxes that were still on shelves. Then she set the camera to low light, wide angle, and programmed it to automatically snap a picture every sixty seconds. She attached a power cord to the camera. Emptied the contents of one of the small storage boxes into another that was half-full. Tore a hole in the side of the empty box and set her camera inside, the lens looking through the hole and the cord snaking out the back. Then she set the box on a high shelf with the camera facing out and pointing down. She ran the power cord from the box to a wall outlet and plugged it in. Turned the camera on, and waited.

Click. Emily cringed. The sound of the shutter was loud enough to alert any burglar. She couldn't mute the shutter—the camera was a DSLR and the mechanism was mechanical—but maybe she could mask the sound. There was already white noise in the unit—the hum of the ventilation system that was blowing cold air on the back of her neck. She checked the thermostat and switched the fan from low to high. The hum grew louder. She waited for the next camera click. She heard it, but she might not have noticed it if she hadn't known it was coming. She hoped it would do.

She took the camera down and checked the pictures, un-flattering shots of herself looking as if she'd lost her best friend. "There," she said, putting the camera carefully in the box and setting the box back on the shelf. "At least now we'll know if someone's coming and going when we're not here."

36

BECCA DROVE OFF, leaving Emily to close and lock the unit. Emily lingered, looking at the pictures of Mr. Murphy's boxes that she'd taken when she was first there. More than a single box of padlocks had gone missing. She reactivated her friend-finder app long enough to see Frank's location come up UNAVAILABLE. She hoped that meant he was in court or in a meeting. She didn't want him to come home and find her again in his basement, which was where she was headed now.

Friday afternoon, it took a few traffic-light cycles to make her way through the Square. Finally she turned onto her street. Both her mother's and Frank's cars were gone, but a black sedan was parked in front of her house. As Emily drove past, she tried to casually inspect it. Any doubt that it was an unmarked police car was banished by the light bars, barely visible through the rear window, and a searchlight mounted beside the driver's side-view mirror.

She continued down the block. As she was about to turn the corner, she looked back and saw a pair of police officers emerge from behind her house and head in the direction of the black sedan. She drove a few blocks away, pulled over, and waited.

Five minutes. Ten. When she circled back, the sedan was gone. She parked in front of the house and grabbed her gear bag. She hurried inside, heading straight for the door to the basement. She dropped her bag, turned on the light, and picked her way down the stairs.

In the musty space, she gave the piano frame, which was now on its side and leaning against one of the Lally columns, a wide berth as she looked around for more stray boxes labeled with Mr. Murphy's characteristic labeling tape. She zigzagged her way between piles, checked above and below the Ping-Pong table, and made her way to the metal shelves that lined one wall and which were stuffed with old games and puzzles and boxes of magazines.

She was about to give up when she found them—two cardboard boxes with green plastic labels. They were hidden under a dusty crocheted afghan in the lap of the seated plastic skeleton. She picked up one box. It was heavy and its label read DRAWER PULLS. The other box was lighter. It was labeled SWITCH PLATES.

Suspecting that she might find these boxes in her basement wasn't the same as actually finding them. No wonder Frank had been so upset when the police took the box of padlocks, an item specifically listed in the search warrant. *Those are mine*, he'd said. Only they weren't.

Frank had to have been in the storage unit Sunday night. Emily had come back from Quinn's house, shaken by the incident at the coffee shop and only slightly drunk. Soon after she drank the cocoa that Frank had made for her, she'd conked out and slept so soundly that she hadn't gotten up once to pee during the night. So soundly that she'd had trouble waking up the next morning. At the time she assumed she'd been sleeping off the prosecco, but now she wondered if she'd been drugged.

Did Frank know Quinn Newell? When Emily introduced them, Quinn had acted as if she despised Frank, as if the very notion of a male attorney gave her indigestion. They'd both made it seem as if they were strangers who couldn't even get each other's name straight.

One thing was for sure. Walter Newell had coveted Quinn's first husband's collections, or he wouldn't have paraded them on his walls. Frank would have coveted them as well. Emily could imagine Frank, thirty years from now, wizened and gaunt, chanting *My Precioussss* as he gazed at his own holy grail, the original art for an early *MAD* magazine cover. Or the cover art for *Creepy*, which he claimed to have found between the pages of a two-dollar scrapbook at a yard sale. It occurred to her to wonder what had been tucked into that portfolio he'd been carrying when he found Emily in the basement, about to be attacked by the piano frame. Another treasure he'd never have been able to afford? What would he have been willing to do in return? And was that all it was, a business transaction? Emily had written off Frank's recent indifference to sex as the stress and disappointment of fertility testing, but maybe he'd been getting it somewhere else. And if he had, for how long?

Just then, car tires crunched in the driveway. Through the basement window Emily caught a glimpse of Frank's car's mag wheels rolling past. A minute later she heard the back door to the house open. "Emily!" Frank called. The door closed. "Emily? Are you here?"

Emily didn't answer, the seething in her stomach curdling into outrage. She heard footsteps overhead. A pause. She looked up at the insulated water pipe that snaked across the ceiling. Footsteps again, moving across the kitchen's tile floor. The door opened, then slammed. Then, silence. Frank had gone back out.

Angrily, Emily stacked the box of switch plates on the box of drawer pulls, picked them up, and carried them to the top of the basement stairs. Frank came bursting in from outside, arms loaded with what looked like empty plastic bags. Emily drew back and watched as he crossed to the utility closet. Dropped what he was carrying on the floor. Snapped open a large black plastic garbage bag and began stuffing the smaller plastic bags into it.

"Hi, Frank," Emily said.

He jerked upright. "Hey, hon. I thought you were upstairs."

Looking at him, she felt cold, as if she were seeing him for the first time. "What are you up to?" she said, holding the boxes of hardware in front of her, daring him to notice.

"What am *I* up to?" He shook one of the plastic bags at her. "Look familiar?"

Emily dropped the boxes on the kitchen table and took the bag from him. The clear plastic was printed with blue block letters: ICE. Frank held the garbage bag open so she could add it.

"Why on earth did you need this much ice?" he asked, swiping an errant bag from the floor.

"Me? What makes you think they're mine?" Emily asked.

"Because they were in the trunk of my car and I didn't put them there. You're the only person who's got a key besides me." This was straight out of Frank's legal playbook: *The best defense is a good offense.*

Emily sat down in the kitchen chair. "Frank, I don't know how those bags ended up in the trunk of your car, but I didn't put them there."

He looked past her to the boxes she'd set on the table. "And I suppose you're going to tell me you didn't put those boxes in the basement, either." That question left Emily speechless. When she didn't answer, he went on. "Light switch covers? Drawer handles? Locks?"

Emily said, "They're from the storage unit that Becca and I are emptying out."

"I guessed as much. But what I can't figure out is why you left them—"

"Whoa." Emily reared back. "I most certainly did not—"

"Didn't you?"

"No!"

Frank's eyes widened. "So I'm supposed to believe that those boxes just magically appeared in the basement?" He shook his head and knotted the garbage bag shut. "Like these bags got beamed into the trunk of my car?"

Emily folded her arms across her chest. "It wasn't me."

Frank straightened and gave her a long, hard look. "If you didn't." He blinked. "And I didn't. Then *someone's* messing with us. Planting evidence that—"

Before he could finish, the front doorbell rang.

Frank shot Emily a questioning look, then headed for the front hall. Emily followed. He looked through the peephole. "It's your mother."

"Ringing the bell?" Emily asked.

Frank opened the door. Lila stood outside holding a pizza box. She looked pale and shaken.

"Mom?" Emily said, taking the box from her.

"What's wrong?" Frank asked.

Lila stepped inside. Behind her stood two police officers. One of them, a chunky gray-haired man with an American eagle tattoo just visible on his upper arm beneath his short shirt sleeve, showed them his badge and gave his name, which Emily barely registered. "Emily Harlow?"

"Officer?" Frank said, positioning himself squarely in the doorway, his arm wrapped around Emily's shoulders, keeping her glued to his side.

The officer said to Emily, "We'd like you to come with us to the East Hartwell police station to answer some questions."

"Police station?" Frank said. Emily felt his grip on her loosen a bit as he exhaled. "Okay, then. I guess that means I'll have to meet you there." Emily looked at him, surprised. Then she realized how relieved he must be that the police weren't here to search the house. It would take two seconds for them to spot the boxes of hardware from Mr. Murphy's storage unit that were sitting on the kitchen table.

For her part, Emily was just as glad not to ride in the car again with Frank. Best-case, he'd harangue her about what she should and shouldn't do once they got there. Worst-case? She wasn't ready to face what that entailed.

Frank closed the door, leaving the police officers outside to wait for Emily. "Well played," he said, giving Emily a hug. She stiffened and pulled away. Frank didn't seem to notice.

Lila appeared in the doorway to the kitchen. "You're not going anywhere alone," she said. "I'm coming with you." Obviously she'd been listening.

Lila's no-nonsense support would have been a godsend, and Emily was about to say so when Frank said, "We need someone to be here in case the police come back with another search warrant."

Sadly, Emily had to agree. "If nothing else, as a witness."

"But—" Lila began to protest.

"Don't worry," Emily said, forcing a smile. "I'll be okay. I just need my gear bag." She didn't want to have it confiscated in another police search.

Lila disappeared and returned a moment later with the bag. "You're sure?" Lila said. Emily gave her a hug.

Frank said, "Go on. Give me ten minutes and I'll meet you there. Meanwhile . . ." He put a finger to his lips.

37

EMILY WASN'T SURPRISED when the backseat of the police car felt like a cage. But now it made her feel safe and gave her the private space she needed to sort her thoughts. As the cruiser drove off, she imagined Frank already heading out of their house, taking with him empty ice bags and Mr. Murphy's boxes. He was right, the police had executed a search warrant the last time they'd questioned her.

Cocooned in the backseat, Emily felt as if her life, like a disordered closet, had been suddenly emptied out, assumptions upended. What to toss? What to keep? As if she had choices.

She thought back: this had all started with Ryan's call to Becca, begging them to help his wealthy friend. Emily had assumed that Quinn was one of Ryan's *wenches*, as he liked to call them. And yet, when Emily saw the pair of them together, she sensed no undercurrent, no spark. In fact, he barely seemed to know her. In the same way, Emily doubted that the man in the green pickup truck was Ryan's client. Which made her wonder: Was Ryan a straw man, set up to receive Emily's distrust while more and more evidence piled up connecting Emily to Walter

Newell's murder? Who had put the boxes from that storage unit in her basement and the empty ice bags in the trunk of Frank's car? The obvious answer: Frank. Or was she overreacting and all those months of futile fertility tests had left her feeling estranged and paranoid?

By the time the police car pulled up to the back of the station, Emily was no closer to deciding which pieces of her life to neatly fold and tuck back in place, and which she was ready to jettison. It all came down to whether or not she trusted Frank.

One of the officers escorted her to a booking area. Just visible through a doorway behind the counter were a pair of holding cells. Empty.

The officer waited while she signed into a logbook. Then he pointed to a camera mounted on top of a computer monitor on the counter. "Please look up there." Emily did exactly what Frank would have advised her to do. She covered her face. "No, thank you." She said it loud, so there'd be no way they could act as if she hadn't objected. She was relieved when the officer took this in stride and herded her upstairs.

The layout of the police department was familiar to Emily now. She continued down a corridor. The door to the room where she'd been taken to give a *written* statement was open. At first Emily didn't recognize the woman inside wearing dark glasses, a white coat, and a red head scarf, despite the warm night. But on a second look she realized it was Quinn Newell. Quinn glanced at Emily but remained poker-faced.

Then Ryan appeared from behind Quinn, blocking Emily's view. He stepped through the doorway and looked past Emily and down the corridor, where Frank strode toward them with yet another police officer.

Emily's officer nudged her on. She looked back. When Frank got to Ryan, Ryan said, "Sidebar," and pulled Frank aside.

No. No sidebars! This wasn't some corporate lawsuit with damages and legal expenses hanging in the balance. This was their life. But Emily feigned indifference and followed her officer to another small, windowless interview room farther along the corridor. Before she stepped inside, she glanced back to where Frank and Ryan were huddled.

Emily entered the interview room and took a seat at the table. Frank joined her, closing the door behind him. He paced the few steps that he could. Up and back. Pent-up anxiety. Emily kept seeing Quinn's glasses-masked, emotionless face as she'd gazed out at Emily. Ryan's *sidebar* repeated itself in her head like a record scratch. What kind of sidebar had Frank and Ryan needed? Were they circling the wagons? Or maybe strategizing, since they could soon find themselves defending opposing clients?

"What were you and Ryan—" Emily began.

Frank shushed her, raising his eyebrows in the direction of a mirror that was installed on the wall facing them. Probably two-way glass. "Remember, they're watching *and* listening," he said under his breath.

"That's sturdy and nice-looking," announced a woman's voice, "and thirty years ago you might have found a buyer." It took Emily a moment to recognize the voice as her own, another moment to realize that it was coming from a small speaker that sat on the table. "But these days, it's what people refer to as . . . 'brown furniture.' Frankly, it's hard to give away. But there'd be a ready buyer for that kitchen set if you put it out at a yard sale."

"What is this bullshit?" Frank said.

Emily stared at the speaker in disbelief and horror. *This bullshit* was the conversation she and Quinn had had on the night they'd first met, a conversation fueled by far too much prosecco. Quinn had *recorded* it?

"Oh goody." Quinn's voice. "A yard sale! And let's not invite Wally." Her throaty laugh.

"Or you could donate." Emily. "There's a ton of charities and you'd get a tax deduction. I can find one that will pick up."

"What I really should do is stuff all of my old shit down Wally's goddamned—" Silence for a few moments. "Think there are any charities that will come over and pick *him* up? Or maybe he's just another worthless piece of—what did you call it?—brown furniture. Maybe I should just chuck him off the roof instead."

The laughter that followed was Emily's. Had she really found that so hilarious? Frank sank down into the chair beside her as the laughter continued and Quinn joined in. Cackling and hooting. Frank stared at Emily, disbelief in his eyes. Emily wanted to crawl under the table.

Quinn's voice picked back up. "Or slip poison mushrooms into his lasagna." A gagging sound. "Or accidentally back over him. *Rrrmm.* Oops! My bad." Emily remembered how Quinn had looked over her shoulder while she pretended to hold on to a steering wheel.

The clink of wineglasses. Then Emily's voice. "To *'til death do us part.*"

"To accidents waiting to happen." Quinn's voice. "Or maybe it's safer to hire a hit man, a complete stranger, and be done with it?" After a pause, "So, could you?"

"Could I what?" Emily had sounded so matter-of-fact, not a hint of shock or even surprise in her voice.

"I'll bet you would. In a heartbeat." Then, in a barely audible whisper, "If you thought you could get away with it."

There was a click and the audio shut off. In the silence that followed, Emily stared at the tabletop, at the speckled Formica that was pockmarked and lifting up at the edges. Slowly she let her gaze rise. Frank chewed on his thumbnail and scowled.

"Frank? I didn't—" She reached out to touch his arm. He pulled away and shushed her.

At that moment the door to the little room opened and Sergeant Stanley stepped in. Stanley looked down at Emily, then across at Frank with undisguised pity.

Frank crossed his legs, folded his arms across his chest, and leaned back. "That tape isn't evidence. My wife never gave her permission to be recorded. It's inadmissible in court."

"I wasn't aware that this is a courtroom, Counselor," Stanley said with mock seriousness. "Still, it's pretty interesting, don't you think? Speaks to your wife's state of mind." He scraped a chair across the floor and took a seat before addressing Emily. "Mrs. Newell knew she couldn't get away with killing her husband. But you, a complete stranger, could. I'm wondering what she promised you in return." He let that sit for a moment, then shifted his gaze to Frank. "Mr. Harlow, I'd watch my back if I were you. Because it sounds as if your wife and Mrs. Newell struck a deal."

Frank sat there, frozen. Emily could tell he was furious, bottled rage, that muscle working in his jaw the only evidence of him talking himself down from taking a swing.

"Test results are back," Stanley went on, still talking to Frank. "Those carpet fibers that we found in the back of your wife's car? They do match the rug that Walter Newell's body was wrapped in. If you'd like to see the report, I'm happy to show it to you. It confirms the CCTV camera footage that shows Mrs. Harlow delivering a body to the storage unit."

"All it confirms—" Emily began.

"Don't respond," Frank said.

"—is that the rug was in my car. Not that I put it there, or even that I was driving. Frank knows. I was asleep."

"'Frank knows. I was asleep,'" Stanley said, repeating her words. "So you're saying that someone, we'll say some unknown person, took your car and used it to transport Mr. Newell's body?" He paused. "Okay. Let's run with that. Who could that have been? Had to be someone who had a set of car keys or who knew where to find them." His gaze shifted to Frank.

"Frank doesn't know anything about that rug," Emily said. "But I do. I can even tell you where it came from. It was—"

"Emily!" Frank's voice echoed in the little room. He squeezed her arm. "Don't be fooled by . . ." he started to whisper, then stopped and addressed Sergeant Stanley. "Can my wife and I have a minute? In private."

"It's up to your wife," Stanley said. "Pardon me, your client."

Emily nodded to Stanley. Stanley got up and went to the door, glancing at his watch. "Five minutes." He started to close the door then turned back. "Mrs. Harlow, I'm telling you this in good conscience. From my experience, it's not a good idea to be married to your attorney. Consider yourself warned." He left and closed the door behind him.

"'Consider yourself warned.' Asshole," Frank said, muttering into his cupped palm. "And that was entirely too easy. He wasn't even recording our conversation. If he had been, he'd have informed us."

Frank fished his cell phone out of his pocket and opened a newscast, turning the sound up. Then he put the cell phone on the table alongside the speaker, turned his chair away from the mirror, and waited until Emily had turned away from it, too. The CNN station was giving the weather report. Heat. Humidity. Chance of occasional thunderstorms.

With the news playing, Emily could barely hear Frank's low voice. "We don't know where he's taking this. What else he's discovered but isn't telling us about. Because, taken at face value, it mounts up. Boxes from that storage unit show up in my basement. And now, come to find out that the rug the body was wrapped up in actually *was* in your car."

"I know where that rug came from," Emily said in a whisper as a CNN commentator took viewers through the home of a cat hoarder who'd been evicted from her Brookline home. "There was one like it in the Newells' garage."

"One like it?" Frank tilted his head and narrowed his eyes, considering. "Is that going to help you?" He chewed on his lower lip for a few moments. "Taken together, it points to you being involved. If not in Walter Newell's murder, then in the disposal of his body. If I were the police and heard that recording of you and that woman talking about getting rid of your husbands? It wouldn't be too big a leap to imagine the two of you coming up with an even simpler plan. Kill her husband and make it look like *I* did it. Two husbands for the price of one."

It took Emily a while to wrap her head around that logic. "I think the rug was planted in my car to incriminate me," she said.

Frank said, "And the boxes of hardware? Planted to incriminate *me*."

For a moment, Emily was speechless. "You can't think that I—"

"Of course I don't." Frank looked at his watch, a reminder that five minutes was all Stanley had given them. "And you can't think that I . . ."

"That you what?" Drugged her so he could slip out at night? Took boxes from the Murphys' storage unit? Helped Quinn hire someone to kill her husband? Helped her himself? At this point, it was scary how easily Emily could have forced the facts to fit any of those scenarios.

"Do you think the police know about Quinn's first husband?" Emily asked. Frank had been reaching for his cell to turn off the CNN feed. He stopped mid-reach. "That collection of advertising signs and illustrations that are hanging in her home?" Emily added. "That all belonged to him, not Walter Newell."

Frank didn't say anything for a moment. "She was married before?"

"Married before. Widowed before. For all I know, she's already got number three waiting in the wings. Maybe that's how Ryan figures into all this. Or Rafe Bartok." *Or you?*

Emily was too focused on watching Frank's reaction to notice that the door of the interview room had opened. Behind her, Sergeant Stanley said, "Who's Rafe Bartok?"

Before Emily could respond, Frank said, "Emily!"

"Rafe Bartok," Emily said, ignoring Frank and turning to face Sergeant Stanley. "He's the man who showed up in a coffee shop in the Square, made up to look like Walter Newell and driving Walter Newell's car. Just to guarantee that he'd be noticed, he hit my car and had someone report the incident to the police."

38

STANLEY SAT IN the chair across the table from Emily in the little interview room. He leaned forward. "Go on," he said.

"That's enough!" Frank looked like he was ready to explode.

"I'll answer your question about who's Rafe Bartok," Emily said, ignoring Frank, "if you'll answer a question for me first."

"Okay. Shoot," Stanley said.

"When does your medical examiner think that Walter Newell *could* have died? Forget CCTV cameras. Forget paint scratches. Level with me, or if you can't, say you can't. What does the body tell you?"

Frank pushed away from the table.

"What are you thinking?" Stanley said, giving Emily a narrow look.

"I'm thinking that your medical examiner has done a thorough job but maybe he'd come to a different conclusion if he had all the facts. I want to know what's the earliest that Walter Newell *could* have died? What's the time range? How certain is he? Because at the time when Walter Newell was supposed to have been at an auction in Hyannis, and later when he's supposed to have been driving back in what you told me yourself was a major traffic jam, and later when he's supposed to have hit my car in the Square and then gotten run down at the town wharf, is it possible that he was already dead?"

Stanley propped an elbow on the table, rested his chin on his knuckles, and gave her a speculative look. "From the autopsy results?"

"This is crazy," Frank said. "Walter Newell was at that auction. He registered, didn't he?"

What happened to *Don't speculate? Don't offer information?*

Stanley tilted his head to look at Frank and gave a slow nod. "He registered."

Frank said, "So doesn't that mean—"

"It doesn't mean a thing," Emily said. "All you need to register at an auction is a credit card. If he had his credit card at the auction, then why didn't he use it later that night to pay for his coffee?"

Stanley said, "You really think someone went to the auction pretending to be Walter Newell?" He sat back. He seemed to be enjoying this. After all, they were doing his job for him.

"Maybe," Emily said. "Smoke and mirrors and men wearing beards and baseball caps and tinted glasses. What I want to know is, from the body and only the body, what's the earliest he could have died?" She looked at Sergeant Stanley. At Frank. "Anyone have a problem with that?"

Frank shut down, his face drained of expression.

"Fair enough." Stanley stood. "Give me a few minutes. I'll be right back."

As soon as he left the room, Frank turned to Emily and gave an exasperated huff. "I only hope you know what you're doing."

Emily shushed him and pointed to the mirror. She was banking on something from Stanley, assuming he was going to level with her, that would account for a whole lot of ice.

A minute ticked by. And another. After five more, Emily glanced toward the door. "What do you think he's up to?"

"It's a technique they use," Frank said. "Vanishing in the middle of interrogations. It's their way of toying with you. Remember when we bought your first car?"

Her "first" had been the Honda that she was still driving, and they'd been rubes when it came to bargaining. The salesman had said he'd have to take their lowball offer to the manager. Then he disappeared and left them sitting there for over an hour. They couldn't leave because he'd taken the keys to the car they'd inherited from Frank's mother and were using as a trade-in. That was before Frank developed a taste for flashy cars.

"You think that's what he's doing? Leaving us to stew?" Emily said.

"More like hanging us out to dry."

But moments later Stanley returned carrying a manila folder and looking somber. He opened the folder and pulled out a stapled set of pages. "Here's the autopsy report. I'll read you the conclusions." He turned to one of the final pages. "Based on body temperature, rigor and livor mortis, and stomach contents, approximate time of death: eight o'clock p.m., Sunday, August fourth, to eight o'clock a.m., Monday, August fifth. Immediate cause of death: traumatic asphyxia due to blunt chest trauma. Manner of death." He looked across at Emily. "Homicide."

Emily swallowed. "Eight o'clock Sunday to eight o'clock Monday," she said. "That's a twelve-hour window."

Stanley closed the file folder. "Generally speaking, we like it to be more precise. But the body had been in water. That delays the onset of rigor. And it was found in the equivalent of a warm oven, and apparently had been there for a period of time. Which accelerates decay."

"So the time frame is really a guess," Emily said.

Stanley nodded.

"And it allows time," Emily went on, "for him to have registered for the auction and for that witness to report him hitting my car?"

"The hit-and-run," Stanley said, "was the last time anyone but his killer saw Walter Newell alive."

"No," Emily said. "It was the last time anyone saw Walter Newell's *car*."

Stanley opened his hands, palms up, allowing that she had a point.

"Could Walter Newell have been killed earlier and his body packed in ice?" Emily said.

There was silence in the room. Stanley blinked. Narrowed his eyes. "It would take a lot of ice."

"It sure would," Emily said. "And if that's what happened, what does it do to the estimated time of death?"

"I'd have to ask an expert," Stanley said.

"Come on. You know as well as I do that it would shift the time frame earlier. How much earlier?"

Frank grabbed her. "Seriously, Emily, we need to talk. This is pretty outlandish."

She peeled his fingers from around her arm and turned to Stanley. "My husband is worried because someone stuffed the trunk of his car with empty ten-pound ice bags. A great mound of them. He thought I put them there."

"But you didn't," Stanley said.

"Of course I didn't."

"Bags." Stanley sat back. "You have them?"

"I handled them," Frank said. "Emily handled them, too."

And so did the killer. "Aren't they in your car?" Emily asked Frank.

"They're not," Frank said. He swallowed. "I got rid of them on the way over here."

"You . . ." Stanley shook his head. "Where?"

"In a dumpster behind 7-Eleven."

"On South Main?"

Frank nodded.

Stanley faced the mirror and gestured to whoever was watching from the other side. "I'm sending an officer over there right now." He turned to Frank. "And I'm hoping for your sake that they're still there. Tampering with evidence in a murder investigation?" He eyed Frank. "I don't have to tell you, that's a felony. Up to twenty years in prison."

He turned his attention to Emily. "So you're suggesting that Walter Newell got back from the auction early."

"Or wasn't there at all. Someone using his ID and credit card could have registered as him."

Stanley picked up the thread, his eyes narrowing as he spoke. "But he was already dead, his body packed in ice. Someone else drove his car to the coffee shop, created a bit of a stir, hit your car, and then drove to the wharf and abandoned the car."

"Rafe Bartok," Emily said. "That's the man who ran into me at the coffee shop."

"And you know that . . . how?"

Emily knew better than to blame a pair of coffee-stained loafers. And she remembered the promise she'd made to Ana Perez. "You can check for yourself," she said. "Look up the purchases he made on his personal credit card. I'll bet he used it to pay for a venti. Hot. Black. At around nine-thirty at the Java Connection."

Stanley nodded, thinking. "So, assuming Walter Newell died, let's say a day earlier, where were you on Saturday?"

Before Emily could answer, Frank was on his feet. "Enough. My wife has been more than forthcoming. Emily?" He was out the door before Emily had gotten up out of her chair.

Emily glanced at Sergeant Stanley, catching an unguarded look of frustration on his face. "You have no idea who killed Walter Newell, do you?" she said.

"We . . ." Stanley seemed taken aback. "Let's just say your information tonight has been extremely helpful. Right now I have no more questions for you. Just one piece of advice." He gave her a long, hard look. "Watch yourself."

IT WAS DARK, and live crickets were chorusing when Emily found Frank sitting in his parked car in the police parking lot. The dome light was on and the windows were rolled up. Frank sat hunched over in the front seat, his cell to his ear. Waiting? Listening. Because a moment later he straightened and turned, talking animatedly and jabbing a finger to make his points to whoever was on the other end. She caught his gaze through the windshield. He held up a finger. Then shifted to face away from her.

Finally, Emily heard a click—the doors unlocking. Frank's window rolled down. "Sorry," Frank said. "I didn't mean to abandon you. I just wish you hadn't told them about the ice bags."

"I wish you hadn't dumped them at the 7-Eleven," Emily shot back.

"I didn't. I was buying time so we could destroy the bags and return those boxes to the storage unit." A police cruiser screamed out of the parking lot. "I think you're right. The ice bags. The boxes. The rug in your car, too? They were planted to implicate you. Or me. Or both of us."

Frank reached across and pushed open the passenger door.

"Come on, get in. It won't take long before they realize there's no bags in that dumpster. They'll be back to search our house and cars. We need to make sure that this time there's nothing for them to find."

Emily hesitated. "Who were you talking to on the phone just now?" she asked.

"Ryan. I wanted to give him a heads-up in case you and I both get pulled in again. We might need separate attorneys. I asked him to make some calls." He made it sound so routine, like lining up a plumber for a stopped-up drain.

Watch yourself. Stanley's warning came back to her. She said, "You're sure you can trust Ryan? He's the one who connected us to Quinn Newell in the first place. Then he told me he was helping Quinn because *you* had asked him to. He left the ball game early. He could have come back and helped Quinn kill her husband and hide his body."

Frank didn't respond right away. "Emily, Ryan is the least of our worries right now. I don't think you realize how much trouble you could end up in. What if it turns out that everything in that storage unit is stolen?"

That was just what it was starting to look like. Emily swallowed hard. "But we're returning everything we can to the libraries they were taken from."

"What do you want to bet that your client will cut a deal in return for testifying against you?"

A breeze had kicked up and Emily's hair whipped about her face as she stared at the open car door. Frank was right about Mrs. Murphy. She'd put her own self-interest first.

"We need to return those boxes and we need to return them now," Frank said. "If they're found anywhere but safely back in that storage unit, you'll be facing charges of trafficking stolen goods. Not just you. Your mother and Becca, all of you could face felony charges and get sent to prison. You're the one who knows how to open the storage unit and where the boxes need to be put back. Come on. I can't do this without you."

He was right. Doing nothing could put all of them at risk. Emily got in the car.

"Which way?" Frank said.

Emily pointed, and Frank pulled out of the parking lot and accelerated onto the main street. "Keep on straight until you're past the wharf," she said. "Then right again over the bridge and come back on the other side."

Frank drove through the center of town. She was relieved that no police cars were parked in front of the Java Connection. Frank put his hand on Emily's leg. "You okay?" he asked. She turned to look at him. She was not okay, but neither was he. Tendons stood out on his wrist as he gripped the steering wheel.

Emily got out her phone and texted her mother.

Almost done. Home in 30.

Then she put her cell phone in the cupholder between the seats, leaned back, and closed her eyes. She thought about the trail of evidence. An abandoned car with a dented front fender. Yellow-tinted aviator glasses. An auction bidder card where it didn't belong. An area rug, rolled up and lying in a puddle of water. Empty ice bags. Boxes of vintage hardware. A cover-up that would have taken two people to pull off—two people who had access to the Murphys' storage unit, Emily's car, and her house. Behind Emily's eyelids danced her business logo: a high-heeled boot kicking a video reel. The unspooling tape morphed into disjoined body parts—her own head, torso, arms, and legs.

Emily opened her eyes as Frank turned and drove through the main gate of Inner Peace Storage, continuing directly to the Murphys' unit. He parked just past it, beyond the CCTV camera. Fear prickled at the back of Emily's neck. How did he know which unit it was?

Frank shut off the engine, popped the trunk, and got out. Emily stayed in the car, panicked. He must have been here before. She realized that no one but Frank knew where she was. She should at least text Lila and Becca.

She reached for her cell phone, but it wasn't in the cup holder. She felt around on the floor. In her gear bag. No phone. The car jiggled as Frank rummaged in the trunk. Emily reached around under the steering wheel, feeling for the car keys, but they were gone, too.

The trunk slammed shut and Frank emerged holding a long-handled windshield scraper with a plastic bag hanging off the end of it. In the other hand he held a pen. Not a pen. From one end of it shot a beam of green light. A laser pointer.

Frank aimed the laser at the security camera as he moved into its field of vision. Raised the windshield scraper. It took three tries to drape the plastic bag over the camera lens. Then he went back to the trunk and returned carrying the two boxes containing Mr. Murphy's hardware. He rapped on Emily's window. "What's the combination?"

She picked up her gear bag and got out of the car. With not another human in sight, the storage facility felt like a cemetery, the units untended graves. She glanced at the CCTV camera, its lens now shrouded by a plastic bag that had once contained ten pounds of ice.

"Frank, have you seen my phone?" she asked.

"Again? You're always losing it."

Emily didn't bother coming up with a response. She remembered the combination Becca had given her. She went over to the storage unit door, bent down, and entered the code. The lock popped open. Frank reached past her, raised the door, and turned on the light. Books and tubes were still on the floor in a dozen or so piles, just as they'd been when she was there this morning.

She hung back as Frank entered.

"Where do these go?" he asked.

She pointed to one of the now-half-empty shelves. He set the boxes down and was starting to turn away when he froze and picked up his head, hyperalert. He looked back, scanning the shelves. Emily knew at once what had happened. Even on high, the fan in the unit hadn't kept him from noticing the shutter click.

At first he didn't spot the box where Emily had set up her camera. But when the shutter clicked again, he did.

"What the hell . . . ?" He reached for the top shelf and carefully took down the box. The power cord plugged into the wall trailed behind it. Frank unplugged it. Raised the lid. He emerged from the unit and thrust the box at her. "Did you set this up?"

"Of course I did," Emily said. She took the box, lifted out her camera, and detached the cord.

Frank stared hard at the camera. "Why didn't the police find it?"

She glanced at Frank. His jaw was tense, his hands fisted. He thought the camera had been set up to take pictures days earlier, back when Emily had first opened the unit, before Walter Newell's body was dumped there and the lock was changed.

"I guess they didn't know what to look for," Emily said, playing along. "One of the security guards told me that he'd seen a woman coming and going from this unit. That's when I planted that camera. We didn't want to get accused of stealing anything."

That sounded plausible. In fact, it would have been an excellent idea, if only she'd been that prescient.

"Did you catch anyone?" Frank reached for the camera.

"Hang on. Let me have a look." Her heart was beating so hard she was surprised Frank couldn't hear it. She turned away from him and carried the camera up the alleyway. She pressed PLAYBACK. The first image, a smeary exposure that looked like a close-up of Frank's shirt, had been snapped as he'd taken the lid off the box.

"There you are," she said. Frank looked startled. "Just now."

"Let me see," he said in a harsher tone.

She turned the LCD screen to face him for a moment and gave what she hoped sounded like an easy laugh. "Your shirt and . . . that looks like your thumb." She pressed PLAYBACK again. The previous image came up: Frank putting one of the boxes of hardware on the shelf. The one before that was a completely black exposure—the dark interior of the closed storage unit, taken before they'd opened it up.

Emily scrolled back through a stream of pictures of the same dark nothingness, the time stamp pacing earlier in one-minute increments.

"What?" Frank said, coming up beside her.

She turned the screen away from him. "Still just shooting blanks." She clicked back more until an image came up. "And . . . wait a minute." There was a person in the image, a silhouette backlit against the partially open storage unit door. The time stamp placed it a few hours ago. "I can't see who it is. Looks like someone's closing the unit. A man."

"Emily." Beads of sweat had popped up on Frank's forehead.

In the next image, taken a minute before, the door to the unit was fully raised. In the foreground, Emily recognized Mrs. Murphy. She was standing by the workbench, opening a document tube. Several other tubes were lying on the workbench.

When Emily saw the next earlier image, she almost dropped the camera. There was Mrs. Murphy again, but now a man stood beside her, in profile to the camera. He was taller than she, and the overhead light gleamed off his silver pompadour. His eyes were in shadow under wild dark eyebrows. He looked like the man in the framed photograph that Mrs. Murphy had on her piano—her supposedly deceased husband.

The image was focused enough to see that they had one . . . no, two documents laid out on the top of the workbench. Two maps, similar in size. Mr. Murphy was holding them down flat.

Emily zoomed in. Even with crappy resolution, the maps looked identical. One old and one new? She remembered what her mother had told her about printing a forgery of an old map onto old paper using digital technology so advanced that even experts were fooled.

"What? What did you get?" Frank said.

Emily clicked back, then ahead again. Mrs. Murphy hadn't been opening the tube. She'd been closing it. And she'd slid one of those two maps inside, keeping one and sealing up the other. It wasn't hard to guess which copy she'd be keeping and which she was planning to return to the library. It was a neat trick, and she probably would have gotten away with it, especially with Lila running interference for her.

"People can really surprise you, can't they?" Emily said, looking at Frank. "And not in a good way."

Frank had gone pale. "You have to destroy those pictures." He grabbed for the camera, but Emily held on as she backed away. He tugged it his way, she tugged it hers. Finally it flew from their hands and landed on the pavement with a thud.

Frank lunged for it. Picked it up. A web of cracks in the lens lit up as he turned the camera over under the streetlight. He dropped the camera on the ground and stomped on it with his heel until the screen shattered and the case came wedged apart, disgorging circuit boards and wires.

Emily gasped as a wave of sadness swept over her. Not for the camera, which could be replaced. Not for the pictures that revealed Mrs. Murphy to be a thief, a swindler, and a fraud. She wasn't even a widow.

No, the grief Emily felt was for Frank—the Frank she'd married. The one who'd bought his first pin-striped suit for their wedding. Who'd stood stiffly in it, his hair refusing to slick down, as they faced the minister. When they'd kissed he'd smelled sweet and musky. They'd made love that night twice, the first time frantic, the second time slow and leisurely. That lazy smile of his that could still take her breath away.

Back then, Emily knew beyond the shadow of a doubt that she was *the one* he'd chosen. Now he could barely meet her gaze. "Emily, I—" he began. For a moment it seemed as if he were about to break down. But if so, he was interrupted by a car that approached from behind her. His face was lit up by oncoming headlights and his shadow, cast against the adjacent storage unit door, grew taller as the car approached and came to a halt. When Frank waved, Emily's heart sank. She wheeled around.

The car's headlights went out, but even in the dark Emily could see that it was a white Honda Civic hatchback with the Clutter Kickers logo stenciled on the door.

THE CAR DOOR opened and a woman got out. She wore a blue cap, its brim pulled down over her eyes. A long, straight ponytail stuck out the back. She had on blue pants and a top, just like the ones that Emily and Becca wore for dirty work. It was Quinn Newell.

This must have been how she'd looked when she'd driven Emily's car to pick up her husband's body from wherever he'd been killed—not the wharf, Emily was pretty sure—and deliver it to this storage unit. Making sure that the CCTV camera got just enough of a glimpse of her to convince the police that she was Emily.

Now Quinn stood, arms akimbo, facing Emily.

"Shall I tell you how her first husband died?" Emily said to Frank. "The one she married before Wally." She raised her voice, adding, "She killed him, too."

"Shut up," Quinn said, and lunged at Emily.

Emily backed up onto the apron of the storage unit. "On her honeymoon—" Before she could finish, Quinn backhanded her across the face. Emily staggered back, tripped over her gear bag, and landed on her behind on the concrete floor inside the unit.

Winded, she sat there gasping, her ears ringing as Quinn stood over her.

"Stop it!" Frank shouted. "This wasn't part of the deal."

Emily rolled over onto her stomach. "She's not good at deals, unless it's the part about 'til death do us part."

"I said, shut up!" Quinn said, and kicked Emily. Emily curled into a fetal position and lay there, her arms folded, pain like lightning searing her rib cage.

Above her, she heard Frank. "You were married before? You never told me . . ."

"What difference does it make?" Quinn snapped.

Emily slowly rolled onto her stomach and dry-heaved. Her mouth tasted salty and metallic. "Big mistake," she said as drops of blood stained the floor. "You were so careful not to leave blood evidence for the cops to find the last two times. Now—" She got onto her knees and spat onto the concrete.

"Cops," Quinn said, her tone dismissive. "They never know where to look. They won't this time, either."

Quinn grabbed Emily under one arm. "Come on," she said to Frank. "Help me."

Frank hesitated for a few seconds before he grabbed Emily under her other arm. Together he and Quinn dragged her to the back of the storage unit. The rough cement floor scraped Emily's back and her arms felt as if they were being pulled from their sockets.

Quinn yanked the overhead door shut. It landed with a thud. The interior went pitch-black for a moment before Quinn turned on the light.

"Your first husband was killed?" Frank asked.

"So?" Quinn gave a slow smile. "Does it matter?"

"It matters, Frank," Emily said, taking a painful breath and

forcing out the words. "He was a collector, like you. Those signs
and prints in her house? They were all his."

"She's full of shit. They were Wally's," Quinn said.

"Know how her first husband died?" Emily said. "She pushed
him off the deck of a cruise ship. Then she marries Wally. He's
not a collector at all. Just, what? Wealthy? And now I guess she's
in the market for an attorney to settle his estate. Someone who'd
do anything to own all those fabulous magazine covers " Frank's
cringe told her she was right.

"Shut up," Quinn said. "You have no idea what you're talking
about." She reared back, about to kick Emily again, when Frank
grabbed her around the waist from behind. "Seriously?" Quinn
said to him. "You have to know it's too late to be having second
thoughts. You're up to your neck—"

"It's not too late," Emily said, struggling to sit up. "Frank?"

Frank looked lost. He'd always been so good at convincing
himself that whatever he was up to, he was on the side of the
angels, even when that meant representing a corporate pariah
whose faulty engineering was killing people. But once upon a
time he'd defended people who didn't have any other options.
That Frank had married Emily in a pin-striped suit. Maybe, just
maybe, he was still in there.

"Frank, whatever deal you've made, you don't have to—"
Emily began.

"I told you the ride might get a little bumpy," Quinn said, shaking free of Frank's grasp. "You just have to hold on. Trust me."

"This wasn't supposed to happen," Frank said.

"What did you think was going to happen?" Emily said.
"You'd set me up to be charged with murder and I'd roll over?"
It might have worked, she realized, if it hadn't been for Rafe
Bartok. If he hadn't realized what he'd gotten himself tangled

up in and gotten greedy, Emily would have gone right on be-
lieving that it was Walter Newell she'd run into at closing time
at the Java Connection, when in fact Walter Newell was long
dead.

She thought back over what must have happened. Quinn and
Frank had waited for a night when Becca was busy and Emily
would have to go alone to meet a new client. Becca had gotten
Quinn's call. Her SOS. When Becca said no, they didn't work
Sunday nights, a man who identified himself as Ryan Melanson had called Becca, begging her to accommodate a new client who needed their help decluttering, and she needed it *now*.
Plus she'd pay double. But that caller must have been Frank,
claiming to be Ryan. Becca wouldn't have been able to tell their
voices apart.

So much of what had happened after that made sense. Of
course, tutored by Frank, Quinn knew Emily almost better than
she knew herself. Frank would have advised her to complain
about a husband who was an out-of-control collector. To have
a few bottles of chilled prosecco handy. To put the Care Bears
atop the pile in the garage. Given Frank's penchant for dragging
back what Emily put out for Goodwill, those Care Bears might
even have been Emily's. Thinking back, none of that junk, piled
high in Quinn Newell's garage, looked like anything that Quinn
Newell ever would have coveted.

Emily heard a muffled cricket's chirp. Silence, and then more
chirping. Her ringtone. Frank reached for his hip pocket and
took out her cell. He looked at the readout.

"Becca?" Emily said, though she was far from sure it was.

Frank gave her a blank look, but she knew him well enough to
know that she was right.

"She knows I'm here. If I don't call back, she'll come looking for me."

Quinn took the phone from Frank and turned it off. "We'll just have to take that risk. Besides, we won't be here long." She rested her chin in her hand and gazed down at Emily. "You know, I'm actually sorry about this. In another lifetime, we might have been besties. Now you need to disappear." She tapped a finger against her lips. "The question is, how? This time, we'll keep it simple."

"I guess you don't have the time you had with Wally to create an illusion," Emily said, "or the convenience of a ship's railing to push me over."

"He sat on the railing, you know. Like he was asking . . ." Quinn shifted her gaze toward the river. "Water," she said, mulling. "I wonder when it's high tide." She took out her phone. After a bit of fiddling, she frowned. "Not for a few hours. We have to wait. Just as well." She turned to Frank. "You need to leave. Go be seen somewhere. And I need to be seen somewhere, too."

"What about me? Shouldn't I be seen somewhere?" Emily said.

"Easy peasy," Quinn said, flipping the fake ponytail attached to her cap. "We'll make sure there are plenty of witnesses who'll swear that they saw you driving around in your car."

"Another hit-and-run, made to order?" Emily said.

Just then there was the sound of movement on the other side of the overhead door. Quinn and Frank traded surprised looks as, with a creak, the door started to rise. Frank raced over and slammed it shut. Quinn joined him, holding it down.

"Who's in there?" A woman's thin, reedy voice. A hand slapped sharply against the metal door. "You don't belong in there. Get out!" Emily had never been happier to hear Mrs. Murphy at her most outraged.

"Friend of yours?" Emily said. Quinn glared at her. "I guess you knew her husband. Charles Murphy? Antique maps, sold at auction? You helped them out, didn't you? Did she know you were going to dump your husband's body in her storage unit?"

"Let me in!" Mrs. Murphy's voice came from outside.

Emily shouted, "Ruth! Call the police. It's Emily. I'm trapped." But her final words were drowned out by Mrs. Murphy banging on the door from the other side.

Quinn glared at Emily, but she couldn't hold the door shut and muzzle her at the same time. The door rattled as Frank and Quinn held it shut. They didn't notice Emily crab-walking inch by inch backward to her gear bag.

"What are you doing in there?" This time it was a man's voice. Sounded older. Probably the white-haired Mr. Murphy. "Open the door. Now!"

The man must have taken over trying to raise the door, because Quinn and Frank were struggling to keep it shut. Emily reached her gear bag and rummaged around inside. She found her stun gun, then painfully rose to her feet. She held it out in front of her and advanced toward Quinn.

"What's that supposed to be?" Quinn said, eyeing the stun gun, straining to keep the door down.

"Frank?" Emily said. "Why don't you explain?"

"It's a stun gun," Frank said.

"Looks like a toy," Quinn said.

"It's not a toy," Frank said. "But trust me, she'd never use it."

Emily put her thumb on the trigger switch. "You don't think so?" She took a step toward Quinn and Quinn shrank back. "It's painful, but don't worry. It won't kill you. But it'll knock you out cold for an hour or two."

Quinn kicked out at Emily, aiming for the stun gun. But she couldn't reach it and hold the door at the same time.

"Mrs. Murphy," Emily shouted. "I'm in trouble. Call the police. Do it now!"

"Emily? Is that you?" Mrs. Murphy asked. "Open the door. This is my unit. I have a right to be inside."

Emily caught a look passing between Frank and Quinn, his questioning, hers a headshake. Emily could only hope that Mrs. Murphy was as surprised as anyone when Walter Newell's body turned up in her storage unit. The woman was greedy, happy to delude herself if it meant turning a profit. But she was more amoral than evil.

"I know what you've been up to," Emily shouted. "Stealing and counterfeiting. Selling fakes. But you really don't want to be charged as an accessory to murder."

Silence from outside.

Emily went on. "I can help you, once I get out of here. But you have to call the police. Tell them to come. Now."

Emily heard low voices, Mrs. Murphy's and the man's. Sounded as if they were arguing, probably weighing their options. They wouldn't be eager to have the police back. There'd be no windfall from selling original old prints and returning their giclée copies to libraries from which the originals had been stolen. Emily hoped the loss was outweighed by the prospect of no charges, no trial, and no prison term.

Finally Emily heard footsteps. A car door slammed. Then another. A car engine turned over and tires sounded on the pavement.

Cautiously, Quinn released her grip on the door and inched away.

"She's calling the police," Emily said, though she was far from certain.

"Maybe," Quinn said. "But I'm guessing not. They've got quite a big investment to protect." She darted at Emily, reaching for the stun gun, but missed.

"You sound as if you know them," Emily said. "They steal. You fence?" Emily backed away, running into the workbench.

Quinn kicked the stun gun from Emily's grip and sent it skittering across the floor. Quinn lunged for it, grabbed it, and backed away. "So this knocks you out for a few hours?" Quinn looked at the stun gun, unimpressed. "Really?" She rushed at Emily, pinning her against a bank of shelving, poking the stun gun hard into her neck and pushing the trigger again and again and again.

All Emily felt was the cold metal of the prongs and a tickle of electricity, the stun gun's feeble attempt at firing. She shuddered and screamed, then slid to the floor, stiffening and shaking as if she were having a seizure. Then she lay there on the cool concrete, eyes open, staring at the ceiling, going from rigid to slack. She let her head fall to one side, her mouth drop open. She had no idea if that was what actually would have happened if the gun had been fully charged, but she was banking on neither Quinn nor Frank knowing, either.

Out of the corner of her eye she saw Frank raising the door. He came over to her and got down on one knee. Hovering, he grasped her wrist and felt her pulse. She knew her heart was pounding. She tried not to blink.

"She's all right," Quinn said. "And there's no mark. We need to get her out of here before anyone comes back. Maybe the river this time?" When Frank didn't respond, she said sharply, "Frank, listen to me. You'll tell them that she was depressed. At her wits' end about the murder investigation. Her reputation shot. Her business failing. I'll say she shared her despair—"

"How can you be like this?" Frank said. "So cold. It's as if she's just . . ." Frank seemed at a loss, but Emily would have supplied the rest: *an inconvenience.*

"And you," Quinn said, "are a hypocrite. You had no trouble helping me get rid of Wally's body. This is no time to get sentimental."

Helping me get rid of Wally's body. Emily couldn't help but feel relieved that maybe Frank hadn't actually killed him. Without meaning to, she shifted her gaze. Her eyes locked with Frank's. He flinched.

"What?" Quinn said.

"I . . ." Frank said. In the pause that followed, he continued staring down at Emily. Was he going to rat her out? She wanted to believe that he'd gotten himself into this situation not with a huge leap, but inch by inch. An attraction. An affair. Imagining what-if. His devotion to Emily weakened by months of passionless sex, the timing dictated by her basal body temperature. Emily knew firsthand how Quinn could hone in on vulnerability and lure you in. She'd gotten Emily to express feelings she'd never admitted to anyone, even herself.

Emily squeezed Frank's hand. She could only hope that he'd remember what they'd been to each other.

"Back the car up to the door," Frank said.

Quinn went out. Frank got behind Emily, hooked her arms, and dragged her backward across the floor and out of the unit. The air smelled of car exhaust as Quinn backed the Honda up to them. Emily heard a click. The tailgate unlocking. Frank reached across and raised it. "Get her bag," he called. "The stun gun, too. And pick up the pieces of the camera from outside."

While Quinn was in the storage unit, Frank positioned himself to block her view and whispered, "Get in." Emily scrambled into her car through the open tailgate. "Stay down and hold on." She lay curled on her side as he closed the hatchback. Seconds later the front door of the car opened and shut. The car lurched in reverse, throwing Emily against the back of the car's backseat. Then it peeled out.

"Frank!" From outside, Quinn's voice pierced the air. "Where in the hell are you . . ." Her voice grew faint until it was gone entirely.

"Emmy, are you all right?" Frank said.

Emily's side throbbed and her face still stung. But she hadn't been run over twice or pushed off a cruise-ship railing. "I'm—" The car took a sharp turn and accelerated. Emily was tossed from one side of the car to the other. She heard the piercing shriek of a siren. Blue lights screamed past in the opposite direction. Emily looked out the back window as the speeding police cruiser continued toward the storage facility. Mrs. Murphy, bless her heart. She must have called the police, after all.

"I'll be okay," Emily said.

Frank tossed her his cell phone. "Call Ryan. Tell him to meet us at the police station."

Tell me you didn't kill Quinn's husband. Did it really matter? Because what was clear was that this had been, in fact, a twofer, as Frank had suggested. Only not two wives setting up one husband to take the blame for the other husband's murder. It was a pair of lovers, setting up his wife to take the blame for her husband's murder. When you looked at it that way, Emily had been Frank's savior. Because how long would it have been before Quinn tired of him? One look at what Frank collected would have been enough to curdle her rosy view of the life that he and she would share.

And he would have insisted on a prenup.

41

SIX MONTHS LATER, Emily sat at her kitchen table with Becca and Lila, the front page of the *Boston Globe* spread out in front of them. "Looks like he's gained a little weight," Lila said. She was taking in a photograph of Frank testifying at the murder trial of Quinn Newell, aka Amanda Quinn Safstrom Newell.

Frank didn't look fat. He looked pasty-faced and miserable in a tie that seemed to be choking him. He'd been in custody since the night Ryan met them in the parking lot of the police station and walked Frank inside to cut a deal with the DA. Frank had agreed to turn state's evidence in return for pleading guilty to a lesser charge. Eventually, when the trial was over, he hoped to be released on time served.

Emily would be testifying soon, the prosecution's other star witness. She was relieved that the tape of her and Quinn, apparently conspiring to kill their husbands, had been ruled inadmissible, and she'd sworn off prosecco.

The media was having a field day, calling Quinn Boston's black widow. Emily tried not to read about the trial, and if something about it came on the radio, she turned it off. It was bad enough that she'd had to play a supporting role as the clueless wife.

Rafe Bartok would take a turn in the witness box, too, testifying that Quinn and Frank had hired him to impersonate Walter Newell. His role was to drive Walter's car to the Hyannis auction, register as Walter, turn right around and drive back in plenty of time to run into Emily at the Java Connection, where he'd make a scene, ding her car, and then abandon Walter's car at the wharf, thereby establishing multiple reliable witnesses who'd swear that Walter Newell was alive long after he'd been killed and put on ice in the Jacuzzi in the Newells' master bath.

The whole operation had gone off like clockwork until Rafe Bartok realized the face he'd been paid to make himself up to look like belonged to a murder victim. Emily couldn't help but feel that it was entirely reasonable for him to feel shortchanged by a mere one thousand dollars, a cash payment Quinn had withdrawn from the bank a few days earlier.

Frank was being held in what they called *low-security detention*. Emily was not paying him visits. She was sleeping in the middle of their king-sized bed. She'd thrown away his pillows along with his shampoos and aftershaves, cigars and Maker's Mark. She'd sold his BMW and given his Chevy Suburban to NPR, then rented three oversized storage units at Inner Peace Storage and hired movers to transport the contents of Frank's office, along with everything he'd stuffed into their basement, attic, and garage.

Most of the time, looking at those newly emptied spaces sparked joy.

"So," Emily said, folding the newspaper and tossing it into the recycle bin, "back to work." On the table she placed a chart showing the timelines for their current projects. "Looks like everyone has a full plate." Business was booming, with Lila now rounding the staff of Freeze-Frame Clutter Kickers up to three and expanding their reach to Cape Cod. Their success was a testament to the axiom that there's no such thing as *bad* publicity. You want to build name recognition? Get embroiled in a scandal. Better yet, get embroiled in two.

Quinn Newell's murder trial, along with the return of prints and lithographs stolen from libraries, had catapulted them into news feeds nationwide. The Murphys' books, alas, turned out to be worthless. Most of them had been purchased in marginal condition as library discards. It was the prints, protected in special tubes that were impervious to the mold and decay, that were priceless. The police had impounded scores of giclée copies that the Murphys had been prepared to "return" to the libraries from which they'd stolen the originals. They'd then sell the originals, netting well over a million dollars.

Emily was convinced that Mrs. Murphy was protecting her husband. Apparently he'd gone underground a year ago, at around the time that the District Collection and others had gotten wind of their losses. Mrs. Murphy wouldn't admit that he was still alive, or that she'd known Quinn Newell, though it must have been Quinn who suggested Mrs. Murphy call Freeze-Frame Clutter Kickers and act the part of the clueless widow who needed their help to liquidate—though the more accurate term would be *launder*—her husband's collection. Quinn must have had a key to the Murphys' storage unit. She'd probably been the woman the Inner Peace security guard had seen coming and going from the unit. She was probably the one who'd disabled the ventilation system in the storage unit, some time before she and Frank dumped Walter's body there. Emily expected it would all come out at her trial.

"Any new leads?" Emily asked.

Lila said, "I got a call this morning from a woman who inherited her mother's collection of dolls. Hundreds of them. She and her three sisters are arguing about what to do with all of them." Lila went on laying out the basics of the project. The dolls, the dollhouses, the clothing, the spare doll parts because the mother had repaired dolls, too. Emily spaced out, envisioning the freeze-frame video that she could put together. Dolls marching around. Saluting one another. Doll parts sorting themselves.

"Four sisters?" Becca said, giving the project a thumbs-down. "It will be a mess, and it won't ever be about the dolls."

ACKNOWLEDGMENTS

I CONFESS, I'VE long been happily married to a man who's addicted to yard sales. There will never be enough bookshelves in our house to accommodate his finds. Though occasionally it makes me want to strangle him when he comes back with more books, he has more than enough redeeming features to make him a keeper. I have him to thank for inspiring me to write this book.

The main character, Emily Harlow, is a former elementary school teacher (as was I) turned professional organizer (never me, not in my wildest dreams). Thanks to Kathy Vines (Clever Girl Organizing), Melanie Cerio (The Holistic Organizer), Muffy Loomis Kaesberg (Organizing 4 U), and Michele Raimondo for helping me understand the valuable role that professional organizers play. Thanks to the New England Chapter of the National Association of Productivity and Organizing Professionals, whose meeting I attended, where I listened and learned. Any errors are my own.

Thanks to my blog mates on Jungle Red Writers for their encouragement, and special thanks to Roberta Isleib and Hank Phillippi Ryan for reading and advising. To my husband, Jerry, who is my final reader and never takes offense when he finds himself in the book. To my agent, Gail Hochman, for her encouragement, warmth, and advice that always make it better.

Thanks also to the fantastic professionals at HarperCollins, including Gena Lanzi, Vedika Khanna, Rachel Weinick, and Kate Hudkins. I couldn't be in more capable hands. And to Katherine Nintzel. Every writer should have the pleasure I've had of working with such a gifted and talented editor.